# The Harrowing of Tam Lin

By L. E. Perry

The Harrowing of Tam Lin

Copyright © 2021 L. E. Perry

All rights reserved. No part of this book may be reproduced in any form or by any electronic or mechanical means, including information storage and retrieval systems, without permission in writing from the publisher, except by reviewers, who may quote brief passages in a review.
The characters in this book are entirely fictional.

ISBN 979-8456269393

Published electronically and in print in the United States of America

uberlark@google.com
https://www.facebook.com/LEPerryAuthor/
Visit www.moonphasebooks.com for further information on the Moonphase world and upcoming books by this author.

## Introduction

This book is based on an old Scottish ballad, as well as on mythology, ancient alien theories, science, and history. Weaving all of these things together seamlessly is like playing a game of Tetris, and sometimes it requires that I twist the pieces a bit so that they fit into place. Which is why good students of Scottish history might notice that I've taken some liberties; Tam's father is an Earl of Moray, and Tam was at the coronation of Robert the Bruce, which should make him the son of the very first Earl of Moray in the very early 15th century. Armor reflects that era, with chain mail covered by partial plate. But other details might not be a perfect match, particularly Turnebull's Phillip Hall and the destruction of Dunbar's own keep. The dates and events might not match on closer inspection. Bear in mind, this is fiction, and that was 600 years ago. I recommend you give the same latitude to the history as you do the science; it should be close enough to pass at a glance, but in a world where the fey are from another planet, and they've created half-human creatures for their own scientific research, trust that it is indeed a slightly different world than the one we live in, and the historic timeline might be just a little bit off as well.

For those who wonder how a character in a ballad became part of my sci-fi/fantasy series, here's the story; I spent a number of years studying the music of Renaissance

Scotland when I was engaging in medieval re-enactment as a harper, and competing in the Scottish harp competition at the Texas Scottish Festival & Highland Games in Arlington, Texas. Which I highly recommend if you get a chance to visit. Bring bottles of frozen water so you have some cold water when they melt.

The first time I heard this ballad, it was the version by Fairport Convention, which focused on the criminal behavior of Tam Lin and the mysterious way he appeared and disappeared. I didn't think much of it. I also listened to the Steeleeye Span version which had the same words but different melody. Since there are numerous versions of the ballad in Child's book, how it starts, who Tam is, and how it ends varies. And Child never recorded a melody. So Anais Mitchell and Jefferson Hamer recorded a more romantic version a few years ago that I found far more captivating, and that's when it hit me; the way Tam changes from human to beast and back again at the end of the song makes him a great candidate for my own Moonphase novels, so I dropped him into book two and he took over quite unexpectedly. His story is very compelling. And his heritage allows for more explanation of what the aliens/faeries (Sh'eyta) are doing here on earth, which is important to understand before book four of the series. So I figured I'd better tell Tam's backstory, then return to the series, so that readers have their footing as the novels draw toward the final showdown between the aliens and the half human, half animal hybrid creatures they engineered.

If you enjoy reading this story half as much as I enjoyed writing it, check out the rest of the Moonphase novels; I'll be writing them for many years, as well as spinoffs, and we'll have a great time getting to know these characters better as they face extraordinary challenges with extraordinary powers.

## 1 – The Invitation

The sundial that protruded from the wall of the tower barely read nine when Tam saw the great black warhorse of Lord Dunbar drawn around to the stables, along with his chestnut riding horse. Being his kin and the son of a nobleman obligated him to greet the man. All noblemen were related to each other at some level, of course, and he had countless uncles and cousins of varying relationships. He straightened his grey tunic and turned his belt so that sword and dagger hung properly at his hips and the buckle hung on center again, then combed his fingers through his short, black hair, tucking back the longer locks that hung down past his eyebrows. He felt his thin mustache and bricf goatee for length as he walked across the yard. He should trim them later if time allowed, he thought as he strode toward the hall.

"Tam!" Lord Dunbar called out from across the yard. The man was impossible to mistake; a large, red-headed and well-muscled Scot, his fashion an odd cross between traditional Scottish leine rather than a tunic, and trews instead of hosen, but with nods to continental finery shown by the lace at the ends of his sleeves and at his throat.

"Aye, my lord?"

"Come here. Look at you, laddie! You've grown another foot since I saw you last, and I can't fathom how your skin became so dark. You were the same milky white as your lovely mother for aye a decade. And how's the new horse you won at the games? Is he coming along?"

Tam strode toward the visiting lord and bowed. They were family, but as a squire he must show respect to the office. Lord Dunbar accepted his courtesy with a serious look, then broke into a laugh. "Well done, lad, but I'll not have you keeping your distance! Let me size you up!" He swept Tam into a great bearhug.

"Let him down, Dunbar, you're going to crush my best squire! Good God, man, he's not a child to be hugged and coddled at will," Lord Douglas berated him.

Dunbar released Tam, who took a moment to catch his breath before answering.

"He's a good horse, my lord, staying steady enough that I best the swinging deadman in nine out of ten tries." He used the squires' slang for the burlap dummies stuffed with sand and straw that they tilted at with lances to practice their polearm skills.

"Well there you have it! He'll be a knight soon enough. On the cusp already if the blood runs true. Come along, then." Dunbar turned toward the great hall doors that stood open to receive the trunks his people would be carrying in shortly. At just nineteen, Tam didn't expect to be raised to knight for another two years, but his heart leapt for a brief moment at the possibility that Lord Douglas might consider him worthy of an early honor. For now, Tam took heart in seeing his kin; the man always brought news of the latest battles and shifting alliances of the borderlands between Scotland and England. The big bruin could be a challenge to keep up with, though, and talk would turn soon enough from the art of warfare to the art of drinking. Tam brainstormed excuses to remove himself from the conversation as soon as he lost interest. He preferred a good hunt to talk of women and wine, neither of which interested him on a practical level. He considered his first duty to be an upright Christian and preferred a clear head any time he might need to fight, which was always, with the English on their doorstep.

"You're untasked today, are you not?" Lord Dunbar looked over his shoulder at Tam. "I heard of the wound Sir Gregor took, he'll not be rising from his bed for some time yet." It had been a horrific gash, the blade having found the section of armor that Tam had told Gregor should be repaired as soon as possible; the chain links had stretched in an earlier blow. Gregor's opponent undoubtedly knew exactly where to strike, driving a sword into the weakest place in the heavy mail. "I'd like a squire in attendance," Lord Dunbar continued, "rather than a page. I have some things to discuss that might need a third mind. I have to know more about the lay of the land where you've spent summers, Tam. Can you come?"

"Aye, my lord," Tam fell in behind Lord Dunbar and his own liege, Lord Douglas, listening as the two great men discussed the family, births and deaths, movements between summer and winter halls. They passed through the great hall where yeasty breads, freshly churned butter, honey, and platters of rashers and fruit disappeared into the hands of hungry folk as they moved through the hall. His stomach growled as he followed them into the library, hoping they weren't planning to talk in some corner all the way through the tail end of the meal. Once the sideboards emptied it would be a long wait until the evening meal. His stomach growled again and he sighed as the two men dropped into chairs on the far side of the room. Tam closed the door behind them, then kneeled on the floor, resigned to a rousing discussion of local politics that would be followed by an unfortunate assessment of a chambermaid's charms, or the quality of this year's whiskey, but Lord Dunbar surprised him almost at once, turning directly to face him.

"So, Tam, what would you say to a bit of hunting? The king has charged me with a hunt in Ettrick to fill his pantry and possibly his dungeon. Thieves aside, I could use a man to butcher while I harvest. The deer produced a bumper crop this year and the herds need to be thinned. Gregor taught you how to separate meat properly by now, hasn't he? It's much easier to carry a hind once we butcher it."

"Dunbar!" Lord Douglas protested, "Watch what you're saying, man! Are you trying to steal the lad away from me? He's nearly ready to be raised and he outstrips even some knights who are fool enough to take him on. I'll not have him go to your house after Gregor's work training him!" but his uncle raised a hand for silence and looked at Tam. Tam blushed and looked at his knees as he listened to the praise.

"Ach! And don't I know it. But think of Sir Gregor's state; he'll be down for some time yet. We can't let Tam get lazy while no one's watching, and a good hunt will strengthen bond between horse and man." The words seemed sincere enough, but the delivery was almost absent-minded, as if his thoughts were elsewhere.

Tam looked up to see Lord Douglas nodding grudging agreement. "As long as it's a short enough trip I suppose it would behoove you to add bow and polearm to your battle skills, Tam. You've mastered sword and lance well enough from what I've seen of you in the yard, but your weakest moments are when greater distance separates you and your opponent." The men sat in silence as they both looked at him.

He sat confused for a moment, wondering why no one spoke, then he realized they were waiting for his answer. Oh dear God, they were both staring straight at him. They expected him to decide? As a squire, decisions about who he served and when, or where, had never been his to make. He quickly assessed the idea; travel to Ettrick would take only a few days and he could be back just as fast if Sir Gregor sent for him. He'd barely started making progress in the list yard with Honor, the well-muscled snowy white gelding he'd been awarded for defeating the other squires in the annual games. But the thought of roast venison had his stomach growling painfully.

Lord Douglas scowled with impatience and Tam felt his face flush. "It would be my honor, my lord, to join you," he said, flustered, and Lord Dunbar nodded as Tam berated himself silently. "Serve" would have been the better word. A simple enough sentence, but he felt like he had to move an entire mountain to get the words out and fell short of proper form despite the effort. He discussed matters easily with squires, and even held his own when he spoke to the knights, but the lords were another matter. They rarely asked him to join them, and there were countless forms to observe to show sufficient respect and understanding of each lord's stature in the kingdom. Tam hoped that was the last question he'd have to answer for a while.

"Get to your feet, Tam. It's time you took a seat in the discussions." Lord Dunbar's voice cut through his thoughts, and he shot up in answer. By the lady, he had hoped to be left alone with his thoughts in due course, at least. Now he had to not just listen to the political discourse, but be prepared to weigh in? He thought longingly of the great sideboard where bread and rashers must be disappearing as he stood.

"Pull a chair around, Tam," Lord Dunbar murmured. Intrigued, Tam reached for a chair to move toward the two lords so the three men sat in a tight circle, facing each other, and he sat back down, leaning forward as the other men did. Dunbar lowered his voice, as if worried that someone might overhear. "That's the story we'll be telling the others of why you'll be leaving here with me, and we'll hunt, surely enough, but there's more at stake," Dunbar said in a hushed voice. "I've just came from Phillip Hall, and I saw signs that someone's been lurking in the woods as I approached your keep."

Lord Douglas rose halfway to his feet. "And you're only now telling me? Surely they can't be close or my men would have caught them!"

Lord Dunbar nodded as Douglas slowly lowered himself back to the chair. "They followed my wagons for several leagues, but they dropped away beyond your men's scouting forays." Lord Dunbar repositioned himself and his eyes narrowed as he continued to look at Tam while speaking quietly. "They seem wary of my men, Douglas, and yours as well; I'd like to string out a fighter as bait for them, one that can hold his own against them but isn't known on the battlefields, to see if we can lure them out. We need someone with good training but no serious rank, an unknown who yet can defend himself well enough while we remain hidden at a distance."

"Good God, you'll be putting him in danger!" Lord Douglas answered.

Tam's eyes were wide now as he listened. The idea of getting a major role in a skirmish made his heart race with excitement.

"There aren't many men I would trust with this, Douglas, but I believe Tam can hold his own, and as the grandson of a lord so close to our king, they'll want to ransom him, so they'll see that they do him no serious harm." Dunbar turned to the other Lord.

Tam sat listening to the men speak and was surprised when once again they were both staring straight at him. There'd been no question this time. Then what they said sank in. His chest grew tight as he asked, "Myself?" to gain time to think, but it was clear this was his mission to accept or reject, they would not make the decision for him. When he answered the first question, he hadn't merely agreed to join a hunt, he'd volunteered to let the enemy capture him, like his ancestral hero Lord Randolph, the first Earl of Moray, many years ago. Now they waited for him to confirm. The two men continued to stare at him as it sank in. Fear mixed with exhilaration as he realized the opportunity had come for his first solo assignment in this great game of nations, minor though it was. He nodded slowly, eyes wide.

"Okay, Tam," Lord Douglas began to talk, suddenly serious. "There are a number of things I want to tell you about holding your own until Dunbar's men descend on the enemy, whoever it is. For you to act as a lure, his men have to be far enough away to embolden the spies. Heed me, you might find yourself severely beaten before you can be rescued. Randolph once told me how he got through punishment by the English when he was taken hostage. There are a number of things he did that helped; I think you can learn from his experience."

Tam had wanted to know more of Lord Randolph's story; the English had captured him and turned him with lies, even had him lead soldiers into war, but Lord Douglas himself reclaimed him. He later led a group of men to retake Edinburgh Castle using information he gained from the enemy and one soldier who knew a back way into the castle. His bold strategy had made him indispensable to King Robert, who rewarded him with the Earldom of Moray.

"Go on! We haven't got long," Dunbar replied grimly. "Tell him everything you know; you're more familiar with Randall's tales, your families are thick as thieves. But Gods, Douglas, I'll need to leave at first light to find these knaves. Egads, I could eat a horse. Was that a meal I saw on the sideboard?"

"Yes, the remains of it," Douglas answered.

Lord Dunbar rose. "I'll be getting a plate of it, then. Have you eaten, Tam?"

"No," Tam's stomach growled loudly.

"I'll get you one as well. Douglas?" The other lord shook his head as Tam rose to protest. Fetching food and drink was the job of a squire.

"Sit back down, boy," Lord Dunbar commanded. "You've got a lot to learn, and little time to learn it. I know how to carry a plate. It's the least I can do for you, before I put you in harm's way with no one at your back. This once I'll be bringing food to you. Don't get used to it."

Tam watched the big man's arms swing as he swept out of the room, shaken by his uncle's dire excuse to act as manservant, then turned back to Lord Douglas, whose eyes were intent as he started speaking again, and Tam focused sharply on every word. The code of chivalry gave him only slight protection; he could be abducted and he might have to endure torture if any of his captors were dishonorable. They all hoped Lord Dunbar retrieved him before the enemy carried him off, but it was a perilous task and no guarantees could be made. As a nobleman's son, he could at least hope to be ransomed if all else failed, but he had no intention of becoming a liability. He listened, rapt, as Lord Douglas told him what the earlier Lord Randoph had endured, and how he made it through.

## 2 – Borrowed

"[A knight] must be generous and give freely and ungrudgingly to the needy… Everywhere he must be the champion of the right against injustice and oppression."
Medieval and Modern Times, James Harvey Robinson, PhD, 1916

Several hours later, after going over details with the two lords, Tam's boot heels echoed through the great hall again as he strode toward the pell yard, where the local squires practiced their skills against the equipment and each other. His head swam with information. He wanted to put a saddle on Honor and go riding through the hills, but the long discussion had taken several hours and he'd missed most of the morning practice. He needed to work on a few grappling maneuvers. He listened to the sounds of boots, hooves, and slippers, aware of maids, pages, noblemen and guards. Being a squire, he had to be ready for anything. Knights and squires remained on guard at all times against possible intruders. If a thief or brigand had snuck through the needle's eye in the dark of night or come in with a wagon in broad daylight, the time it took to hear an alarm could be long enough to take a dagger in the back as the miscreant escaped. He grabbed an apple from one of the barrels in the hall and bit into it. He'd been interrupted while on his way to check on his horse earlier. He passed Sir Gregor's other squire as he entered the musty darkness; James worked diligently in the stall with a horse Tam didn't recognize, scraping a huge hoof with the iron hook to dislodge mud and stones. Tam nodded as he passed, then spoke quietly as he came around the rump of his own horse to alert Honor that his master had arrived. He checked the horse's limbs for heat that would indicate a new sprain. Countless things worried a horse at all times of the day and night, and the only way to know if his limbs were sound was to check. Honor snorted at him but there was nothing amiss, so Tam went to get the pitchfork from James, who was through with it now. After he mucked out the stall he sped the big beast through a few of the standing commands he'd been taught before pulling the apple core from the hook he'd hung it from when he arrived and let Honor lip it gently off his palm as a treat, rubbing the long nose with affection.

He headed toward the door and saw James still in the stall with the horse, barding halfway on. "Is everything alright, James?" With Gregor down, Tam oversaw James' work with the horses. James was much younger and not as experienced with horse care, having taken over from Tam only recently when Gregor decided it would be helpful to have a separate squire for his horse. When Lord Douglas raised Tam to knight, heaven forbid Gregor should have to cut his own meat at feast, they laughed.

"Can you check this leg, Tam?" James wrung his hands. "Does it feel right to you?"

Tam ran a hand along where James indicated and felt the twitch of flesh that told him the horse found it uncomfortable. He felt something rough in the skin. He searched the area with his fingers, and found a tiny bump which he scraped with a fingernail until it fell into the palm of his hand. "Tick," he said, showing the tiny creature to James.

"I thought they were like little balls!" James said, looking at the squirming pest.

"Only after they're gorged; you caught it early. You did well to notice it." Tam pinched the creature tightly between his fingernails, cutting it in two, then dropped it on the floor. "Wash the place you found it with clean water, lad, and keep an eye on that, make sure it doesn't get infected. Come to me if it does so I can show you how to treat it, but it should be fine. Have you any other worries?"

"No, that was all. Thanks, Tam!"

Tam nodded and went back out into the yard, happy to see James developing a bit of confidence. He'd spent his days as a page under a cruel lord, where the ladies were always looking for someone to blame their own issues on, and James had been beaten without warning for things he hadn't done. Sir Gregor had rescued him from that fate and had pulled Tam aside to make it very clear, one of Tam's jobs would be to assist James not only in teaching proper horse care, but to be gentle with him until the boy learned that he could trust his new family. Sir Gregor already treated the boy like his own son. The diligence James showed was encouraging; soon enough Tam would trust the boy to care for the horse alone.

He hoped to practice with his sword today. Against one of the other lads, if they could be spared; he could gain strength, even dexterity, working with a pell, but he needed someone fighting back to keep his senses sharp, and he spent most of his time lately working with the new horse instead.

"Finn! Would ye care for a match?" he called across the yard.

The stocky blond turned toward him. "Against who? You? Gads, Tam, I've still got a limp from the last round I went with you, and that was days ago!"

"You'll never best me if you keep avoiding me. Come along! You're twice my size, man, and some of it muscle."

"I may have you on flesh but you're hardly a twig yourself, and hard as a rock. At least where it counts, from what Gregor's wife says."

Tam reached for his sword in fury, and a knight came out of nowhere to grab his arm. "Hold there, squire! If you let him best you with words the fight is done before it starts." He almost fought against the bigger man but stopped himself. The knights discouraged drawing a sword in reply to an insult. If needed, a duel could be arranged, but the squires were expected to keep their tempers in check, fight only in battle, and guardedly in games and practice. He'd almost drawn live steel in the pell yard, for which he could be called in front of Lord Douglas for judgment. Men had found themselves shackled in the cellar for less.

Tam dropped his chin with contrition, but he couldn't keep himself from blurting out, "There's nay bit of truth in it, the swine deserves to be run through for disrespect to a lady, and Sir Gregor's wife at that!"

The knight released him. "And well I know it, squire; they were wed less than a month ago and they're in each other's arms enough no man could squeeze between them, even with Gregor's wound. Go now and I'll forgive your worthy offense." Then he called out to the other squire, "Finn, you go too far! I'll not have you calling out the goodly wife of a knight. Get over here, I'll have a talk with you."

Tam dodged out of the yard before the knight reconsidered whether Tam might need a lesson himself. The so-called "talk" mentioned had nothing to do with words. As he approached the stables, he considered taking Honor out anyway, wanting to give the knight how had stopped him time to forget what Tam had almost done.

"Oyez, squire!" a voice rang out behind him. Tam swung around. "Come here, s'il vous plais!" a big man with a strong French accent bellowed at him. "Are you on a task?"

"Nay, I was just going to check on my horse, but he is in no need of immediate care, Sir," Tam replied. It was Sir Philip, one of the French knights that had been making the rounds through Scotland. He came from the court of a strong ally, but Tam was frustrated that he couldn't remember the name or rank of the lord he served. Sir Gregor had impressed upon him the importance of knowing which knight served which lord. Tam could recite allegiances of every knight and lord in Scotland, but as soon as he went beyond his own country his memory failed him.

"I need a man to get me into my steel. I've been asked to show my skill against one of your own men and my squire is busy getting my other set of boots repaired. Come with me." Sir Philip turned, expecting Tam to fall in behind him, and Tam strode to his side. Untasked squires were expected to assist any knight who asked in whatever was needed, at a moment's notice, and Tam responded without thought. It was a good way to practice thinking quickly in battle. Combat changed without warning, and a knight that couldn't keep up with change faced a quick death.

They entered the small shared room Sir Philip had been assigned to as a visiting nobleman and Tam started checking sections of plate for secure straps and dents, then lifted and fastened the heavy sections into place on Sir Philip himself, who had pulled his heavy padding on, over which he donned mail. The French man's armor looked much like what Tam had become familiar with, for Sir Gregor, but Sir Philip schooled him in the differences. Tam checked each part for breaks, deep dents, or loose straps. If any of the armor came off Philip during the rigorous joust it was on Tam, and he had no intention of letting the smallest detail slip past him, after watching his own knight go down with what could have been a fatal wound, in what should have been a safe display of prowess. He would be Sir Philip's body squire for the rest of the day. There would be no wrestling or tilting for him today, but that was fine. He could think while watching Philip charge forward on his steed, then check his armor again after each round and verify that it was still secure before Philip charged again.

"Have you a squire handling your horse, sir?" Tam thought of all the men it took just to see a simple jousting match through.

"Sir Gregor offered his horse squire to me when I stopped to visit him, so my own horse should be on the field before I arrive. I am surprised that you Scots have so many squires that even a horse gets his own! Sacre Bleu, if I had known I would have come to Scotland long ago."

Tam nodded with a grin; so James had tacked up Sir Philip's horse. It would be the two of them assisting Sir Philip today. It made sense; they were both free and experienced with these tasks. "Aye, my lord. James is a good lad. I've trusted him with the barding for Sir Gregor's steed for some time now."

Sir Philip stopped moving for a moment, and Tam froze in place. Had he made a mistake? Had he missed a sharp edge and gotten Philip injured?

"I did not know Scottish squires were so attentive to the work of their peers," Sir Philip mused. "How does it happen that you have attention to spare for another boy's efforts?"

Tam's mind raced. What had he done? "Sir Gregor says a body squire should take everything into account, sir. James takes care of the horse, but he's young yet; if he makes a grave mistake, my own work is for naught. I handled the armor for both man and horse before James arrived, and I'm expected to see that James has my support until he needs it no longer."

Sir Philip looked surprised. "You're Gregor's, then? I've taken both of his squires?"

Tam nodded, stiffly, still wondering if he had inadvertently offended the foreigner. Was there some sort of French etiquette he had unintentionally failed?

Philip roared with laughter, and slapped Tam on the back so hard he nearly fell, surprised by the sudden act.

Philip was outrageously strong and seemed to enjoy demonstrating that fact. "Sacre bleu, it is a good thing I'll be in my own armor, or they would all be mistaking me for Gregor when I'm out besting your knights! What is your name, squire?"

"Tam, Sir."

Philip looked surprised yet again, as if he knew the name. Tam couldn't imagine why the man would know his name yet not his face. He must have imagined it. Clearly Sir Philip didn't recognize him, today, in spite of the times he attended Sir Gregor while the knights exchanged stories of their conquests in one town or another, but that was how it should be. A squire served his knight without drawing attention to himself. If Tam had gone unnoticed, it meant that he was doing his job well.

## 3 – Waylaid

Tam left Sir Gregor's room with his sweaty clothes after securing the knight a fresh change of tunic and trews. The sun had gone down while he cleaned and polished Sir Philip's armor after the long series of jousting matches the foreigner had been put up to, but he'd be up for some time yet scrubbing Sir Gregor's clothing out and hanging it to dry over his bed. Gregor didn't like lying about in his unmentionables, with lovely ladies waiting on him hand and foot, so Tam had to be sure he kept the man well-groomed as he recovered from his injury.

"Tam!" a voice yelled at him from the shadows by the courtyard wall. He peered into the darkness, then sidled over to see who had called him. He stepped between two bushes and suddenly he was thrown to the ground face first, crushed under the weight of two men who had driven their bodies into him, one on each side. He kicked his heels out, hoping to make contact, then tried to twist his body, trying to get his knees under him enough to push himself back up to his feet, but a third man, the one who had called to him, fell across his legs and pinned him to the ground.

"Off!" Tam grunted, but the man on his chest made it hard for him to breathe, much less talk. They had his arms and were pulling his wrists toward each other behind his back. He squirmed uselessly but managed to keep his wrists apart with an incredible effort.

A voice hissed. "Dammit, Tam, you're being trussed whether you like it or not! Stop fighting us. It's three on one. Do you really think you can best those odds?" and a fist struck him hard behind the ear.

"Get your pissing paws off me, you swine! I don't have time for this shit," Tam cursed them.

"You earned this shit, you're gonna take it, meddler!" Tam recognized Finn's voice; clearly the young man had been censured harshly, and blamed Tam for it.

"Quiet, you fool! This is back-alley work."

The French accent caught Tam by surprise, and he caught a boot to the abdomen and found himself struggling to catch his breath as his wrists came together against his will. A coarse rope dug into his flesh as they were tied. The weight of the bodies shifted as one of them worked at the knot, which gave him a chance to press his knees into the earth and shove his body upward, nearly dislodging Finn. They soon had him trussed like a pig, wrists secured and legs bound together up past his knees.

Tam wondered how the big knight had gotten involved in the pell yard argument. Tam was thrown over the back of a horse, landing painfully on his ribs with an "Ooof!" One man had his arms and, on the other side of the horse his legs were pinned by Sir Philip, whose hands were so strong he thought he already felt tingling below the tight grip.

"Are you aye so weak the three of you can't haul a trussed man yourselves?" Tam queried.

The big knight answered, "We're saving our strength, my friend. It's going to be a long night, Tam, and you're not going to like the dance steps we're about to school you with. You'll think again before crossing my cousin." Tam recalled then that Finn's father had married a French woman. He was dismayed to think that a full knight with years of battle experience had singled him out for private punishment, along with two other men. Tam had been on the battlefield before, but only as shield bearer for Sir

Gregor. The foreign knight could surely overpower him alone even if he broke free of the ropes. How was he going to get out of this?

The afternoon had been brilliant; Sir Philip showed the Scottish knights some French jousting strategies. He'd learned a few tricks himself that he was eager to practice. It had been a great day! Or so he'd thought.

The big horse came to a halt in the stables, and someone stretched a cloth tightly over Tam's eyes as he heard a lamp being lit for the other men. His body was thrown down onto the ground, hard, and as Tam rose the first kick came, the toe of a heavy leather boot driving into his side, then the heel of another boot struck his ribcage. He grunted as he fell again and tried to roll away but a boot came at him from that side as well. He was soon twisting and turning, tucking his head down to protect his face, bringing his knees up to protect his belly as one foot after another flew at him, none of which he could see. They focused on his midsection, mostly his ribs, but the occasional foot hit him on the back of the skull. His back took several well-aimed blows and he was afraid a rib would snap in the rough bludgeoning. He grunted in pain, but the next boot struck him on a shoulder, then several feet pounded his thigh. Ice water splashed over his face and he spluttered, having taken a sharp breath as it poured down on him. A piece of wood caught him in the back, then another bucket of water splashed onto his face and he coughed and spluttered again. They were intentionally tossing water on him as he tried to breathe. But their ministrations had moved from his midsection to his thighs, with the distressing addition of water aimed at his nose and mouth to make it harder for him to catch his breath. Relieved of the need to protect his gut so much he was able to pull his feet toward his back and he used his fingers to tug the tight curves of the knot at his calves every chance he had. He could feel the knot slowly unravelling, but every painstaking advance on the knots was accompanied by a dozen or more painful kicks.

The drumming of boots and sticks continued for what seemed like hours. He continued to work on the leg ropes, which were wet now along with the rest of him, still tucking himself together when they moved painfully again to his belly and back.

"Enough!" Sir Philip cried. "Sooth, he's nearly broken free, and he'll fight us like the devil if we don't get away before he turns the tables on us."

The siege ended finally, and he was happy to hear the other three panting as heavily as he was. At least he made them work for the punishment he received. Someone grabbed his hair and his head was wrenched around, the cloth yanked up, and he found himself staring Sir Philip in the face.

"Sir Gregor is going to throw you out on your ass, Sir!" Tam blurted.

Philip shook his head, emphatically. "Gregor will never hear of this."

Tam glared at him. "Why wouldn't he?"

Sir Philip reached a hand down toward him after the third man untied his hands, and he reluctantly reached up to let the knight pull him upright. Tam groaned as he tried to stay on his feet. His thighs were weak with bruising and his ribs and back felt like he'd gone far too many rounds on the list field, outmatched against a stronger foe.

"Get out of here, you two," Sir Philip said to the other squires. "I'll speak to him alone," and the other two man ran from the barn as he continued to speak in his thick French accent. "I swore to my mother I'd watch over Finn, and he wrested a promise from me to punish you if you crossed him, but I'd never have taken that oath if I knew he planned to set you up. I'm not at all pleased that it put me at odds with a young man who can fight as hard as you. I have not seen a fight like you gave us when we brought you down with three trained men on top of you.

And you'd have freed yourself in another minute while we beat you from every side, blindfolded. I have fought against the best knights in several kingdoms. I had to call an end because you were coming near to getting hands and legs free, and I'm not sure Finn would have survived if you did. You are a beast, man! Two beasts!"

Tam stared at the black-haired gentleman and waited for an apology, but Philip was listening to the sound of booted feet walking away from the stables. When the night was silent again but for the shifting of weight by horses in stalls, he continued. "I'm sure that Finn came crosswise of you knowing I'd have to atone for anything he got himself into. He came to me as soon as he received his punishment. But that sniveling fool didn't tell me what a fighter you are. I'm not proud of this, and I'd ask you to keep this to yourself, by the code; for all that I hated this task, I swear I'll be back to finish you off if you breathe a word of this outside this barn. For your silence, I will see that Finn understands this is the last time I'll defend him against you, and if he comes crosswise of you again it will be himself that receives my punishment, and it will be far longer before I call it off. To seal my word I give you this," and the knight reached into a pouch secured to his belt, drawing a glass vial from it. "This is the strongest antidote for pain I have ever used. It was given to me by a sailor who died in my arms returning from Jerusalem, and I have used it sparingly, because I have no idea where I can get more. But a few drops is enough to suffice. Consider this my apology for carrying out a task I did not enjoy. God, man, what a fight you gave us! When you make knight, and I know that you will, it is my prayer that, if I ever see you on the battlefield, I have you at my back and not at the end of my sword." Philip thrust the vial into Tam's hand, pressing Tam's fingers closed over it with his other hand, nodded once, then turned to jog out the stable door. Tam had no idea, at that moment, that it would be many years before he saw the man again.

Tam stumbled backwards, unable to stay on his feet any longer, and winced as his hip struck the wall. He pressed himself against the wood to remain upright at all, and, in a painful crouch, pulled the cork from the top to sniff the contents. He almost spilled some of the precious fluid as he thrust it away from his face again, overwhelmed by the strong scent of cloves and peppers. He recapped it and stumbled forward, limping as he went back to the yard and found the clothes he dropped when he was attacked. They were right where he'd left them, and muddy now as added insult. He was nearly immobilized with soreness but he had work to do yet. He leaned down to grab the bundle of clothes, then rose again with a cry as his ribs shifted against each other in protest. It had been a long night and it wasn't over yet. Chores had to be done, regardless of his condition.

## 4 – Hunting

"Deep and drowsy was the sleep on my poor body fell."
Child Ballad 39: Tam Lin

Tam kneed his horse across the shallow stream, his hips low as he was taught, reins tight in his gloved hand. He needed the horse to learn his signals, but his ribs were still painful and his bruises weren't healed yet, so he jumped down periodically, to walk stiffly, giving his body a break from the rocking motion of the horse's stride. Fortunately his uncle was preoccupied and didn't notice the occasional wince and limp.

The pain failed to cut through his euphoria as he remembered the quick ceremony that had lifted him from squire to knight that morning. Lord Douglas had insisted, stating that Tam's suitability for the mission was the very reason he deserved the honor, but the early hour and secret mission required it to be a simple affair. Lord Dunbar had assured him that some men became knights with no more than a touch on the forehead on a battlefield, but he still felt cheated of a vigil or sermon on the virtues of a proper knight. He was assured there would be a more public ceremony once the current objective was achieved, but for now it was enough to know he had been lifted to the station he'd desired all his life.

"Hush!" Dunbar hissed, and Tam dropped his reins. The horse recognized the signal and dropped a lifted hoof then stood stock-still at the edge of the stream, eyes rolling as he tried to see what danger might lurk in the shadows around them. When the horse started chewing at the bit Tam slapped his neck to draw his attention, then caressed him gently when he was quiet. "Good boy," he whispered, continuing to rub the great, heavily muscled neck as he watched his uncle draw a long arrow silently from the rawhide quiver and knock it to the huge bow. It took a highly experienced archer to use a longbow from the saddle and Tam watched, fascinated at Lord Dunbar's form. He held the bow at a wide diagonal. There must be a deer in the thicket beyond but Tam couldn't see it from where he sat. The shadows had grown long in the cool evening. The wagons were far behind them by now, it was just the two of them along with the woodland chatter and Tam watched his uncle's steady grip, thumb to his ear as he leaned far to the right side of his mount, assuring the bowstring was well away from the animal. Slowly the fingers released the sinew, and the arrow was launched through the air. Something moved in the bush beyond just as the fingers uncurled and the arrow missed its mark, as evidenced by the furious crash of a body through the underbrush. "Stay with me, Tam, it's on the run!"

Tam jumped onto his horse, lifted the reins and urged the gelding to a gallop, following his uncle through the woods. Pain faded into exhilaration and he had to focus his mind on the task at hand; watch for the leaping deer ahead, listen for his uncle's commands, and stay on the horse. His spirit soared as his legs gripped the heaving sides of the beast, and he rejoiced as Lord Dunbar let out a hunting whoop and crashed through the brush ahead of him. It was a good day!

The deer increased its lead and Lord Dunbar slowed, then stopped. Tam looked at him, confused.

"Are you alright, sir?" He hadn't seen the horse stagger, but he couldn't fathom any other reason to stop the hunt when mercy required that they put an injured animal down quickly.

Lord Dunbar swung his leg over the barrel of his horse and dropped to the ground, motioning Tam to do the same, holding Honor's reins securely in his gloved fist as the two men walked toward each other.

"This is it, Tam. I need to leave you here. We've been followed, and this is our chance to lure them in."

Tam stood for a moment, still confused. "But what about the deer?"

Lord Dunbar shook his head. "My arrow flew over it, just close enough to startle it. The deer was never wounded, it was an excuse to have us get far ahead of the wagons yet leave a trail that can't be missed. I'll circle back with my men while the enemy is distracted with you."

This had to be it. Of course. Much farther and they'd be in the next town.

"Are you ready, laddie?" The big Scot asked, anxiously. "I don't know when we'll get a better shot. Are you up to it?"

The man's eyes measured him up, and Tam nodded. "I'm ready, my Lord! May God bring them down upon me. But can you take my horse?"

His uncle chuckled. "That's thinking like a true knight, always others first even down to your horse. But no. If you send your horse away they'll know something's wrong; you're too good a man to be separated from the beast. You'll have to keep yourself free until we get back to you, lad. It won't be long, I assure you." The man peered at Tam. "Pretend to be asleep and they'll not have to fight you. You might be safer that way. We'll be back swiftly; what we want is to take them by surprise. If they feel they have time to assess the situation, it might give us more time to circle around."

Tam reached into his saddlebags to pull out his cloak. He worried about how Honor would be treated if the enemy took him. Tam stretched out his heavy, oiled plaid on a pile of leaves under one of the trees and tried to keep his nerves from jangling as he prepared to fight whoever came for him.

"Good lad," his uncle said, then gave him one last swift embrace before leaping up onto the back of his own huge horse, pressing the beast forward with a good kick, and Tam watched them thunder away through the trees. Suddenly a deep weariness came over him from a restless night due to the pain of his recent injuries. Fearing the pain would prevent him from defending himself, his hands sought the small vial Philip had given him, desperate for relief. He pulled the small cylinder from a padded pouch. Looked at it curiously, then tilted it until he felt several drops fall onto his tongue. He capped what remained, then lay down on his cloak. He decided on a minimum dose until he knew how it affected him.

He pulled a corner of the cloak over himself as if he were just taking a quick nap. Would they fall for it? His head began to swim as he realized how powerful the potion was. He struggled to keep his eyes open, but soon lost the battle. In moments he drifted into a dreamless sleep.

## 5 – Abducted

*"Then by it came the Elfin Queen, and laid her hand on me; And from that time since ever I mind, I've been in her companie." Child Ballad 39: Tam Lin*

Tam woke as hands grabbed his arms and legs, bringing the memory of the recent attack flooding into his mind, and he tried to launch himself to the side, hoping to escape. He felt as if the world tilted as a flash of bright light blinded him. Something grabbed his boot and yanked him backwards, but he rolled over and kicked. For a moment his leg was free, then a man fell on the lower half of his body. He tried to pull an arm free but he was still weak from the potion, and the two men at his shoulders had his arms behind his back. He continued to struggle but they trussed him up much like the other men had done before, though the ropes were only at his wrists and ankles this time, his knees still had freedom to move separately. He tried to shake a strange, fuzzy feeling from his head as they unbuckled his sword belt and relieved him of his weapons, even the short dagger he kept in a sheath on his boot for throwing. Damn! He'd hoped to give a good accounting for himself, at least.

Furious with himself for falling asleep, he resigned himself to a humiliating defeat. Lord Dunbar would have to overcome them to get him away. What could he expect from the enemy until then? Would they take care to leave him alive and free of permanent injury? Being trussed rather than unconscious was a good sign, at least.

They wrapped him in his cloak then threw him over the back of his horse, pulling his arms down on one side and his feet on the other, to tie his wrists uncomfortably to his ankles under Honor's belly, who carried him from the scene of his capture. There was no blindfold over his eyes so he took the opportunity to look at his captors as best he could. The nondescript men wore odd clothing; loose black silken tunic and wide trews under tabards that undoubtedly covered chain mail. Who wore silk in the forest? English dandies, he supposed. He didn't recognize the design on their tabards, which surprised him; he'd studied all the houses on the British Isle and he was sure he'd never seen this one. Of course, his uncle had been clear; those that followed were the enemy. But what nation were these men from? He had expected to see recognizable English styling. Worry ate at his belly; who were these men?

On the long ride through the forest Tam had plenty of time to think, but nothing to think of. He prepared for an attack but none had come, beyond the fact of his capture. Should he speak?

"Hey, swine," he yelled at the men in front of him, but there was no answer. "How about you, you filthy oafs?" He called out to the two men at the rear, but they said nothing. "Can someone get me some water?" he continued. "How about a nice bottle of wine?" Nothing. "Your wives? I'm due for a good dip in the favors of lesser men." No response. He had to get filthier, which he found extremely distasteful. He tried to put the thought of his sainted mother and his dear sisters from his mind as he stepped up his game, recalling the foul language he heard the other squires use while their charges were slowly wasting themselves at a feast. "Hey flat-top, where's your sister? She was delightful last night. A man can't buy lips like that, and I rose to the occasion—" He heard a light clop of hooves increase in pace. Out of the corner of his eye he saw a delicate arm make an abrupt gesture, and a man kneed his horse to come even with Tam, then kicked him in the head, stunning him for a moment. Tam tasted blood and found that he'd bitten his tongue. He continued. "What was her name? Mary?" The man kicked him again, quite hard, knocking him senseless this time.

Tam's head throbbed when he regained consciousness. He was being pulled down from Honor's back and he felt sick as he tried to shift upright again, struggling against the pain from the cracked rib. As he rose, he leaned into the horse, his legs tingling from the long, uncomfortable ride. He gained what courage he could from his contact with the gentle steed he'd known for just a few months now. "Where are we?" he asked, not expecting an answer, but a lady stepped down from a slender riding horse to his left and he swung his head around to look at her, regretting the sudden motion. She was dark skinned, her hair pinned up under a small, lacy hat. She wore an ornate bejeweled gown of the palest silver over a white silken chemise with yards of lace at her throat, over which sat a torc that hung from a delicate chain. Several charms shaped like men hung from the torc. Intricately jeweled brooches were pinned to each breast. He recalled several gowns just like it, worn by English ladies, but much brighter in color. The men snapped to attention as she appeared so she had to be their superior. He watched her move and marveled at how her skin was the color of deep, muddy water, darker even than his own had become when he grew into manhood. He once asked his mother if there were Moors in their lineage, but she just laughed and told him that he spent too much time in the sun since he became a squire. He accepted the explanation, though he wondered that the other boys seemed pale from the waist down, while he was the color of milky tea over every inch of his body.

"Tam," she said. "It's good to meet you." She held her hand out, and he took it gently to kiss, as a gentleman ought to when meeting a lady, despite his misgivings. She smiled. "I've looked forward to this day."

Tam frowned. This wasn't what he expected at all. "I'm sorry, milady, I'm at a loss. Do I know you?"

"Not yet, my love, but I look forward to correcting that omission. My name is Morgan and I'm your mother."

Tam stared at her. He knew his mother well and she was pale skinned like his father. Like he was as a child. Her eyes, though, were wide and dark, like his own, and her brows were straight lines across her forehead, just like his as well. His mother and father both had arched brows. They'd told him he must have a great-grandfather with such brows, but never saw a single portrait to match. Both the shade of her skin and the shape of her eyes were a match for his own; this woman, though, was barely older than himself, if that. Even if he'd thought himself adopted, she wasn't of sufficient age to be his mother.

He thought it best not to point out the obvious flaw in her deceit, but he couldn't allow such a claim to stand. "My mother is many leagues from here. What makes you think you and I are related, my lady?"

"Because I gave birth to you, my child, then placed you in the crib while your mother slept, removing her own child so that she would raise you as her own. I cast a spell on you to look as she expected but it fades with time, and you have come into your true features over the years."

Tam stared at her, speechless. Of all the things Lord Douglas had lectured him to expect, this never come up. It was, however, the first story he'd heard that explained why his skin had darkened, unbelievable as it was. Stories of Changelings were just fictions women told to explain strange children; more likely the result of adultery. But how had she known he was born light skinned? Why did she have enough interest in him to know him both as a child and now that he was living at Lord Douglas's keep? "Does my father know?" he asked her quizzically, buying time as he tried to figure out why she abducted him and who she was.

She laughed. "Oh, he surely remembers our dalliance, I would be hard for such a man to forget, but no, I never said a word to him about you." She leaned toward him and whispered, "It's our secret, Tam! None of your people know it."

Tam realized they stood outside a walled tower. Where had the structure come from? This was just a clearing in the woods a moment ago.

Tam's thoughts raced, and he pieced his knowledge together. "Why have you been spying on Lord Douglas' keep?"

"We were watching for an opportunity to bring you back home, my dear."

Tam released a sharp burst of air. This was going nowhere. He abandoned the deceit. "My lady, I'm afraid I need to leave and get back to where you found me."

She looked shocked. "Oh, no, you can't go back! No, Tam, you're with me now. This is your new home, and, humble as it is, it is far superior to where I found you. I apologize that we've had to restrain you, but it often takes time for a changeling to understand his true place in the world. My son, don't you understand? I only left you with them so they could raise you; that's not something we do well. But I never intended for you to stay with them, they're far too primitive. There is work for you to do. You'll come with me; I'll explain more inside. This beastly outdoors is dreadful. I don't wish to remain here any longer than we must."

The men had him surrounded since they arrived, he couldn't escape. He'd been captured, but the English didn't seem to be involved; her accent wasn't British. It was foreign in an unfamiliar way. This woman seemed to command them, but she was out of her mind to think he was her son. Perhaps she saw him in a tournament and noticed he had similar features to her own, then decided she wanted him for whatever reason. Young ladies assailed him at every event, to his distress, though their intentions were nothing like that of a parent. This was going to be awkward.

He could see now the tower that rose up beyond the high walls where a portcullis rose, across the bridge from where they stood. He noticed how rapid the river ran as it curved around the wall. He shook his head, wondering how he was just seeing this now; the knock to his head must have been harder than he thought. The guards were pushing him forward over the bridge but he took a moment to assess the structure for vulnerability. Perhaps siege towers could work on the side and the back—

He felt the guards that were right up against each side of him go stiff. The lady had gestured for them to stop. "Come with me, Tam, let the men take care of your horse. I'll show you where you'll be staying."

"For how long, my lady?"

She looked surprised. "Forever! Unless we move. I've just rescued you from a dreary life, Tam, you should be grateful. Oh, I suppose you know nothing yet of who you are, where you come from, or the great destiny you'll fulfill."

Two more guards flanked him while another led his horse away. Even if he overcame them the mounted guards would run him down within fifty paces. He would bide his time and find a better opportunity. The men apparently considered him more of a threat than the lady did; they wouldn't disobey her, but they took great care to keep him immobilized. She may prefer to treat him as a guest rather than a captive, but he was under no such illusion that the guards would do the same.

As he passed under the portcullis he assessed the small yard; stables to the right, garden to the left, nine wide stone steps and a huge set of wooden doors. She swept up the steps and the doors opened, letting out a strange glow. Someone must have been watching for her. He followed her in as many of her people peeled away to take the wagon to the stables or around the side of the tower; he heard the portcullis closing behind them.

The grand entry here and the great hall she showed him into was half the size of Lord Douglas's. There were two sets of doors on either side, and tables down the middle. She turned around with a wide smile, beckoning him with one hand. Tam scoffed. "I need to get back to Ettrick Forest, my lady. They are expecting me there."

She scowled. "Tam, there are insects out there."

Tam realized the place was empty of flies, gnats, and mosquitos, or insects of any sort. It baffled him. As he stepped into the eerily bright room, he smelled a fresh sharp scent coming from the candles that were lit along the walls. It seemed far brighter inside than candles alone should make it, with no windows, but he found nothing to explain that.

"Come, I'll show you to your room. I'm sure you'd like to rest."

Having little choice, he followed her. "My lady, you said you would explain. Perhaps now would be a good time for that?"

She looked at him and placed a hand on his arm. "If you insist. You have been raised by humans. We're not human. And you are my son, a half human. I've simply brought you back to where you belong."

Half human? And half what? This abduction was becoming quite frustrating, with no valid reason given. Where were the lords to oversee his captivity? Surely they intended to interrogate him. He was only known to be a squire, publicly, and all this trouble for a squire made no sense, especially if he wasn't to be questioned about the placement and tactics of the Scottish defense. A squire wouldn't be expected to know much, but surely they intended to find out all he knew. He watched her carefully; the dark skin was really the only thing different about her, but he knew others with skin as dark. She led him a few paces past the stair to a room that had a bed with a canopy, a footlocker at the end of it, and two windows with heavy curtains, a small washstand sitting in one corner. She beamed at him. It was much better quarters than he'd known since becoming a squire and joined the barracks. Squires had no privacy until they were raised to knight, then reclaimed their heritage. With Sir Gregor serving Lord Douglas directly while masons built his own manor house, Tam slept with the servants. His father might grant him lands from the family estate someday, but Tam preferred the camaraderie of his peers and took his duty to watch over the younger boys quite seriously. He was accustomed to lodging with boys and men of various ages, seeing to the care of the younger ones and doing as the older ones told him to. A loneliness struck him as he looked around, facing the prospect of a night with no other voices, no scuffles to break up, no late-night arrivals or early morning departures by boys and men with various duties at all hours.

A man appeared in the door, Tam's saddlebags and bedroll in one arm and his sword in the other. "Your highness, shall I secure the sword in the armory?" he handed the bags and bedroll to Tam.

"That's my grandfather's sword! The sheath as well. And the belt I won in my first tournament. My lady, I object to my personal belongings becoming common property!"

"That's quite alright, Tam, I'll see that the sword is secured for you, and you can have the belt as long as there are no weapons on it. Tam, this is my captain of the guard." The captain bowed briefly to Tam, tucking the arm carrying the sword behind him first, and Tam nodded in return. As a nobleman he outranked the captain of the guard, but the man's deference clearly didn't include subservience.

"I would prefer the sword where I can see it, my lady," Tam prodded.

Morgan raised an eyebrow and the captain said, "I believe I can see that the sword is secured within his eyesight." He bowed again to Morgan, turned on his heel and strode out the door with the valuable weapon.

She looked at Tam, saying, "Well, I'll let you get your things put away," and she turned and left as well. That would only take a few seconds, thought Tam, as he walked to the foot of the bed and dropped everything into the chest.

## 6 – Captive

"And pleasant is the fairy land, but, an eerie tale to tell . . ." Child Ballad 39: Tam Lin

Tam lay staring up at the ceiling and considered his situation. His sword had been shackled high on the wall of the great hall below him, higher than he could reach but visible as promised; at least no harm had come to it. He made sure they cared for his horse as well and that Honor had a suitable stall. The strangeness of the place became more familiar; it looked like another nobleman's keep from the outside, though there were strange devices within. But he needed to find an exit.

The sleek wall around the tower was high and thick, flaring at its base, with a river surging around much of the structure. If Lord Dunbar had come after him, it would be hard to breech the defenses. Tam would have to get beyond the walls and seek those who sought him.

There was a quiet tap at the door and he whirled, reaching for a blade that should be at his hip.

An elderly balding man in silver robes stepped in, looking disdainfully at Tam's hand as it hung over his thigh, reaching in vain for a sword that wasn't there. Tam dropped his arms to his sides with chagrin.

"The lady would like to have you join her for dinner in the lesser hall. Do you need anything?" The colorless man asked.

Tam searched his memory to picture the layout of the floor below them. "That's aye the hall below, with the portrait of a lion in gilded chains by the fireplace?"

The man's long, wispy eyebrows rose, but his eyes remained lidded. "Yes, my lord. That's the one."

Tam looked around the room. "I have nearly everything I need," his eyes turned floorward, as if he could stare through the wood plans and see the great hall below. "I'll just be having you bring the sword to me?" He looked up at the man's face.

The man shook his head with contempt.

"Then I'll take what I'm allowed." Tam frowned. "How do I control the light?"

The man raised a hand and pressed it against a gold sigil on the wall next to the door, and the room darkened, then he turned and waited for Tam.

He followed the man from the room, tapping the sigil as he went; the room lightened again.

In the hall, Morgan sat across from him at a small table. "Are you finding your room comfortable enough?"

"It's quite comfortable."

She asked him many questions about himself but gave cryptic replies to his own questions, a scene that would repeat daily. He chafed at the solitude between meals that offered no companionship and kept his answers short.

"Why am I here, my lady?" he asked yet again one evening.

She sighed. "Your duty is to provide another generation of offspring. Our young women have been notified that it is time for them to come to you so we can replenish our population." She tore a piece of bread from the small round in front of her and used it to pluck a piece of meat she'd cut from the chicken sitting on her plate.

Tam's hand stopped halfway to his mouth, the drumstick hanging in midair as he stared at her. "I beg pardon? Are you saying I'm to marry one of your lasses?"

Morgan laughed, the delicate sound ringing pleasantly off the near wall. "Oh no, you are not meant to marry, Tam. Not among us; marriage is for humans, though you're half that. But you will have... a series of... concubines then. Enough to keep you quite happy. Surely you seek concubines? I understand it is a tradition among men."

Tam lowered the piece of chicken, still staring at her. She seemed to be toying with him, which made him angry. She held him captive but treated him as a guest. What did this conceit gain her?

"I'm to be put to stud, my lady?"

She smiled. "Yes, Tam. That's why you exist. We need to breed back into the human population periodically or inbreeding causes the bodies of our newborns to return to our original form, which is adapted to our homeworld, not yours. You were produced to bring human traits back into our bloodlines, because humans are native to this world." Her eyes were bright, as if he should be delighted. Well, he could see the allure of a steady stream of young women.

"Is this a problem for you?" Her gaze landed on his shoulders, then his waist, then dropped below it, with a worried look.

"God be damned, woman!" Tam snapped, then closed his eyes and breathed for a moment. He drew his hand from shoulder to shoulder then forehead to navel. He opened his eyes again to level his dark gaze at her. "Where on earth have you come from that such a proposition seems acceptable?"

"Not from earth," she answered bluntly.

Tam sat without moving as she told him she had come down from the heavens. Not Heaven, she was clear; heavens, as if there were more than one. She mentioned stars but he knew that the only thing beyond the stars was Heaven, singular. And she claimed that her home was in the stars, not beyond them. She persisted in this strange conceit that her people were not humans, yet they must reproduce with humans, namely himself, and she would see that these ladies were brought to him. Which made her no angel. Was she charging someone for his services? Or was it something more mythological? He thought he remembered his great-uncle telling him a story about Roman gods mating with human women, but he couldn't quite remember if the discussion had actually happened or he'd just dreamt it.

"So, you're not human?" He said finally, when she had finished saying much and nothing.

She rolled her eyes. "Oh come now, Tam, this is a simple thing to understand. I'm Satan."

He froze in place. "I beg your pardon?" He listened intently to her answer.

"I'm Sh'eytan," she said again, and he heard the subtle difference in pronunciation that allowed him to continue this discussion. She hadn't said what he thought, but he still struggled to make sense of her actual words.

He searched his memory for a people with such a name. He tried to piece all her statements together as if he were wrestling with a blacksmith's puzzle, but the whole story just twisted in his mind, refusing to come together. He shook his head; this was ludicrous. He needed time alone to figure out her game. He rose to his feet. "May I be excused, my lady?"

She looked down at his plate, then back up at his face with concern. "Tam! You've barely touched your food. Are you feeling ill? I'm told humans need more nourishment than I've seen you take."

"I don't seem to have an appetite." He thought quickly. "It's the inactivity, I think. I need to exercise. I'm accustomed to practicing with weapons, wrestling, and taking my horse for long gallops across the moors. Sitting around all day, I can't work up an appetite. Is it possible for me to do something more strenuous? Could that be arranged?" He named activities that would give him a chance to get away from this place.

"Oh," she said, "Of course! You've been separated from your usual activities, and it has put you out of sorts. I've read about this kind of malaise. I'll talk with my captain and see what we can do." She smiled at him.

After a brief discussion with the captain, Tam was allowed to take Honor out for exercise with guards at his side and given a weighted, padded cane for sparring with the guards to the side of the garden. The captain insisted that he must not make any attempt to go beyond the edges of the glen; his entire realm was the narrow valley between two low ridges. Four men would guard him as he went, and he pushed Honor to see how fast their horses were, but he couldn't outpace them.

He spent hours a day wrestling and sparring with the uniformly nondescript men that made up Morgan's guard. There were usually several that seemed to be milling about, and the Captain allowed him to exercise with them as long as there were no visitors and the portcullis was down, so Tam made a point of testing their strength and fighting skills, which were formulaic, and he would best them easily if it weren't for their tirelessness. Tam was accustomed to being one of the strongest and fastest young men in any pell-yard, so it came as a surprise to him, but soon he was holding his own, at least, against the strangely silent warriors.

Tam stepped back and twisted sideways, then feinted to the left before slinging his elbow at the solid man's head, and the move was blocked but it gave Tam an opening to connect a swift kick with the man's shin. Most men would have bellowed at the pain, but he fought in complete silence and threw a fist at Tam's lower back before stepping out of the way of Tam's next blow.

Stripped to the waist, Tam sweated as he sparred, but kept going for another two hours. The man never spoke, never sweated, never took his shirt off. The men's tactics were identical to each other. He remembered hearing of twins that fought identically, but there were at least four of these men, and Tam could find no difference at all in their styles.

He went out daily to exercise his horse and become familiar with the area, and realized he recognized a line of blackthorn bushes. The rowan tree at the end seemed like the very same one his distant uncle's daughter, Janet, had climbed when he and his brothers had come crashing through the brush, attacking each other with new wooden swords they received as gifts from their great-uncle when the Scots crowned their new king. She surprised them by dropping out of the tree and yanking a large stick from the ground to join in the fun. What a day that had been! The thought of the girl with such brazen strength and vigor brought a smile. She was surely tormenting young men with her tempestuous self-confidence by now.

He found it strange, though, that day after day he rode out and returned without seeing a single man, a deer, or even any trace of them. The tower seemed to exist in a shadow world like that of the Sidhe, the treacherous faeries that would steal a man away and force him to dance to their music, sometimes killing him with exhaustion and leaving him back in his own world, his body to be found by his family. But there'd been no dancing as of yet.

Every evening the lady sat across from the table from him and watched him as he ate, asking how his exercises had gone. All day long he did what he could to maintain his strength and training, but none of the men would say more than yes or no when he asked questions. He had everything he needed except companionship. Until the day the lady provided that as well.

# 7 – Purpose

> "There's nane that gaes by Carter Hall but they leave him a wad, either their rings, or green mantles, or else their maidenhead."
> Child Ballad 39: Tam Lin

"Tam, come meet our guests," Morgan said to him one afternoon as he sat in the manuscript room to study the strange texts he found there. He followed Morgan into the great hall where two delicately dressed and perfumed young women entered the room, measuring him up quite openly.

"Come, Tam, the ladies have come a great distance to meet with you," Morgan admonished.

Tam looked at the woman who claimed to be his mother but seemed to have no understanding of the relationship, then he looked at the younger women. No names were offered, and they didn't raise a hand toward him in greeting, they just stared at him as if he were a shopkeeper and they expected him to show them his wares.

He'd sat in a manuscript room all afternoon, now suddenly he had to navigate a very odd introduction, and Tam felt a bit dizzy as he looked into the deep blue eyes of the paler one with blonde ringlets escaping from under her silken hat. Who on earth were these Sh'eyta? Did he need to teach them how to be properly introduced? He turned toward the two young women and bowed slightly, unsure of their rank; they were dressed, coifed and perfumed as noblewomen but they offered no titles. "Ladies, you may call me Tam."

They each gave their names but he was watching their eyes and their lips. Both were lovely young lasses, and he found himself captivated by their lilting voices as they all sat down to dinner together. They asked him about his profession as a knight in training (his knighthood not yet a matter of record) and took great interest in hearing how he handled armor and trained his horse. He was sure he drank the wine only moderately, but it wasn't long before his head was swimming.

The next morning he found himself in bed naked, the covers askew. He wished he could recall the evening better because it had ended quite well for him. He remembered the dark exotic eyes of the black-haired lass. What was the name she gave him? He looked around the room and sat up abruptly. She was gone, but he knew he remembered her being there. Between her sweet perfume, plump bosoms, and the strong wine, he did exactly what Morgan had said he must. All in all, he couldn't complain, really; as bidden tasks go, it was a pleasant one. He rose to his feet and found that the pitcher was full of water and a waxy bar with a light cedar scent sat next to the basin. In a few minutes he felt somewhat refreshed and ready to face the world again.

"Ah, there you are," Morgan greeted him, beaming as he came down the stone steps into the lesser hall. "Will you be completing your obligations today? I would have preferred you saw them both last night—"

"Good grief, woman! Would you have the decency to at least pretend you know nothing of my fornication?" He turned toward her.

"But Tam, that's why you're here! We need a healthy, intelligent man to sire this generation. Come. Take Gruoch to bed and be done with it—"

"You can't give me orders to bed a woman," Tam said, aghast. "It's an abomination! A man makes his own choice in such matters!"

She gave him a shocked look, then patted his shoulder. "Oh, that will be fine. You send for her when you're ready then. But don't wait too long or I'll have to put you under compulsion again. It's such a bother!"

Tam grimaced in frustration as he considered her words. Compulsion? Had she done something to him? He felt embattled, but not in a way he could fight against. He didn't understand why she believed he was her son, nor why he was required to mate with the women she brought him, but she was relentless. He longed for a simpler imprisonment. Where were his real captors? When would they speak of his ransom? And why on earth was this fey woman foisting lasses on him—

His blood ran cold. Fey. Sidhe. Sh'eyta. Satan. The words repeated in his head, and he kept staring at her as pieces of the puzzle fell into place. He recognized the similarities between this place and that of the Faeries, the Sidhe, and why it had seemed like he was beyond a veil, in some unreal kingdom where one could walk the same earth as another man and the two not see each other. Why there were no deer in these woods and no sign of people even though he recognized the very trees he rode under and the tower he slept in. Could it be that he was in the underworld of the Sidhe, the Faeries? He hadn't believed in them since he was old enough to wield a sword. The stories said they were wicked creatures, no better than demons. Horror drew every nerve taut as he wondered if what Morgan had told him could be true; that these were no humans. If so, he knew no way to get back to his own world until they were done with him. And they wouldn't be done with him until he damned himself to hell doing their bidding. He'd already done it! He'd consorted with the Fey. With a sinking feeling he looked into her eyes and realized Lord Dunbar would never find him; he was no longer in Scotland proper, and he was far from safe. He recalled again the tales of the Sidhe commanding humans to dance, and the hapless humans did as they were told, unable to stop until they died of exhaustion. The dance had begun.

## 8 – Bring Me A Priest

"O I hae been at gude church-door, an I've got christendom;" Child Ballad 39: Tam Lin

Tam stared at Morgan's dark face as his mind raced. He began to doubt his conclusion. "I'd heard the Sidhe were tiny creatures, and pale as frost. Why are you such an unseemly color?"

He felt a strange, feathery touch in his head and her image wavered like a reflection in a rippled pond, then she appeared in perfect stillness, but with skin like alabaster. "I told you we can change appearances. If you like, I'll inform the ladies you prefer pale skin; they can appear however you wish. As for me, I prefer not to bother with the artifice. We're a dark-skinned people, and taller than your species." Her image wavered and her skin turned dark again.

"But your height…"

"Really, Tam? Yes. In the past many of my people thought to appear small so they didn't appear threatening. I assumed your warrior training would prevent you from feeling too threatened."

Tam took a deep breath and tried to still the pounding of his heart. The "wee folk" had powers beyond man's reckoning. He wondered if the strange feeling in his head was related. He felt as if he almost understood what had happened in his mind. That was where her spells were cast.

He stopped his thoughts. This didn't matter. His need to escape mattered. What could he use against her? What were her weaknesses? She claimed not to be human, and the more he spoke with her the more he felt that her knowledge of humans seemed limited to broad generalities. If it were true that she wasn't human, and he was right that she had an inaccurate view of humans, perhaps she underestimated people. By her words, she considered them little better than beasts. And sometimes she expected him to behave like she thought a human should, sometimes like herself. If she were Fae, and underestimated him, he might feign an expected human weakness and slip under her guard to get away. Also, the Sidhe had no defense against anything holy. He grimaced. He had nothing in his possession that was holy. And no way to get to a church.

Well, if he couldn't go to church perhaps the church could come to him. The Sidhe were adept at capturing humans, obviously. He took a deep breath. "My lady, I cannot fulfill this responsibility you've given me unless I can see a priest. I must be able to confess my sins."

She folded her arms and tilted her head toward him.

He squared his shoulders and spoke adamantly. "You must know this about humans; the only fate we consider worse than death is condemnation to Hell. If I must commit a sin, I must cleanse my soul, and for this I need a priest."

Tapping an elbow with her fingers she sat silently for some time. "I will allow it, but you will be guarded; do not attempt to leave the glen." A slight breeze traced his arms as she turned away swiftly. A wave of relief followed the chill of her departure. Yes, the safety of his soul required it, not that she would agree. But more importantly, the Sidhe couldn't abide the presence of the clergy, and he would find a way to make that work in his favor.

The following day the captain led him to the edge of a clearing, near the blackthorn hedge and the rowan tree that reminded him of young Janet. A shadow of a building stood on the left side of the field, but the captain led him straight to the Rowan on the far edge of the meadow and dismounted, gesturing at Tam to do the same. He felt a shift, the air flashed brightly, and suddenly a man in black robes stood in front of him. A part of him felt as if he almost understood how the shift occurred; if only he could feel it again. He thought about the feeling it had given him—

"Are you no longer in need of a priest?" the captain's voice was sharp and he lost his memory of the strange sensation. He tried to reach for it again but found nothing there. He came back to his senses and saw a priest standing in front of him. He lowered himself to his knees and bowed his head. "Forgive me father, for I have sinned."

The priest was silent for a moment and Tam looked up to see him looking around in wonder and muttering. "The tree is quite the same here, but it seems to be summer." The captain directed the man's attention to Tam. The robed man jumped. "Where did you come from?"

Tam realized his request had put the man in danger. "I apologize, father, I should not have asked you to come. I felt the need of a priest, but…"

The priest shook himself, then turned to glare at the captain before stepping forward. "Then I have work to do." He looked around once more, then cleared his throat and stood up taller. "What do you need, my son?"

"I have sinned—"

"Do you have a rosary?"

Tam shook his head. "I am in need of one, Father. I've been brought to a strange place and I have nothing to protect me."

The priest cast a questioning glance at the Captain, who said, "He is in our care. We will do him no harm." This seemed to be enough for the priest, who drew his own rosary over his head and handed it to Tam. "My son, you have more need of this than I." Tam was dismayed by the priest's quick acceptance of the captain's words. Did he have some sort of bargain with the Sidhe? Could he be trusted?

Hiding his misgivings, Tam reached for the circlet of beads and the silver cross that dangled from it, and the priest's hands closed over his as he took it. He listened in awe as the man instructed him to recite a prayer and bade him repent.

"But Father, this must be strange to you," Tam said, determined to know what justification the priest might give for his complacency.

The man looked at his feet, nodding. "God's ways are unknown to us. Wherever I find myself, it is my duty to serve God."

"But why—"

"I am not here to answer your questions," he interrupted. "Go, and sin no more."

"But they've ordered me to…" Tam's voice trailed off as he realized he couldn't keep such a promise.

The man raised an eyebrow. His voice was unsteady as he replied. "I have done what you asked. I expect to be returned to where I belong. If I am summoned again, we will speak" Finally his shoulders dropped. "It is my own penance that I must come if I am called. Long ago, when I was a foolish young acolyte, I believed myself immortal and tested myself against the fae. The released me only because I vowed to stay near and come if summoned. The lady had questions..." he said with a shiver. The man eyed the captain as he stepped backwards, away from them both. The captain gave a slight nod and the priest's robes swirled as he left. Tam watched, mouth agape, as the world tilted and the air shimmered. He was alone with the captain again.

Could he trust a priest that seemed to be in league with the devil? He looked at the pile of beads in his hands and rubbed a finger over the cross reverently, then lifted them over his head.

He went cold from head to toe as he realized how completely the captain had controlled the entire exchange. Recalling the priest's wariness, he was sure the man feared the captain. With all his holy powers, the priest feared the Sidhe. He clutched the rosary, but fear crept into him as he wondered if it could protect him at all. If it could, the captain would have denied it.

He recalled the way the air grew bright and the world suddenly shifted. He felt dizzy.

"Stop that!" The captain shouted and struck him across the jaw. Tam's arm swung automatically toward his foe, but he had to lurch backwards as the blade of the captain's dagger came up between them and two of the guards pulled him to the ground. The captain stepped forward and looked as if he was going to kick Tam, but he stopped himself with a growl. "I'll remind you that Commander Morgan ordered you to obey me. You are not allowed to control the passage between worlds. She gives you too much freedom, you ungrateful wretch. My people have need of you or I'd drop you in the deepest well. You have no honor! No sense of responsibility. Get up!" The guards released him and he rose to his feet. "The veil is locked to humans, no passage is allowed unless I myself command it. Neither the priest, nor soldiers, guards, noblemen or peasants. No mere human men!"

The captain's vehemence intrigued Tam; for some reason he'd commanded Tam not to open the passage himself. He was lumped in with "human men," in spite of Morgan's insistence that Tam was of the Sidhe. The captain didn't seem to think so, though he'd revealed that he believed Tam was capable of opening the passage. It must be related to the moment when Tam recalled the shifting sensation, which had been immediately followed by that same shifting sensation. He tried again to feel what he felt when the world had shifted, but the captain clouted him with the heel of the dagger and knocked him senseless.

He awoke in his room. He recalled his attempt to open the passage and reached for the sensation, then the walls of his room wavered as he felt weightless, and the bed disappeared from under him. He grabbed for the wall and prayed it was solid; the room steadied around him. This told him two things: when he tried to practice opening the passageway, he could do it, but he should be on solid ground first. The thought of finding himself in the air as the walls and floor of the tower disappeared terrified him. Realizing he just remembered the same thing without the effect, he wondered what the difference was. Sensation; if he just remembered that it happened, there was nothing. If he tried to remember what it felt like, the world turned upside down. He marveled at this newfound ability; on the one hand, he was dismayed to find that faeries and magick were real. On the other, it seemed he had some of that magick. He thought of how he might use it on the battlefield. Not the list field, or during games; he didn't need to expose himself as kin to the devil. Thoughts of causing men, or even battalions, to disappear took up the rest of his afternoon, and he wondered if it had to be in certain locations, or could he do it anywhere. He heard the doors between worlds only occurred along ley lines, and were strongest where the lines met.

God save him, did this mean he was really half Sidhe?

That evening he ignored the rap on his door at the normal time for the evening meal, and the old servant's face appeared as the door creaked open.

"It's Roscoe, my lord. Will you be coming to dinner?"

Tam realized it must be late by the angle of the sun. "Nay, Roscoe, but thank you, I have a headache and I'd rather rest." Tam looked for any sign that his status had changed, but the slender grey man's face bore no expression at all.

"Shall I bring you a plate then, sir?"

Tam nodded. When it came, it bore little meat and a great deal of root vegetables and cooked greens with onions. Perhaps he would only eat meat if he joined the others. Well enough, then. He still felt a bit nauseous from the blow the captain gave him, and he chewed carefully while continuing to parse the strange book-like object he'd lifted from the manuscript room. He opened it, and the single, glassy surface, like a polished obsidian tablet, showed the very text where he'd left off, but it was written in the strange symbols again. He placed his hand on the page, hoping to see words he could read, and the words changed into English; as he read, he traced the text with a finger and the lines of text moved slowly up the page so that new lines appeared at the bottom of the page, just like before. He had no idea what made the magic work, but he intended to understand these creatures by any means he could. He bit into the starchy bulb of another turnip, wiping his fingers on the square cloth he used to wash his face before gently sliding the text upward with a finger. It seemed to be a history of sorts. Perhaps it would tell him how to kill them.

## 9 – Control

"I had to stop him from crossing back into his own world." The captain stood at attention in the sparsely adorned room.

"But you DID stop him, did you not?" Morgan tapped a finger against her elbow as she paced, arms folded. "As long as he is with you, you will prevent him from any attempt to escape."

"When he is on foot he can be outrun, but his horse is another matter. It's surprisingly swift for such a muscular breed."

Morgan crooked a brow at him as he considered his complaint. "Are you saying we need to hobble the horse?"

"I recommend you do nothing to hinder or harm his steed; he treats it like his own child. Humans are closely related to beasts, of course."

"What do you recommend?"

The captain stood still for a moment, staring at a table. "Harness him with Rigellium."

Morgan scowled. "Rigellium is precious and takes too long to breed enough to make an entire neckpiece for a beast of that size."

"Not the horse! The man."

Morgan's eyebrows lifted slightly. "We haven't enough to do that, but I can have the smith start a new colony of it; there might be enough for a set to hold hand and head in a few days' time, but it will come at a dear cost." The

Rigelliumsmith had been painstakingly clear with her that Rigellium was both a metal and a colony of creatures; they had to be grown with care and harvested and trained in a timely manner. Each grouping had to be grown together so the tiny living metal cells bonded with each other and performed whatever task they were given, seamlessly. Like all life forms from her home planet, they had a degree of telepathy, but being so primitive meant they had to be coaxed into each shape and task they were given. It took time and resources, and so was not lightly done.

"I would prefer not to wait days. I can spare one of the golems for some time if you would remove its heart and have the smith recast it as shoes for the horse. That would be enough for our immediate needs, while we wait to have enough grown to chain him and create another heart to replace what the golem lost. He goes nowhere without the horse, that will give us a measure of containment at least."

Morgan's eyes narrowed as she considered the plan. "I will see what the smith has to say about it. Will the golem work at all without the transmitter?"

"Only for basic tasks. The one that has been feeding the animals can continue to do that without new directions, though his ability to guard will be reduced. With proper horseshoes, I'll have less need of a full cohort of guards. There is only the one human to guard, I'll make do."

Morgan tapped the sheer, glassy panel on the wall. "Smithy," she said quietly, and the dark form of a man appeared, bending over a tank of water. A chime sounded, and he turned toward her.

"Ah, Commander! What do you need?"

"Shoes for a horse and chains for a man."

He nodded. "And how soon?"

"The shoes, for now, but we can provide the Rigellium for that."

He chuffed. "Have you started your own colony, then? Who is tending it?"

"No, we can spare a golem transmitter. I'll have you recast it into horseshoes."

"Madam, it would be far easier to grow a new colony! Once trained to a task, they can be quite stubborn, they'll likely refuse a new shape, much less purpose. Why do you need Rigellium horseshoes?"

"My son, our new breeder, is proving difficult to contain. We need to prevent him from running, and until we can get the chains to keep him in place, we'll need to keep the horse from transporting him beyond our reach. The task will be similar to that of a golem; he must stay within our boundary, and receive and follow directions even when out of sight."

The man's jaw dropped open and he lowered himself to the bench beside the water tank. "Why would your son be trying to escape? Have you not told him he must provide the next generation or our race is doomed to extinction?"

Morgan fluttered a hand at him. "This is always a problem with our changeling program. They become too much like humans before we bring them back. If I had any patience for having undeveloped younglings about, I'd put an end to changelings, but humans are convenient caretakers."

The smith pursed his lips and nodded his understanding. "Well," he sighed, "I suppose the task is simple, and near enough the former task. I'll start the new colony immediately, of course, so you have the chains as soon as possible, and I'll do what I can to change the heart transmitter to horseshoes. If you'll be using it to curb the distance the horse can travel, and to locate and control, I suppose I can use most of the transmitter routine they were bred for. You understand that if I can get the horseshoes formed and functioning correctly, it's unlikely they'll ever work as a golem transmitter again. What will you do with the golem?"

"We'll need a new transmitter."

He paused for a moment. "So, you're asking me to convert a transmitter to horseshoes, grow control colonies for the man, and grow a new transmitter for the golem?"

"Can you do it?"

"On what timeline?"

"I need the shoes within a day. As soon as possible for the chains, and we are short one guard until the new heart is made."

He frowned. "I'll need a cask of cream, twenty pounds of straw, a fiddler and a full cohort of dancers."

"You can't drink on duty!" Cream had an intoxicating effect on all Sh'eyta.

"On the contrary; if you wish me to get the shoes made in no more than a day, we'll have to get the Rigellium to consume the straw at an enormous rate. For that, we have to convince them they need the energy. The best way to do that is for a group of us to exert a great deal of energy, so we'll need to dance all night long; that will telepathically excite the Rigellium. To dance all night long, we'll need to forget how tired it makes us. For that, we need cream."

She nodded, unable to find a flaw in his logic. It was often easier to abduct humans and make them dance instead, but on such short notice it would be hard to get enough of them.

"And if you want the chains within a few weeks, I'll need the same again tomorrow, and every day until the work is done."

Morgan frowned. The straw wasn't a difficult request; stealing tools, food, and other items from farmers was great fun for most of her kind, but it would be hard to find enough cream from buckets of milk that were set out to separate overnight. "I can't promise more than a single cask of cream."

"I suppose that's fair. I can't promise I can make four horseshoes out of one transmitter. But if you can't get me enough cream, I'll need twice as many dancers, or captured humans we can force to dance, so that there's a full cohort on the floor without pause."

"Two horseshoes will do; if we can control the hindquarters, the forequarters won't be going anywhere else."

Morgan tapped the glass on the wall, and the smith's image disappeared. The man's job seemed quite frivolous at times, compared to her own, and she didn't like it. She couldn't fault his product, though; if he weren't one of the best Rigelliumsmiths this world had known, she'd have limited her use of Rigellium to what had arrived on board the spacecraft that had brought her people here ten thousand years ago. And she'd cannibalized all of that not long after she replaced her father as world commander. She knew there would be a reckoning with the home planet overlords when they arrived, but she intended to blame that on someone else.

## 10 – Escape?

"The steed that my love rides upon Is lighter than the wind; With silver he is shod before, with burning gold behind." Child Ballad 39: Tam Lin

Two days later, Tam hummed a dance tune that had come to him in his sleep, and groomed Honor, running his hands down the horse's legs to be sure they were sound. He was puzzled to notice that Honor now had golden horseshoes on his rear hooves. He inspected the metal, sure it would be soft like gold, but it seemed as hard as steel, maybe harder. Frowning, he vowed to ask Morgan why his horse's shoes had been replaced. Why had a farrier been called to handle his steed? He didn't like them becoming so familiar with his own animal. Honor became restless, blowing and stomping, and Tam forced himself to relax. "Sorry, lad, don't fret about it, it's for me to worry about, not yourself." He reached for the tack hanging at the front of the stall and began to fit the well-oiled leather pieces onto the horse, humming to himself again. A horse picked up every emotion his master felt, and Honor was no exception. A good horseman led with calmness, no matter the situation.

Ever observant, the captain had noticed Tam tacking up the big horse, and two guards were at Tam's side before he left the barn. He wondered if they kept their own horses tacked up the whole time, and why. And where they kept those horses. Much of what happened here in this realm seemed as if by magic, and he didn't understand it, but wasn't sure yet how deep he wanted to probe where their powers came from, nor how they worked.

He led Honor out, then, standing beside him, placed both hands on the back of the horse as he put a booted foot into a stirrup and vaulted himself up, rotating to slide one leg across the saddle. Once seated, he lifted the reins and cluck gently to prompt the beast forward. They approached the gate slowly as the portcullis was raised with a foreboding clank of chain. Two guards were right behind him. One stepped his horse around in front of Tam and they proceeded across the bridge, Honor shaking his head and stamping as Tam insisted that he remain at a walking pace, but once they were on the dirt road that led away from the tower he gave a slight kick and Honor took off, powerful legs driving against the ground and propelling them past the leader, who'd been taken by surprise at Tam's sudden charge. He twitched the reins and Honor turned to the left, the thunder of hooves following behind as the two men forced their horses to catch up with him.

After several weeks testing the men's fighting skills and relearning the area, Tam was ready to see how far he could get if he ran for it. He circled the tower walls to view the entirety of his prison, then stopped and spun Honor on his heels to face the surprised guards and plunge back between them. He wanted to lash out at the nearer one as he galloped past them and into the forest, on the overgrown trail that had brought him to this hell born place, but he kept his arms to himself, seeing how swiftly they reacted to his change of direction. They were on his heels almost immediately, and they stayed with him as if glued there.

The trees thinned and he reached a rise that marked the edge of the glen. Tam took a deep breath and urged Honor over the top of the little hill and across the clearing to charge through the hedge, then suddenly the horse was falling out from under him as if the great beast had been struck in the chest with a lance. Tam was surprised to feel himself flying through the air and he twisted to roll across the underbrush that scratched and tore at his clothing. He lurched up and saw that Honor had rolled to his feet as well and stood snorting and tossing his head. Tam shook his own head at the strange sensation; he'd been hit by a lance before, in the chest, and remained in place as the horse sailed out from underneath him while he dropped to the ground. This experience was the exact opposite but just as disorienting. Then he turned toward freedom and ran.

It seemed like mere seconds before he was thrown to the ground, suddenly pinned under the great weight of Morgan's guards. He twisted away and kicked the man in the face, hard, then punched him in the nose as well, before turning again and launching himself to his feet, but he was still slightly disoriented as well as bruised and battered, and he was brought down hard this time.

In another instant, the other man was trussing him like a Christmas pig, and they threw him over the back of his horse and led the two back to the keep. Tam felt every bruise he received on his tumble through the brush, but he was relieved that Honor didn't appear to be limping at all.

"Really, Tam?" Morgan said as she eyed the procession that passed under the open portcullis.

Tam refused to say a word to her but winced as the two men dumped his body on the ground. The portcullis was lowered before the rope was untied from his wrists and ankles, his horse led away. He rose, dusted himself off and limped to the stable to verify that Honor wasn't injured in the sudden fall. One of the big men was lifting the saddle from his back and Tam slapped him away. The man gave no response and Tam was left to remove the thing himself, running a hand over every inch of Honor's body. There were no scratches on the horse, and no tenderness anywhere. What had caused him to fall? He wondered, and scratched his head at the strange, itchy feeling inside his skull.

"It's the horseshoes, Tam. They're made of Rigellium, and they can't be removed. They will bring your horse down if he ventures past the edge of my land. You were told to remain within bounds."

Two successive attempts over the next few days resulted in the same experience, but only because four guards were sent with him now. The fourth time he dropped down off the back of the horse and made it to the hedge before they stopped him. The last attempt was too much for the fey lady. The following day the captain addressed him sharply. "The Rigelliumsmith has finished your chains, and in record time. Any freedom you could have had will be gone. You are a stubborn and incalcitrant knave. Your life has a purpose, and you would throw it away for your own selfish concerns."

Tam ignored the rebuke. But what were these chains the captain was talking about? Was he to be pinned to a wall, or thrown into a cell? How could he perform his "duties" if it were so?

## 11 – The Chained Man

"We don't wear these by choice, and they're not for looks either ... She can track us across any land by these wicked things." Tam Lin, in Kindred Moon

As Tam awoke, he saw gold glinting from a wrist. He drew the arm toward his face and saw gold chains around both wrists, like a lady's bracelet but heavier. Then he reached up to his neck and confirmed that a loop of chain had been fashioned there as well, as tight as a ribbon on a dandy. How had it been placed over his head? It was barely larger than his neck. He was struck with a chill as he realized the chains had been placed there in spite of the rosary that still hung down against his chest, without the silver cross. They could handle the cross but didn't want him to have it. Yet the rosary had given him no protection from them, confirming his suspicion that the priest had no defense against them either. The wristlets, as well, weren't large enough to be pulled off.

"And there you are, Tam. Chained like a pet tiger that wants to escape its luxurious palace, where he is pampered and fed, to return to the harsh wilderness he came from. I was told humans were intelligent, but it seems not." Morgan stood in the doorway, looking down at him. The sun coming in through the windows had that gilded quality that occurred only when the sun sat heavy on the horizon.

"And why have I been adorned with jewelry?"

She sniffed. "They aren't decorative, they're for control." She touched a new charm that hung from her gold torc, and Tam felt the neck chain lift slightly and tighten on him. He tried to pull his hands toward his neck to force it away but they wouldn't move. When his hands were suddenly able to move again, he was breathing hard in panic. He didn't understand the strange experience, but whatever had just happened he was sure Morgan was to blame.

"Distance, my child. Now I can discover what you're thinking even when I can't see you, if I so choose. Also, the Rigellium were taken, as always, to the perimeter of your captivity to be taught their boundary; if you attempt to go beyond, the chains will prevent you."

Tam was gradually regaining control of his breathing and struggled to understand her. "What boundary?"

"No farther than the river on three sides, and Carter Hall on the fourth."

"Where's Carter Hall?"

"The meadow where you met the priest. There was once a small manor that stood on the grounds, but all that's left is the main hall. You will know when you try to go beyond it by the chains, which will incapacitate you. And if you try to defy me, there will be pain. I don't even need to enter your thoughts to punish you; I can connect with the Rigellium and bid them punish you. If I choose, once I've located the Rigellium, I will know where your mind is, and can enter your mind at will to know your thoughts."

Tam cried out in surprise as a thousand tiny daggers bit into his neck and wrists. He lifted his arms and saw ruby beads of blood growing all the way around where the chains had drawn tight against his skin. He reached up and felt a slight wetness on his neck as well. His fingertips came away red with blood.

He looked at the chains; the links seemed smooth, so what had cut him?

"You can't escape the chains, Tam," Morgan said from the doorway, and he turned to curse her.

"You vile creature! What have you done to me?"

"Only what I must. You were told we need you and that you must remain. We've given you what you asked for, even freedom, and you repay us by attempting to run. You were created for a reason, Tam, and you have an obligation to your people—"

"You are NOT my people!"

"You have an obligation to your people, Tam. Stop fighting your destiny—"

"This is NOT my destiny!"

She sighed. "Think of it what you will, but you are here for a reason, you are needed, and you will stay."

Tam growled in frustration. "When will I be allowed to leave?"

Morgan shook her head in aggravation. "We are all expected to fulfill our responsibilities as long as we live. For you, it will be as long as the women of this generation need to produce offspring, or until you are necessarily replaced to avoid further inbreeding. When you are retired you may leave."

"How long?" He asked through clenched teeth.

"At least a century—"

"DAMMIT, woman…" he cursed.

"You tried to shift between worlds when you were taken, in good faith, to see a priest, and nearly succeeded from what my captain tells me. Yesterday you tried to run past our borders. I'm surprised you are so powerful. I would have thought a half-breed would need more instruction, but you have an unfortunate aptitude, so you are bound to us by Rigellium instead." She stepped closer and leaned down to inspect the chain around his neck, measuring it with her fingers. "Yes, the smith did well. You are bound to us. You cannot leave now. The Rigellium will control you, and it will allow me to look in upon you wherever you are, whenever I wish to do so."

Tam gaped at her. "You can't keep me here for the rest of my life!"

"Oh, we most certainly can. Try as you might, you will find that the chains will defend themselves against any attack you launch on them."

"How can chains FIGHT?"

She sighed again. "You have experienced it. Don't be obtuse, child. It's Rigellium; both metal and a living colony of creatures, stronger than any metal you have here on earth."

"Enough, demon!" Tam closed his eyes and pressed his hands over his ears, trying to shut out the thoughts that spun through his head. This place operated by rules he had not even begun to understand, and the power she had over him seem to grow daily. If he didn't get away soon it might be too late, he thought with horror. "Get OUT of my room! Leave me be!" Tam shouted, opening his eyes and glaring at her. Morgan looked at him for several moments, then turned and walked away, and Tam went to shut the door behind her, wishing he could lock it.

He found himself sitting on the bed and staring at the floor some indeterminate time later. He regretted losing his temper. She had been telling him things he needed to know. He inspected his wrists again, several times, and couldn't understand what had happened. The links were perfectly smooth; how had they seemed so sharp?

"Dammit! What is this vile material?" Tam pulled at it, but the response was the same every time; the material couldn't be compromised but his flesh could and was. The metal would change shape and cut into him but remained as strong as before. He yawned, realizing that it must be late. His stomach growled and he thought it was likely Morgan had come to see why he skipped dinner. He frowned. She usually sent one of her lackeys.

An entire lifetime, here in this castle, with no one to converse with. No one to play chess with. No one worthy of wrestling with. Jousting with. The dreary years stretched out before him in his thoughts, and he lifted both arms to pound his wrists against the stone wall in frustration. The chains bit into him. "Stop your devilment, you wretched fiends!" he cursed.

A hundred years? Could these creatures be immortal? He supposed they could. Sidhe were said to be so. A cold, sick feeling grew in the pit of his stomach as he wondered how long he might live, if it were true that he was half-Sidhe himself. He dropped onto his bed in resignation and yawned. He had no idea what they'd done to him, but apparently he hadn't slept. He would try again tomorrow. His stomach protested his decision to go to bed and he lay under the covers for a long time staring upwards into the darkness before sleep overtook him.

## 12 - Gruoch

There was a tap at his door, and he looked up. It was the blonde, fair-skinned lass. "May I come in?" She stepped into his chamber.

"It seems you have, my lady." Tam shifted away. She looked like a tiny bit of a girl, but nothing was as it seemed in this wretched place.

She chuckled. "Well, I'm not accustomed to being denied."

Tam found that quite believable. She was quite attractive. Then he frowned. "You make a habit of entering men's chambers, then?"

"No. I have work to do, and I make reasonable requests of people. I'm accommodated by reasonable people. Are you reasonable, Tam?" She walked over to his bed and sat down on the edge, the rich mauve silk of her gown touching the back of his hand. Her fingers were long and delicate. "You haven't called for me. Are you reluctant to do your duty?"

This woman's skin was pale, almost translucent. Her eyes were a deep blue-violet, mesmerizing, her lips the pale pink of tea roses and well-rounded. The mounds of her breasts lifted and fell against the ermine trim along the wide neckline of her gown as she breathed. It was cut so low he was sure he could almost see the darker skin around her nipples. He wondered if any of her appearance was real. He looked up into her eyes again; she was frowning.

"Duty, lass? Do you think yourself mere duty?"

"Tsk, don't be a boor. We have few needs of your people—"

"I was told you are my people?"

Her eyes rolled as if she were human. "You're half Sh'eyta, but more importantly half human. That's why this is your duty."

He found himself reaching toward her shoulder, just beyond the edge of the fur. "Oh? Is that all I am here?" He succumbed to temptation and stroked the back of her neck. She bowed her head so he could reach it more easily, and he ran his hand across her upper back, appreciating the softness of her warm skin.

"Well it's not as if you need to find joy in it. It's as much a task for me as for you, but I don't shirk it."

He pulled his hand back. "Is it utterly joyless for you, then?"

Her eyebrows drew together. "It's not that we don't experience pleasure, but we aren't motivated by it the way humans are. Our vocation is what drives us, not the sensation of our bodies. That's a thing for humans and other animals. Do you not understand?"

He folded his arms. "Do I not understand what, exactly? What you expect of me, or that you consider me an animal?"

"Why it is expected." She turned her head and kissed his wrist and peered at the skin of his hand before looking into his eyes; it was more assessment than desire.

He leaned back, seeing her actions now as more studious than interested. "If passion doesn't drive you, why are you here?" He asked.

She tilted her head. "To mate."

"No, why are you HERE?" he studied her face.

She stared at the wall a moment, then shifted her gaze to meet his. "To mate," she said again. "Because there can be no offspring of my generation but through you, or else they will all be born sickly and will die."

He'd heard this before. "I've been told I am to call for you when… ah… when…" he paused in frustration, unable to find words that seemed appropriate to speak to a woman. "I was told you would wait to be called for. So WHY are you HERE?"

She smiled slightly as his meaning became clear to her. "Because you are quite the strangeling! It has been centuries since one of such birth has been available to us. I want to know who you are, how you think, what you're capable of! That's my job. That's MY purpose."

Tam was surprised. "So, it's not just the coupling you're after? It matters not whether I've called for you?"

She shook her head, still smiling. "Maybe the other ladies feel that way, but I'm responsible for our xenobiology. And you fascinate me!" Her voice dropped into a husky whisper on the last words.

His head jerked up. "Zena balalogy?" He tried to fit the strange word to his mouth.

"Xe. No. Bi. Ology," she answered. "Xenobiology," again, but slowly.

"Zeno by AWE luh jee?" The syllables seemed both familiar and strange.

"The study of creatures from another planet."

"Another what?"

"Another world."

Tam frowned. "There IS no other world. It's The World. What do you mean?"

Her head dropped as if she were tired, then she lifted it to look at him. "I know many still believe the sun, moon and stars revolve around the Earth, but that's not the case. Earth isn't at the center of the universe. The earth travels in a circle around the sun, and the sun is a star, just like all the other stars in the sky. It just looks big because you're so much closer to it. The other stars have worlds that revolve around them just as the earth you live on revolves around your sun."

Tam stared at her, mouth agape. Being educated, as all noblemen were, he certainly knew the earth revolved around the sun, but the idea of other worlds that spun around stars was preposterous!

She leaned over to pick up the strange tablet that sat by his bed. When she opened it, the page was different. He watched the images that arose and moved across the page as she showed him images of the solar system, then zooming out and back in, other solar systems. It was an incredible tale, but she seemed to believe it. He had to admit, the pictures made a sort of sense, if you could conceive of some force such as magnetism holding the bodies at a prescribed distance from each other. Well, something made the planets orbit the sun, why shouldn't there be other places where the same thing happened? But God created man on Earth, not on distant worlds. It was said that the Sidhe had their own world, but it wasn't in a different place, exactly; it was only different by way of magick.

Tam looked at the tablet suspiciously, wondering how it had shown her the different text. He found the changing words strange enough, but he realized his hunger to understand this strange place, this different world, had blinded him to the dangers of the magick it operated under. He wondered if she could make the tablet tell her what he'd read. Would she trust him if she knew? "You're from one of these other worlds?"

"Yyyyessss," she drew out the word as if to a child.

Her tone of voice snapped him out of his trancelike musings. "Lass, I'll not have you patronizing me," he grumbled, tired of feeling like he was at a complete disadvantage every time he spoke to these strangers.

"Oh?" She chuckled. "What will you have?"

The flirtatious question caught him off guard. Her wide blue eyes and half open mouth enflamed him. She was as luscious as she was infuriating. Was she actually being coy? Could she even understand what that was? He found himself reaching for her again, wanting to make her stop talking, and he pulled her into a tight embrace just to shut her up, but the feel of her curves against his well-muscled chest, belly and thighs overcame him with lust. His attempt to redirect her attention had redirected his own. When she wasn't talking, she was exquisite. She opened her mouth, and without thinking he covered it with his own, kissing her deeply. It was no less than Morgan demanded of him. He bridled at the thought of obedience to an enemy, then decided if he was going to be imprisoned for a while, he might as well enjoy what entertainment they offered him. And so he found himself doing exactly what Morgan wanted him to do.

## 13 – The Changeling Dilemma

Tam held Gruoch close after their bodies were spent. He was still breathing hard when it occurred to him to ask, "Where will the children be raised?"

"It will be done as usual," she said.

"And that is?"

She began to get her clothing in order. The simple practicality of her movements reminded him this was no human lass; mating was a task, not an act of passion. "They're raised by humans, like you were. A newborn babe is disguised to look like a human babe, then dropped in a crib after the human infant is removed from it."

"Changelings," he sighed. Of course. That's what Morgan said. He hoped he'd misunderstood. "And what of the human bairns?"

"What do you want us to do with them?" she demurred.

Tam wasn't sure. What did he want? He'd asked about the human infants, but now he thought about what were to be his own. Someday he expected to have a wife, and children. To see them as they grew before sending them to a cousin's keep to learn skills, like Tam. But he grew up believing he would live among men. If he fathered the children the Sidhe expected him to, he would be here, away from his people. That's what they planned for. He stroked his thin mustache and tried to imagine… he didn't want these creatures involved in caring for innocent children, but he couldn't do it himself. At a bare minimum he needed a woman, and a normal size family. All the more reason to leave, and soon, before he lost the ability to leave, if it wasn't too late now.

Which brought him back to the dilemma of his imprisonment. He hardly noticed her leaving the room as he tried to imagine his future. He had enough to think about for now. He pulled himself together and stood, then paced the length of the room and back. Six steps in each direction. Back and forth he went as he thought about his predicament. Somehow he had to get more information. He needed to know more about the strange sensations he felt; the shimmering and shifting when the veil between the two worlds thinned to let someone pass through, and the blanket feeling in his head when Morgan had changed the appearance of her skin. He felt the world tilt and, fearful his thoughts were creating a passageway, he immediately thought of something else. The demons told him he was half human, half Sidhe… Sh'eyta, as they called themselves. Dear God, they said he was half demon. If so, was there any shame in wanting to learn how to do what they did? He glanced at the tablet. Such strange things they did, seemingly with no more than a thought. There were no wands, no potions, no waving of hands, no words. It happened in his mind. He could use the tablet, and it seemed he had some power over the passageways. The captain thought so, and had stopped him, before he was chained.

He stopped pacing. Yes, the captain had definitely stopped him, which meant he had some skill. He kept pacing. If it was something Sidhe could do, and he was half Sidhe, he must have some ability. But now, they said he would be stopped by the chains before he could get past their borders. He needed to disable the chains.

He was still thinking about it when he went down to the evening meal. Gruoch sat alone at the table, studying him. Morgan must be involved in something important in the room in the back that he wasn't allowed to see. How long would Gruoch stay and study him? If he could tell her what she wanted to know, he might be able to ask his own questions of her, but he'd need to be careful lest she realize his plans. He remembered their conversation before she left. He considered the worst possible answer to the question he asked. "The infants; do you murder them?"

"Of course not! We place our offspring in the cribs of humans to be raised lovingly by them."

"I mean the human bairns!" He snapped.

Gruoch tilted her head. "What happens to the humans is not important. Our own children require care."

"Don't try to convince me you have a care for your bairns if you can't even concern yourselves with raising them."

"That is actually evidence that we DO care for our children. Humans are much more adept at raising children."

"That may well be true, but what care do you take to be sure the child will be raised by the best parents? And how can you thrust a Fey child into the crib of innocent parents and make them raise your children while you discard theirs like a cuckoo? You don't even bother to ask the parents if they're willing to foster these changelings!"

"Do you ask your horse permission to place a saddle on its back?"

The bluntness of the answer took him aback. To these creatures, humans were no better than beasts. Did they think of him as half beast? Was he? With a sinking heart, he realized his comparison was apt; they had no more interest in the infants they disposed of than a cuckoo that kicked a wren's eggs out of the nest. He tried to compose himself. He still wanted answers. "Lass, you asked me what I wanted done with them. If they must be replaced with your own, at least…" well, they couldn't take them to a church. Or could they? He reached for his rosary. "Take them to a church," he said, watching her eyes to see if she flinched at the thought.

Her gaze was steady. "We can do that, if it is important to you."

Leaving babies with clergy was better than abandoning them. But if it didn't bother her at all to think of crossing holy ground, he had to discard the notion that they were afraid of anything holy. He'd learned something of them, then.

His thoughts returned to babies. "How do you know your own will be raised well?" He asked.

"Humans make good parents. Your noblemen see that their children are raised well, as you were."

"Nobility doesn't guarantee a good home," he objected.

"I was told humans were good at child-rearing," she insisted.

"Not all humans. Some are atrocious at it." He thought of James and tried not to grow angry with her, but the thought of dropping a child off as if it were clothing to be washed struck him as cruel.

She gazed at him in puzzlement.

"Do you truly care?" He meant to sound commanding, but he fell short and it came out as more of a plea.

"Of course I care. This will be my child. But I can't raise a child while continuing my work."

Work? This woman had work to do, other than caring for her husband and children. "You mean the zena byologee?"

"Yes. I have to review reports of our research creatures throughout the world, to see how they fare and be sure that they haven't broken the laws."

"What creatures?"

"The human-animal hybrid creatures we created when we were studying the best methods for integrating genetic material from two disparate species. We had to learn how to use native species to blend our chromosomes with, so that we could adapt ourselves to the planets we colonize, and before we performed the procedures on ourselves we did so on animals to perfect the process."

Tam tried to wrap his head around the mouthful of words that had just spilled out of her lush, pink lips. "Can you say that again, with smaller words?" Colonize worlds, she said. Like his own. She said there were other worlds, out there among the stars he saw at night. How did they stay up there? Well, how did the stars stay up there? He thought they were affixed to the firmament. He didn't understand how the planets were able to move between them, though. But even if other worlds existed, they couldn't possibly be large enough for people to live on. Nonsense.

She thought for a moment. "Have you heard of mermaids?"

"Yes," he said. "Women with the tails of fish."

"Yes. My people created them when we were studying how to combine our bodies with that of humans. We had to test our methods on humans and animals first. We made fauns, minotaurs, werewolves, all kinds of creatures. It's my job to monitor their development and inform our scientific community if the creatures change in any way. They're also required to report to me if they encounter any difficulties they can't handle themselves."

Tam was stunned. What she was saying suggested that the strange creatures his nursemaid had told him about when he was just a toddling child were real. Could it be? Some of what she said was impossible. All of it, really, except that this building had appeared out of nowhere, as had the priest. His horse had fallen out from under him without being struck by anything. Magick existed, of that he was sure now. And the Sidhe... they existed? Yes. He was looking at one of them. He needed to know more.

"What other creatures have you created?"

She tilted her head. "I might have already said too much. Humans aren't to know of the creatures; that's a law. Of course, you're only half human. You're one of us, in part. But you mustn't speak of this to other humans. We had to exterminate minotaurs for having been irrevocably identified by humans. One of them lived among humans for years, though they had him imprisoned."

"But I'm not human, not entirely." If they were to use the apparent duality of his nature against him he could learn to use it as well. "You can tell me more. Tell me about these other creatures, the other half-human things your people made—"

"Engineered. We engineered them, crossed the genes—"

"Whatever!" He waved his arms. Words. Strange words. It was the same thing. "What creatures? What animals did you use?"

"Oh…" she said, "Well… wolves, seals, cows… horses, goats… bears—"

"Selkies?" he said with surprise.

Her eyes locked onto his. "Selkies, yes. Human-seal hybrid creatures."

His thoughts were far away, where the ocean waves beat against the dark rocky cliffs of the rugged Scottish coast. Others had seen them, the people of the sea, selkies; sometimes seal, sometimes man or woman. Like him in a way: half human, half other. He wondered if they felt so estranged from their own kin. He often felt like there was another place he should be, then he shook it off.

"Tell me more," he said, "How did you make them?"

"Oh, I don't think I could begin to explain that to you."

Tam frowned. She was going to use more words he didn't understand, then. He changed tack. "How many are there?"

She thought for a moment. "At last count, oh, that depends what species—"

"Last count? Do you mean it changes?"

"Well, yes! They reproduce. And the change culture can be transmitted like a virus—"

"Transmitted?" he asked, alarmed. That word he understood, and feared what it might mean to her.

"Yes. We had to use a gene-editing organism to get the genes of one creature to combine with the genes of another, since different species can't mate directly. But then the hybrids become carriers of the organism, and they can pass it on to normal humans if they're not careful. And, of course, they are often irresponsible, as they're just animals, really…"

Organism. This was an important word, but what did it mean? Trying to avoid more nonsensical words, he was frustrated to find himself tripped up anyway. But among all the incomprehensible words, a few things seemed clear; it sounded like it was possible for a human to become half-beast, or a shapeshifter. He wondered what kind of life that would be. To be able to turn into a seal and swim away.

The tower sat right on a river. Perhaps, if Tam couldn't escape, a seal could.

"If you can cause creatures to reproduce without mating, why do you need to mate? Why can't you use this thing?"

"That was done long ago, by our superiors, and they took the sequencer with them to make sure we couldn't further alter ourselves. We must reproduce naturally. We're still trying to find a way to inseminate ourselves instead of live mating; it would be easier. So far, Sh'eyta are unable to reproduce in vitro."

No, then, for whatever reason she gave. He really wanted to understand what this "organism" was, though. "How is it done?" Her answer confused him. He tried to imagine what it would be like to be a seal.

"Tam?" she had stopped talking some time ago, after telling him how she kept a vial of some kind of substance for each of the species they created. There were so many! Bears: some were half man, half bear. THAT would be a powerful creature! If he were part bear, he would need no weapons. There were stories of berserker warriors that turned into bears on the battlefield, but he scoffed at the stories. What if it was true, and he could become a berserker bear? To become a bear in battle would be a great advantage!

He saw her staring at him, concerned. "A bear?" he asked, and she nodded.

"Why?"

"If I could become a bear—"

"No! Oh no, Tam, if you mutated into homo ursanthrus you'd be no use to us!" She lurched to her feet. "Don't even think of it, Tam!" Her fierceness was stunning.

"Shh, shh, shh," he said. "I was just curious." *Homo ursan fris?* Ursa… bear… but where had he heard the word "homo" before? "Lupus est homo homini." Man is wolf to man. Homo means man. Lupus was wolf.

"Tam . . . promise me you're not serious. What if we couldn't reverse it? We've never had to consider it! If you soil your genes we have to wait twenty years to replace you! You are already our second attempt; the first mating resulted in a female, and we needed a man. We can't afford to lose so much time. As it is we've waited longer than we should. We aren't immortal. Not anymore."

Now she was warning him against getting dirty? What did that have to do with anything? That they weren't eternal beings struck him as important, the rest of it was more gibberish. Probably just as important, but he saw a new wariness in her eyes and thought better of pressing her any further for now. "Hush, lass, I'm just dazzled by the thought. It means nothing to me, really…"

He turned his attention to the plate before him and tried to finish his meal as if he had no further interest in the idea. But he stroked the gold chain around one of his wrists as he imagined his body changing shape. Was it true? And what would it take to become such a thing? What would it gain him? What would it cost?

He sighed. The point was probably moot. He could barely remember the words, much less understand how to perform the process. Besides, even if he could use such a transformation to escape, that made him half animal for the rest of his life. What a horrific thought!

He squeezed his eyes shut for a moment. No, there must be another way to escape. He would find it.

After the meal she followed him as he went back to his room again. "You mustn't think of the creatures, Tam. I should not have mentioned them. You are too important to think of such things."

He grimaced. If he was going to ask questions, he'd better do it more deftly. "I have no desire to become an animal, lass. What would I do with such strange powers?" he scoffed. "It's distressing enough to find that I'm half Sidhe. But lass," he said, taking one of her hands and tugging on it, "you want to learn more about me. I want to learn more as well. Perhaps if you taught me to use these fae powers, we could find my limits?" The more he learned to use whatever powers he might possess, the sooner he would have the choice to stay or to go.

She frowned. "We don't teach, we just know."

His heart sank. He didn't "just know." Or did he? "Am I particularly obtuse, then? More so than a full Sidhe… a Sh'eyta?"

She shifted her weight, silent for a moment. "Perhaps a little." His eyes sought confirmation from her. "Well, it was so long ago, I can't be sure how I learned, actually. And you're half human. The last time I studied someone who wasn't full Sh'eyta it was only one quarter human, as your offspring will be. More astute, I think, but maybe not."

"Did you not say you want to know what my abilities are? Perhaps you could teach me and find my limits."

She looked into his eyes, but he couldn't read her expression. The warmth was gone, she was just studying him now. "We'll see," she said, and before he could formulate another question she had left.

He looked at the tablet that was lying next to his bed. Demon magic. But if using it was going to curse him, it was too late. It had answers; perhaps easier to understand than Gruoch was. He picked it up, opening the cover. There was the strange runic text; he didn't touch it, he just thought of seeing the words he saw before and there they were, in English. Just like the appearance of the creatures themselves, they did not appear as they really were. He wondered again if, in their true form, the Sh'eyta were his size, or very small. He reached out and touched it; the gold chain on his wrist touched the edge of the page and the words changed.

> *It is considered good practice to appear small; this will reduce any apparent threat so that you can garner their good will. Once they agree to what you propose, they will believe they must do it, and you can make them do anything with little effort.*

Tam stared at the words, reading them several times. It was like an answer to his thoughts. He concentrated on the text and tried to think of another question.

"How do they move between worlds?" He whispered. The text wavered but didn't change.

"How can I move between worlds?"

> *You must hide your existence from the humans; if they know they are being observed they will not act naturally. Use a fourth-dimension door to create your dwelling in the fourth plane so that they are unable to sense your presence. When you need to observe them, pass through the door into the third dimension, where they exist, and observe them there.*

Tam closed the tablet with excitement, then opened it again. It responded to him even in this, though he didn't understand the answer. "How do I open a fourth-dimension door?" he asked, but the words remained the same. He touched the edge of the screen with the gold chain on his wrist, and the text wavered and changed.

> *If the door doesn't open easily, be sure that you are in the right place; the doors are strongest where ley lines cross and can even be activated by humans there in many cases, when ley tides are strong. There are certain plants that are more plentiful in such places. You can connect with the power by placing a hand on such a plant, using it as an activator of your power, and see through into the other dimension; relax your gaze so that you are focusing on a more distant point.*

Tam read and re-read the passage. This was it! And he knew the right place. But what did it mean "relax your gaze?"

## 14 - Carter Hall

Over the next week Tam queried the tablet. The half-human creatures fascinated him. Pictures of men and women in half and full animal form swam to the top of the page, often naked. He still didn't understand the actual process and had to wade through long dissertations describing things inside the human body that made his skin crawl, then he read a passage about how transforming from animal to human healed most wounds. What an advantage that would be in battle!

Another woman appeared in the hall, in addition to Morgan and Gruoch, and sat at the table one evening when he came down to dinner. He shot a glance at Morgan, who was staring at him. He pulled out a chair and sat down, ignoring them.

"Tam, you'll see to your duties tonight," she said sternly.

"Ah," Tam said, looking across at her as he cut a piece of meat from the roast, "I had other plans…" he joked, but his head grew fuzzy as the chains drew tight on his throat. His eyes bulged as he tried desperately to free his hands and reach for the necklet. He couldn't move his hands, and the metal rings developed teeth that stabbed into him.

He heard Morgan's swift intake of breath as pleasure combined with pain.

*Oh my,* Morgan resonated inside his head, *what is this that you're feeling?*

He fell to the floor struggling against the bonds, furious at how helpless he was against the metal until the chains released him, changing back into simple links. Tiny droplets of blood beaded under the necklet where they bit into him like a swarm of ants.

*Is this what you call pain? How exquisite!* Morgan's gaze seemed far away.

Her lips didn't move, she seemed to have spoken to him within his head, and he was sure she caused the chains to tighten on him. He rose, watching her warily, and moved the chair back to its place at the table, biting back a furious retort. He lowered himself onto the chair, still watching her. Finally, trying to focus on the task at hand, he finished cutting a piece of meat away from the joint of mutton, then said, coldly, "If you had any understanding of humans you would recognize the humor in my statement. Your reaction is primitive and uncivilized—"

The chains immobilized him again, and this time she moaned as her eyes rolled back in her head. As before, he couldn't move his hands. He saw thin threads of blood trickling from his wrists. The intensity of the pain combined with pleasure again, and she seemed to be experiencing some sort of bliss.

Berserkers threw themselves into battle, laughing as they were cut and stabbed, seeming to revel in the pain, but he preferred to avoid it as much as possible. It was no more than a necessary evil to him. Her words suggested she was feeling what he felt, and he thought it might go both ways; he was feeling her own pleasure somehow. Their minds seemed to be linked. He had never enjoyed any kind of pain, though Gregor taught him to ignore it while fighting. Searching his memory, he recalled her saying that telepathy went both ways; her connection gave him access to her mind as well, but he had no idea how to turn it to his advantage yet.

The pain subsided, and the strange pressure in his head disappeared. She composed herself as he glared at her.

"Lady, you cannot compel a man to do what you ask in this manner!"

Gruoch entered the hall at that moment and scurried to his side. She lifted his wrists and gasped at the tendrils of blood that led to tiny droplets that fell to the floor. She looked up at Morgan. "What are you doing to him? This is counterproductive. For a male, a certain willingness is essential; he's right that you can't compel him this way."

Morgan crooked an eyebrow at her. "Has he convinced you of this?"

"We haven't spoken of it. It's in the texts. This is my scientific advice to you."

The two women faced each other silently; he felt a presence slip from his head, and there seemed to be a conversation passing between them, but he heard nothing.

Gruoch turned to Tam. "She is… well, emotion is rare for us, but she is angry with you. Disappointed. You're not what she expected, and your disobedience is unheard of."

Tam was floored. "I have no responsibility to be—" and again his head filled with a presence and he was fighting the chains.

"MORGAN! LEAVE HIM BE!" Gruoch screamed.

The neck chain released from him and his hands were free to move, but fear of the crippling strangulation gripped him and he dug his fingers into his neck, trying to get under the chain to rip it away from him even if he had to tear his neck to do it. He had faced countless opponents, but never one that rendered him so powerless. It was more than he could bear. If he couldn't control his own body, what was the point of living?

"Tam! Stop!" Gruoch cried, as his mind half-emptied and Morgan swept from the hall, but with a new mincing sway of her hips.

The new lady watched with both fascination and horror as Gruoch held Tam's hands. Her grip was strong for such a slight girl. "Tam, you mustn't resist her, nor can you now that you are chained. You must know that." Her calm voice got through to him. She was right, of course, but did he even care? He remained tense for several seconds longer. He reconsidered his actions and he found himself looking into her eyes, searching for any sign of kindness, and perhaps he found it. Maybe there was hope. She was different from Morgan, more humane. More human? They claimed they weren't human, but even by their own tales they were indeed part human. Surely if he looked deep enough he would find something of her humanity.

He rose to his feet one more time, looked at the roast, glanced at the other woman, and decided to go to his room. He'd had enough humiliation, he just wanted to be alone more than he needed food. He climbed the stairs and dropped onto his bed.

Soon Gruoch stepped into his doorway, startling him. She'd seen him completely incapacitated; shame flooded him. "Damn you, woman, GET OUT!" Tam spat, but she didn't move, she just stared at him. He was powerless here. He leaned back against the wall in resignation, at which point she stepped into the room.

Her boldness infuriated him, but no good could come of admitting it. "Enter if you will, then," he said, with a wave of one hand. "You care not a whit for my objection."

She shrugged. "My only concern is that you help us birth another—"

"I'll not have it! You're evil."

She sat down next to him. "We're not like you. But I want you to know I'm trying to help you. And I'm trying to understand you; your reluctance is strange to us."

"Morgan has no desire to understand me."

She shrugged. "It's not her job to understand you."

"Then perhaps it shouldn't be her job to govern me," he said bitterly.

She tilted her head. "That's an interesting idea."

Tam waited for her to explain.

"She is accustomed to obedience."

He grimaced. "Have I not done what she ordered?"

She frowned. "Not easily. She sees your reluctance as resistance. It's unheard of."

"Then maybe she should stop watching me."

Her eyes seemed to look right though him. "She knows all that happens in this hall. And now that you have the chains on, all she has to do is think of you and she can learn where you are. And, if she chooses, what you're thinking. Normally we can only do that if we can see the person we want to monitor."

Tam frowned. "Does she feel what I'm feeling?"

Gruoch nodded. "When she is reading your thoughts, she experiences whatever you experience."

"Does she like it?" he probed.

Her eyebrows lifted. "She did seem to be deriving some sort of pleasure from it. That's an artifact of her particular humanity, I think; she seems to have more emotion, experiences more sensory input. It's unusual. I'll have to ask her about it so I can record the anomaly."

"Ach! If she has begun to find pleasure in my pain, my life will soon be naught but misery!"

Gruoch frowned. "I would hate for her to fall prey to an unsightly temptation. If she's seen as too human, our administrators would be compelled to replace her, which would be shameful." She stared at the floor for a moment. "It might be best if we found a different place for you to stay. But you would be subject to the same responsibilities."

"I didn't ask to be here. I'm not inclined to do as I'm bid by a woman who enjoys my suffering."

She frowned. "So your objection is that the order comes from her?"

"And that she thinks to use force on me," he said, pointing where the tracks of blood were drying on his skin.

She looked at him, then went to the pitcher of water and wet the end of one of her sleeves. She came back and dabbed at his skin, tenderly removing the crusted blood. "Well, let's deal with what we can, then."

He let her care for him, watching her in wonder. "How can the two of you be so unlike?"

"I told you, it's my job to understand the hybrids, not hers. To understand the hybrids, I have to understand humans, as well as the animals they were combined with."

Tam felt his gorge rise as he thought of humans coupling with animals and he shut the thought away, focusing on her ministrations. He reached out and stopped her hand. "Lass, you'll ruin your gown."

She chuckled. "Don't worry, it will be fine. It's you that concerns me right now. You have no idea how important you are to us."

"I'm important to my own people."

She stopped for a moment, then continued. "What if there was a place you could live that allowed you to be away from Morgan and where your own people could meet you if they chose, certain nights of the year?"

Tam sat up straight, setting her hand aside. "Where?" he asked, suddenly hopeful.

She smiled at him. "There is a place on the edge of our protected land called Carter Hall; it's a liminal place, between the worlds. The structure of the hall remains standing, though the rest of the hold has fallen away. I think the captain took you there to meet with the priest."

He touched the beads of the rosary that hung from his neck, and she reached up to touch it as well, dispelling any question that remained of whether it was possible for Sh'eyta to touch holy objects. "If you like it, you could ask to stay there," she said.

"And my horse?"

"Him as well."

"My sword?"

"Of course not!"

Tam marveled at the idea. He would be that much closer to getting away from these lands. That would be good. He might escape if they weren't monitoring him.

"I can suggest that it would be better for all if you weren't so underfoot, and the Rigellium will prevent you from going farther than she allows. But you must promise you will not shirk your obligation! Our continued existence depends on it."

Tam slowly nodded. "If you will get me away from this imprisonment, I will do what you ask," he said, though his goal was to find a way to escape. He looked at the chains on his wrists, wondering if he could protect his flesh while applying heat.

"If you don't, you will have to come back here," Gruoch whispered, then left.

Soon the other young woman appeared at his door with a carafe of wine. He suspected Gruoch had thought to send it with her; he wasn't sure the others would understand how wine affected people. He wondered if they were capable of enjoying inebriation. His stomach being empty, the wine went to his head, and he soon found himself laughing at her silly questions as she asked how a man could ride a horse while wielding a sword. He felt very little rancor in spite of knowing he would do as he was bid before the night was through. Well, Gruoch was a clever lass. But whose side was she on?

A few days later, Gruoch led him back to where he met with the priest. Tam looked around at the meadow. From the corners of his eyes he thought he saw a shimmering that ended just past the trees. If he stared straight at the shadowy grey shape toward the west, it resolved into a stone structure with a roof and a vacant hole that once held a door.

"Carter Hall," she said. "This is the edge of our lands. Can you see the difference? It should be visible to you."

"Aye, it shimmers," he waved toward the silvery hedge.

She nodded. "If you try to go beyond the blackthorn the chains will stop you. But you can learn to open the passage so that your people can visit you here, and those that know how can open it from the other side in this place. Aside from that, the passage only opens a few times a year."

Tam nodded absently. He had to know how the restraint worked. He strode across the field and into the trees until he felt the neck chain tighten around his windpipe when he pushed into the underbrush. He tried to reach up, but his hands wouldn't move. He struggled to breathe and the chain kept tightening. He backed away; the chain released its grip on his neck and his hands were free to move. He turned around to see the amusement on Gruoch's face.

"Am I your plaything?" he said crossly.

She shook her head. "It's nothing I've done, Tam. The chains act on their own in this. I told you as much, yet you insist on trying it for yourself. Is this because you're unable to delve my mind and determine the truth? We're unaccustomed to guile, Tam. We have no use for it."

They returned to the tower, and that evening, over dinner, he brought it up with Morgan.

"Give me a place of my own," he said.

Morgan's fork stopped halfway to her mouth and she looked up at him, mouth open. "You HAVE a place of your own, Tam." She frowned.

"No, I'm in YOUR place. I mean let me live at Carter Hall."

She tilted her head at him. "You're welcome to go wherever you want, within the boundaries, at any time, just not beyond it," she answered.

"I want to STAY out there, in the field where I went today."

"But Tam, it's a FIELD!"

"There's a building."

"And insects!" She shuddered.

"All the same—"

"You humans are so primitive! So be it, then; if you want to sleep in the fields of Carter Hall, do so. Lay down on the grass, put your head on a rock for all I care. Sleep there whenever you wish. And don't bother to bring the gnats and fleas with you when you return to us; we'll just send the poor women to meet you in Carter Hall." She rose from her chair and walked away stiffly.

It was as easy as that, in the end? Even if the building was a ruin, the weather in this realm was always temperate, somehow; the flowers bloomed early, while at the same time fruit ripened, as if it all happened at once in an eternal summer. He could pretend the ladies they sent were his new wives. Why not? All the while he would press against the boundaries, looking for ways to escape. Gruoch had said his own people could meet him there on certain days. He yearned to know what had become of Lords Douglas and Dunbar; perhaps someone would come with word of them. In every way, the field would be better than here.

He finished his meal and rose to get the pillow and blankets from his bed and rolled them, along with the tablet, into a bundle. He went to the stable, put the saddle and reins on his horse and strapped the bundle on, then leapt on his back and trotted to the meadow as the sun colored the sky violet and gold. After untacking and tethering Honor, he paced toward the stone building. It was empty inside, but well-built. The magick of the gentle prison seemed to slip into him, and he sighed as sat down on the flagstone floor and rolled himself in his cloak once again. This was better. Cruel and hard in its own way, yet better than the strange tower full of aliens.

A short while later he heard the crunch of gravel under horse's hooves and went out to look. Gruoch had come over the rise, leading a pack horse. "I'll leave you with a bit more comfort if you will have it," she said, drawing the horse up next to him.

"I'll take what I can get, as long as I can stay here, as far as possible from her."

She started to unload the horse, and he stepped past her to do it himself. Soon the pile of equipment was on the ground. She looked as if she were going to jump up on the back of the horse, and he lifted her up instead; the feel of her lithe body enflamed him, but he restrained himself. She was his only ally, he needed to stick to business with her.

Then again, he was bidden to mate with these beings. "You won't be staying, then?"

She shook her head. "I've no taste for this wilderness, Tam, and there is a great deal of work I need to attend to right now. I'll visit when I have more questions, if that's alright with you."

He nodded. She drew the horse around and left.

He rummaged through the stack of things she'd left him, finding a small cot and a pad to place on it. There was a small pot to hang over a fire, along with a bowl and a few utensils, as well as twine to make snares with.

It was thoughtful; just what he needed, though nothing more. His lips curled in a wistful half-smile. Morgan didn't care if he were comfortable, but it seemed Gruoch did.

He pulled the valuable tablet from his bundle on the ground. He needed to find a way to deactivate the Rigellium. Or to get away from this place in spite of it. Remembering what the tablet had said earlier, Tam walked over to the rowan tree and placed a hand on its trunk. He tried to recall the sensation that had heralded the appearance of the priest, and his vision blurred as the world seemed to tilt sideways. Then nothing; nothing had changed. The tree was still there, the hedge was still there, Honor was still there. Even the pink flowers of the laurel rose still waved in the breeze. With a sigh, Tam opened the tablet to see what else he could learn that might be of any use, slightly irked when he felt a brush against his mind.

*I see you have a more suitable dwelling,* Morgan's voice jeered.

*Leave me be, witch,* he replied.

She chuckled, and he wondered how she could experience mirth yet be so baffled by other human behaviors. With a whisper, he sensed her disappearance and took a deep breath, relieved.

Over the next few days he tried to make the world shift so that he could see his homeland, rather than this otherworld, but he never saw evidence that it worked, for all it made him feel as if the world was turning upside down when he did it.

But he never asked himself how he would know if he'd succeeded.

## 15 – The Ball

Janet sat perfectly still behind the shrub, watching the young girl who stared intently at a rabbit hole. She had already been shushed by the girl, who told her if they sat still enough it would come out, and the little girl thought she could grab it as it went toward the meadow. She wanted to know if she could be faster than a rabbit. Janet knew the headstrong child would only be convinced by experience. She had learned by now that she couldn't outrun the dogs or horses, but she insisted it was because they were bigger. There was only one way to prove to the girl that speed was for animals. Janet thought it best someone give the girl a chance to learn, but be near at hand in case she hurt herself tripping over a root or stone.

"Janet!" Jack said, behind her, and she jumped.

"Hush!" She said, turning angrily to the tall man who had crept up on the two.

"Are you still getting down in the dirt in your gown? And teaching bad habits to other young girls as well! I thought you were in the hall with the other ladies," her brother said with a knitted brow. Little Margaret just stared at the man, wringing her hands together worriedly.

"We're doing no harm!" Janet shot back. "And you know how I hate the endless afternoons in the hall with all those women, sewing and spinning, gossiping and whinging. They've got no sense at all. I'd rather be out here in the garden with the roses. It's a beautiful day, why should I be stuck inside with a bunch of wrinkled women who've got nothing better to do than talk about the latest fashion? I've no interest in silk ribbons!"

Jack had bent down and took her hand, pulling her to her feet, and she sighed with exasperation. "I could tell you to go get me a glass of water so you'd leave me alone while we escape, you know."

Jack looked hurt. "I'm just trying to make sure you're alright, Janet. Please don't make it harder on me. Your guard is already in trouble with father for having lost sight of you. Why do you have to be so difficult? You know the ball is only three days away, and you're expected to dance with all the sons of the noblemen father has invited. He's intending to find someone to wed you to, Janet! And I'm told you've been skipping out on the lessons the dance teacher has arranged, all week now. I was tasked with seeing that you didn't miss another, and I've failed in that already."

Janet rolled her eyes at him. "Egads, Jack! Grow a spine. He's hardly going to dismiss my guard. He's been serving us since I was young enough to be playing in the sandbox. I remember the day he brought my ball back, after it went over the wall."

"I remember that day as well, Janet, and it was many years ago. You are too old for games, lass. And he's not as fearful for employment as for his hide. Our father has ways to punish the men that you can't understand; he might only be father to you and I, but to the rest of the land, he's Lord Dunbar. Please try to behave! And come inside. For me, Janet. Please don't make me carry you. I'm not sure I could explain that, but I'm at wit's end what to do with you."

Janet pulled her hand out of his grasp, grabbed Margaret's tiny hand and flounced toward the great stone building, but her shoulders sagged as she heard him groan at her stubbornness. The ball was coming up so soon! And she was torn between spending these early days of summer out in the gardens, with the tulips and the birds, or stuck inside practicing enough of the dance steps to avoid making a complete fool of herself. But she hated being stuck inside the cold, stone walls of the ballroom on a glorious day like this; winter had been too long. She sighed and lifted her skirts as she trotted down the dusty path toward the wide steps of the hall her family had moved to while their castle was rebuilt. She hoped the dance master still waited for her. Her father would be furious if she had missed yet another lesson. She wished she could learn from the ladies, like the pages did, but nothing was good enough for Janet but the man renowned for perfect form. As a dancer, at least. As a gentleman, his form was deplorable.

The fiddlers were lounging on the floor, and the dance master was nowhere to be seen when she arrived, breathless, her chest heaving.

"Ah, there you are. So kind of you to join us." She spun around to see the lanky man pull himself out of the shadows in the corner of the hall. He was primped and coiffed like a prized dog, with velvet and sateen and ornate plumes extending for a full foot off of the ridiculous chaperon that sat on his brow. He strolled languorously toward her as if expecting her to swoon at the shapely curve of his leg. She sighed at his buffoonery, and he seemed to take it as a sigh of unrestrained longing.

"Please focus your attention on the lessons," he said, remonstrating her for staring at what he thought was an irresistible physique. The fiddlers had clattered to their chairs and were rapidly checking their strings to be sure they were in tune. There was a subtle, rakish half grin on the horrible man's ratlike face. Janet resigned herself to an impossibly grim hour of disturbing innuendos and vowed to endure the insult as she focused on learning enough to avoid being humiliated at the ball.

In the end, she was still practicing the steps of one of the dances three days later while her maid tried to pin up her hair for the evening, and Janet had to rush to the hall, late for her entrance to the festivities. Her father had a long-suffering look on his face as she slowed down and tried to look stately as she stepped into the hall with a measured pace. She heard a tiny whimper from her maid as one of her hairpins came loose and a long wavy lock of red hair dropped to her shoulder.

She barely had time to think of it as she was soon swept into one dance after another. She took a moment to breathe as she enjoyed one of her favorite dances. She rotated her hips with each of three steps forward, her arms in the air, then clapped her hands, and stepped back the same way, three times. She tried to ignore the man across from her who leered at her chest. She wanted to clap her hands over his ears and kick him a few times for good measure, but she just arched her brow and smiled primly at him, looking forward to a change of partner. As the next man moved toward her, almost tripping over his feet with eagerness to arrive at his place in the circle, she groaned silently. It was a recently widowed baron who had hurried north before his last wife was set in the ground, quick to find a fresh replacement, the younger the better. The official story was that his wife had fallen down the stairs, but Janet knew the woman was more surefooted than that, and his first wife had met the very same fate. Beyond him was the snaggle-toothed son of a duke, then another lord of some sort, she wasn't sure of what type because the breath with which he had assailed her when they spoke was so fetid she thought she would have to excuse herself to empty her stomach out the window.

How was she to choose a tolerable man among such churls?

## 16 – Passages

> "When she came to Carter Hall Tam Lin was at the well,
> And there she fand his steed standing, but away was
> himsel." Child Ballad 39: Tam Lin

Ada flounced up the hill, hoping Duncan was watching her. She was furious at finding him with another maid, heels up behind the barn. She'd planned to tryst with him this afternoon when she discovered his betrayal.

"Ada," she heard him call, but she refused to turn back. She imagined him dressing himself to race after her, and she took big strides to distance herself from him, betraying herself with hopeful glances over her shoulder.

She found herself far from home, following what was little more than a game trail through the trees, and was surprised to see a lovely meadow open up before her. She blinked as she suddenly noticed a huge white horse grazing at the edge of the grasses. Rubbing her eyes, she looked again and saw a darkly handsome young man with his hands against a rowan tree, cursing to himself. He looked up and fell silent as he saw her staring at him.

Refusing to show how flustered she was, she strode toward him as if she belonged there.

"You sir! What is your name?"

He gave her a crooked smile. "They call me Tam, of course. Who else?"

Ada tried to place the name but couldn't. "And where are you from?"

He sighed. "Right here. The Glen. Formerly the tower. Are you looking for me?"

Ada frowned. A forester, then. She refused to be cowed. "Well then, Tam o' the Glen, have you water? I'm fair parched."

He nodded, and stepped inside the tent for a moment, coming back out with a wooden cup. She took it from him and drank deeply, then handed it back to him with a coquettish curtsey. "Well?" she said, having no idea what else to say.

"I beg your pardon, we can get started if you wish," he murmured, "I made a promise to the lady and I'll honor it." He paused, brow furrowed, for just a moment before he reached for her bodice, and studiously pulled on one of the laces that secured it.

Her eyes flew open at his brashness, but her cry of alarm turned to sighs of pleasure as he also brushed the nape of her neck with his other hand. The gentle touch of the extraordinary young man's strong hands brought to mind the mischievous thought that Duncan might yet be following her. She hoped he found her just as she'd found him, and she leaned into the strange fellow who seemed well acquainted with a woman's body. Soon he had her gasping in ecstasy, right there in the sunlit field, Duncan driven from her mind.

Her back arched as they reached a climax together, and his body drew taut as a wire, then relaxed against her. She knew it was wrong, but she'd known so with Duncan, and he was never as attentive to her as this handsome stranger was. She was breathless, but took just a moment to look around, wondering if they were still alone. They were.

"What are you looking for, lass?"

"Ahhh… just wondering at how… lovely your field is…"

He gave her a wry grin as he pulled away from her. "A place as grand as the lady's tower in that it's my own," he said cryptically.

She shivered as a light breeze crossed her shoulders.

"Here, cover yourself, lass," he said solicitously, helping her back into her clothing.

She looked at him in wonder as he drew the strings of her gown back together. She straightened her skirts, realizing belatedly how rash she'd been, with a man who was a complete stranger to her. What if he were a common brigand? Nervously she scanned the edge of the forest, afraid she might see his mates lurking, awaiting their own turn.

Far be it from her to say she regretted the afternoon, but she it occurred to her that the man could be dangerous. She'd been so focused on her fury at Duncan, then the pure pleasure that had overcome her, that it wasn't until now that she wondered what the handsome young man's motives were. And she decided, rather than ask, she'd simply leave. If he let her. She cleared her throat. "Well, Tam o'Glen, I thank you for your attentions, but I must be going now." She jumped to her feet and ran back toward her home, fearful that her rash decision could have led her to harm. She cursed herself the entire way. What had she been thinking? A complete stranger! And a wild one, at that.

By the time she arrived back at the tower, she'd convinced herself she'd been waylaid by the dark man. She spun a tale for the other lasses of the way he insisted on her jewels and then, when she had none to give him, had forced himself on her. But it was hard to keep the breathlessness from her voice as she told how he removed her clothes, and when they questioned her, the faraway look in her eyes and her soft smile made them ponder whether she was as reluctant as she claimed.

It wasn't long before another lass crept away to find the handsome young man who had so charmed her friend, and then another. It was strange, though; sometimes he was there, sometimes he wasn't, but the headstrong young women of the keep soon had their own stories of the young rogue who took advantage of them, always claiming he stole what they never offered. And yet they kept finding reasons to creep over the hill, each explanation less credible than the last; an herb that didn't grow in their own garden, mushrooms the cook required, chasing a squirrel that had stolen a comb.

And Tam kept trying to find the key to open up a passage between the two worlds, pressing his hands against the Rowan tree and trying to sense the shift. He remembered how the shimmering air brightened, but he was flummoxed at how his surroundings remained the same no matter how many times he practiced. Still, he would learn nothing if he didn't keep trying, and try he did, never realizing how successful he was. It was only from the outside, looking in, that someone else would notice the horse and the man appearing and disappearing over time, only to appear again later.

## 17 – The Decree

"Carter Hall it is mine ain, my daddie gave it me; I'll come and go by Carter Hall and ask nay leave o' thee." Child Ballad 39: Tam Lin

Janet stood reverently as the priest swung the incense, passing her on his way out of the chapel. Her father fell in behind the man, and she behind him; the service was over and it was time to get to business. Her slippered feet whispered along the flagstone corridor. She was not looking forward to the meeting he had called her to. He had told her to give him an answer the morning after the ball, but she had dodged him for days. He had finally called the entire court to hear what she had to say, and she could dodge the question no longer. Not a single man was even tolerable, much less desirable. She sighed as she passed through the ornate, gold-leaf doors and into the great hall. She stepped past the rows of benches provided for anyone who wished to hear the proceedings, dismayed to see that most of them were full. He had made it easy for everyone to hear her answer, and she had no idea what that might be.

"Come forward, Janet," Lord Dunbar's voice rang out through the hall, and she flinched, moving reluctantly forward, keeping her head down as a respectful daughter should. She came forward until she was three feet in front of him and dropped into a low curtsey, hoping to give herself time to think. Here in the hall, in front of all the gathered crowd, how could she tell him she couldn't stand the thought of a single one of the ill-favored men and not sound petulant? She searched her memory for a single thing to commend any of the suitors who had arrived to woo her, but every one of them had been so repulsive, so reprehensible, she found no redemptive value in any of them. This was not going to be pleasant and her heart went out to her father. He was a good man, he deserved a more obedient daughter.

"It's kind of you to bless us with your presence," her father said, with an arch of his brow.

"Blessings upon you today, father, you're looking well," she rose from the curtsy and smiled at him.

"Enough with pleasantries, Janet. What say you?"

"About what?"

"Janet!"

She jumped at the loud crack! as he slammed his book down on the arm of the large chair he sat in at the front of the hall. "Don't suggest you don't know why you're here! Speak."

Janet felt like her stomach was going to leap out through her throat and she swallowed hard. "Um, thank you for bringing such a... an impressive array of men... of all ages... to the ball, father. Um, it was a joy to—"

"Which one?" he interrupted, but quietly.

"Ah... well, you see..."

"Please don't tell me you found not a single man to meet your requirements?"

"Well... ah..."

"Enough! You would insult all of the lords that came to the festivities by suggesting that you would rather become a spinster than put up with any of them, is that right?"

Janet looked at her feet in shame. Of course she didn't want to be a spinster! But she wanted a man she could respect, at least.

"Answer me; is it true you will have none of them?"

Janet nodded, then jumped again as he slammed the book on the arm of the chair a second time. "That's it! I have had enough of your insolence. You cannot remain here for the rest of your life, and I can't continue to have the hall upended to provide balls for you to peruse your options."

"But father—"

"SILENCE!" Her father's face turned bright red, then slowly faded. "I would prefer you be a willing bride, but this cannot go on. I give you twelve months, Janet, not a day more. If you can't find a man that is agreeable to you, I will find one myself, and you will be married by decree."

*Oh dear God,* Janet thought, feeling a bit faint at the thought of being forced to marry any of the foul-smelling, boorish or decrepit creatures her father had scared up out of the surrounding lands like so many chickens running for kitchen scraps. Her eyes dropped to the floor.

"Anyone I choose?" she said, not brave enough to look up and see the disgust she knew would be written across his face.

"As long as he's a nobleman and trained in the art of war. I'll not have a peasant or a dainty for a son-in-law."

Janet released the breath she was holding.

"And on that note, I've given orders that you're not to receive further lessons in any of the weapons you've been studying."

"But Father—" she gasped.

"Silence!" He said again, but in a more measured tone. "I'll have you learn to sew like all the other ladies do. You'll start behaving like a woman, Janet; no more of this childish play."

"And what will I say of my dowry?" She attempted humility.

There was silence, and Janet worried that she went too far.

"You will have a sufficient dowry. I intend for you to receive Carter Hall; it's not far from here, in fact. Anyone who wishes to view it will find it a pleasant walk or a quick ride. Plague me no further; you are dismissed. Get out of my hall."

He might as well have whipped her as speak the last sentence. It was unnecessary, after she had been dismissed, and proof of an intense fury that he otherwise contained. She had never felt so alone as she backed, then turned, almost running to get through the doors before her tears spilled down her cheeks.

Voices rose around her and her father's voice cut through the sound like a scythe through a stand of wheat as he called for the next order of business. She had expected his disappointment, but had no idea he could be so angry with her! He had doted on her for so many years. Yet it wasn't his betrayal of her that hurt so much, but hers of him.

She went to the children's room and collected a number of them to go outside for a game of tag, as she so often did when the world weighed on her. She wanted a large family of her own, but for that she needed a man, preferably one less repulsive than the current options.

Sew? She was to learn to sew? The thought mortified her. Were the days of running about with the children over? Well, not today. She led her small charges out past the kitchen into the vegetable garden, where several of the cooks were pulling carrots for the evening's stew. Today she would enjoy the sunshine and play with the children. Tomorrow would be soon enough for sewing.

## 18 – The Traveler

"Cast your green mantle over me, I'll be myself again."
Child Ballad 39: Tam Lin

"Oh my, look at this russet silk," one of the ladies sighed as she let the cloth flow through her fingertips. Janet looked up from wondering what the blue linen she held was suited for. The other three ladies were admiring the ribbons at the back of the trundling wagon that had stopped in front of the high wall around the keep.

"Only the finest, brought back by the silk road through the damned lands by my best journeyman," the traveler said. "But if you want a truly fine cloth, I should show you what I keep in the bound chest, hidden away from all but the most discerning eyes, my ladies." The man's face lit up with anticipation, and all the ladies cooed and nodded eagerly. He ceremoniously unlocked a huge chest in the back of the wagon, levering the top up as they crowded against him to see what lay beyond. The sun struck the bright white cloth and they gasped as they all saw gold sparkling throughout the brilliant fabric; he reverently placed a hand under a pleat and lifted it so they could see it fall in pliant folds. Janet herself gasped at the incredible beauty.

"It's cloth of gold!" One of the ladies said, and he beamed at them as they tried to reach for it, but he restrained them with an arm.

"Oh, I must ask that you not touch this, miladies. I'm sure you understand; it is such a rich fabric I cannot take the chance that a speck of morning toast or a bit of honey besmirch it."

"Oh, but I MUST have it!" a plump noblewoman said.

"The cost is dear," he made as if to put it away and all the ladies began to beg and plead to know the price of such fine material. And so the haggling began; he refused to cut it at all, so the only thing that would do was to buy the entire length of cloth, and for that each of the ladies had to speak up for a portion. Janet thought it was lovely and spoke up for a piece. Enough to make a brat, the simple kilted cloak many highlander women wore. If she had to learn to sew, she would start with the simplest thing she could think of.

It would be weeks before the cloth began to turn pale green, after being measured and cut on the fulling tables, then worn in the damp and rain. The man was nowhere to be found by then. The longer pieces were cut into shorter lengths, and in the end they laughed as each tried to outdo the other with embroidery to try to draw attention from the unfortunate experience as they were turned into simple shawls. Janet decided to keep hers at full length, determined to have a garment like her mother had worn when she was young, even if the fabric wasn't all it had promised to be.

## 19 – The Warning

"I forbid ye, maidens a' that wear gowd on your hair to come or gae by Carter Hall, for young Tam Lin is there."
Child Ballad 39: Tam Lin

Janet sat with her back to the tower room, looking out the window toward the piece of land her father had said would be hers as soon as she chose a man to share it with. She could just barely make out what looked like a small stone building in a field bordered by a stream. She pricked her finger with the needle once again and cursed sharply as she put the offended digit into her mouth to ease the pain.

"Janet!" Her father's voice interrupted her thoughts, and she looked up in surprise.

"Father?"

"I'll have you watch your tongue! You sound like a mercenary. Could you at least pretend to have the habits of a lady?"

Janet tried not to roll her eyes, but his expression darkened as he watched her anyway. "Father, I didn't expect to see you here," she blurted.

"And I wouldn't have disturbed you all," he said with a slight bow to the ladies, "But I've been hearing reports of a most grievous situation in Carter Hall that I must warn you of—"

"Oh dear—"

"What's amiss--"

"Has someone gotten hurt?" The ladies' voices spilled over each other.

Her father held up a hand to silence them, and Janet watched his eyes. She'd never seen him so serious.

"No fatal injuries, miladies; it's a brigand. I'm told he goes by the name Tam o' the Glen, and he's been rising up out of nowhere to take young women… ah… well, he seems to have a taste for the lasses, if you understand me." He looked supremely uncomfortable. An unintelligible babble arose again, and he held up his hand once more. "Hush, there is nothing for you to be afraid of here in the hall, but I must insist that you all stay away from Carter Hall until I can spare men to find this dastardly creature. He only seems to appear when there is a young lass, alone, out seeking herbs or mushrooms."

"You don't mean for us to go without mushrooms, do you?"

"Oh, you'll have your mushrooms, one way or another. I'll not tell the cooks to curtail their gathering of whatever they cannot find in our own gardens, and perhaps the potboys would best be sent for them, but I've let them know I cannot guarantee the safety of any of the lasses. And those of you who are old enough to make your own decisions, you are free to do so, though I need you to be apprised. However," and now the lord looked straight into Janet's eyes, "I am forbidding all the unmarried ladies who aren't servants from venturing anywhere near the ground of Carter Hall until this is dealt with. Do I make myself clear?"

Janet nodded, still sucking her finger, eyes wide. After he left, she ran to her room, found the spyglass she received two years ago as a gift, and ran back to the lady's hall, where the brat she was hemming had fallen to the ground. She leaned out the window, putting the glass to her eye, and strained to see what kind of man might be lurking about on the grounds of Carter Hall. How dare he!

Did he not know the land was hers? Someone must tell him to leave.

Seeing nothing but long grasses waving in the sunlight, she lowered the spyglass, but remained at the window as she considered what she might do to fix this problem. The stranger would only show up when some slight girl he could easily overpower came alone through the glen? Well, we'll see what he does when a lass trained in wielding a fencing foil could do! She knew where her brother kept his epee, always sharp as a pin and well oiled. We'll just see what this Tam Glen says to having the tip of a sword at his throat!

## 20 – An Auspicious Meeting

"She's let the seam fall at her heels, the needle to her toe,
and she has gone to Carter Hall as fast as she can go."
Child Ballad 39: Tam Lin

Janet lifted the spyglass to her eye again, and this time she was taken aback. There was a black-haired man in the meadow! He was brushing the mane of a huge white horse. She broke the thread she was sewing with and dropped the needle to the floor, not caring where it landed as she set the spyglass on the sewing stand. She pulled her skirts up with both hands so she could hurry out the door. One of the ladies looked at her, jaw wide open, as she scuttled down the hallway to the stairs, and Janet supposed she might be watching out the window as Janet ran down the coach trail toward her dowry land. Watch as they would, but she would have words with this young man!

She could see that one of the guards was turning her direction, so she ran through the garden and hid behind the tall arborvitae until all the men's eyes were turned the other way. They were more concerned about keeping people out than keeping them in. She slipped out the end of the gate and edged along the outer side of the wall until she couldn't be seen by them, then began to run again, stretching her legs and exulting in the sense of freedom the fresh air gave her. It had been far too long that she'd been cooped up inside the heavy walls of the castle, and she laughed as she felt the wind in her hair and the sun on her shoulders.

When she came to the meadow, smiling and panting with the effort, she realized she still had the cloth in her left hand, and she laughed, then looked around. There was the horse, standing steady and looking at her, but where had the man gone?

"Lass, are you alright?" a man's voice said, from over her shoulder where he leaned against a tree.

"Ahhh!" She cried and dropped the fabric, realizing she'd left her brother's sword behind. What on earth was she thinking?

He plucked the fabric from the ground and handed it to her with a flourish. "Your shawl, milady?" he said, bowing low before her with a wink.

She had been about to say something, but she found herself mesmerized by the darkly handsome stranger. His intense grey eyes were the color of storm clouds in winter but lit with a fire that seemed to burn her up without consuming her. He lifted her hand and led her to a heavy cloak that lay on the ground. She tried to get another good look at him but the sun was in her eyes, and she had to shade them with a hand. Still speechless, she watched the roll of muscles on his naked arms as he pulled the green fabric over them both as if it were a tent so that the sun couldn't bother her. He smelled of bruised grass and rosemary, and every move was as graceful as a cat on the hunt.

"It seems you'll need a moment to catch your breath." He took her hand and brushed a lock of hair away from her cheek. "Perhaps we should just talk for now."

"Oh, yes," she whispered, "That would be exquisite!" Her cheeks colored as she realized how eager it sounded, even to her.

He turned his head in surprise, looking sideways at her as if trying to determine what she was up to, then he laughed. "Well, milady, just when I thought I knew what to expect, I find myself at a disadvantage. You are nothing like any other I've met in this realm. Tell me, what does such a one as you enjoy *talking* of?"

"Ahhh…" she said again, and he leaned over to kiss her lips; it took her breath away so completely she knew it would be some time before she could speak at all.

He smiled again with amusement. "Well, would you like to hear a story of how a young man learns to wield a sword?"

"Oh, I know how to carry an epee," she said excitedly. "But tell me what you can of great swords. I've never held one."

His eyes widened. "Lass, where did you get an epee?"

"My brother is quite skilled, he taught me much."

Tam tilted his head, pursed his lips briefly, then narrowed his eyes. "I don't suppose he's the Captain of the Guard?"

"Certainly not! He oversees our land use."

"No! Your brother spends his days out on the moors?"

She laughed. "I would tag along if I could!" She sighed. "But I'm obliged to sew now." She leaned toward him. "So tell me, how does wielding a great sword differ from an epee?"

Perplexed, Tam indulged the eager lass until they were both surprised by the growing dark. Janet jumped to her feet. "Oh dear!" she said, as she heard the galloping of hooves from a distance, growing louder, and she grabbed the length of fabric that had fallen to the ground again. Lifting her skirts, she ran toward the sounds; she would be punished for being away so long. She didn't want to be found where her father told her not to go, and she met the men just over the rise; she looked back over her shoulder, but the grey-eyed man was gone and his horse stood alone again, grazing just a few yards from where he stood when she arrived. When one of the guards dropped down to the path and lifted her to sit side-saddle on his broad-backed stallion she made both of them swear not to tell her father where they had found her. She looked back one more time and saw that the horse was gone as well.

## 21 – Exposed

*"When I use the Faraday shawl, she can't find me to control me." -Tam Lin, "Kindred Moon"*

Tam was chopping wood when he saw Morgan come over the rise toward him, with the four guards following closely behind. He continued lifting logs into place, striking them with the axe until each was the proper size to build a fire and cook a small meal, but the memory of the astonishingly beautiful red-haired lass that had visited yesterday remained.

"Where did you disappear to yesterday?" Morgan asked him as he lifted the axe again. Her voice was calm, but her eyes were hard and sharp, like split obsidian.

"I was in my field, where else could I be? And prepared to perform my duties for any who came," he added, in case she came to berate him. He would have if the young woman didn't leave so abruptly. "Why do you ask?" Tam kept his voice light, but every nerve along his shoulders, arms, and back seemed alight with tension, preparing him for an attack which didn't come. He rested the head of the axe on his boot as he watched her. He knew he had let time get away from him, the conversation had been so delightful with the fiery red-headed lass. She had come to him with such imperiousness and humor that his head had fought with his passions, at once wanting to bed her as he was ordered but also to keep her at a distance so he could watch the way her lips curved against the freckled paleness of her skin. There must have been an additional enchantment on her, which bothered him, but not so much that he didn't wish to see her again. He realized he had no desire to discuss the woman, both because he knew the punishment that would follow if she suspected he shirked his "duties" again, and because he wanted to keep the details of their visit to himself, to pretend that Morgan knew nothing of the charming creature. He finally felt Morgan's presence in his head again.

"I looked for you, but I couldn't see you," she pressed him. "I was too busy to investigate until just now; you've forced me to come in person to see what you're doing that has blocked me!"

She seemed to be ignoring his dereliction of duty, focusing instead on her inability to latch onto his mind through the Rigellium. He reminded himself that it had been the young woman who had chosen to talk rather than act, and it was she that ended the visit, and suddenly at that. "I took a nap on my cloak. I was right there," Tam pointed to where his cloak was spread out again.

Her eyes narrowed. "I delved for you, but you were nowhere to be found. I was just going to speak to my Captain when you became detectable again." Her lips thinned. "I haven't delved since, so that you would not be warned of my visit, but I see no explanation." Her voice lowered to a growl. "You have found a way to hide from me. I don't like it. Don't do it again."

Tam was baffled. He eyed her speculatively.

She peered around the field, looking for something, went into the hall, then came back out. "Do you have iron? Copper? Did you use it to shield yourself?"

He felt the tickle of her mind in his and, not wanting her to know his thoughts, he concentrated on the foot positions of an intricate dance so she would find only useless thoughts. Two steps forward, then slide to the left, weave between the lasses then whip around.

*How are you hiding the truth from me?* Her voice resonated inside his head. He didn't move, concentrating hard on the dance steps to occupy his mind. He looked straight into her eyes, thinking about how black they were to further distract himself, and she scowled at him. That he could hide his mind from her was an extraordinary revelation. Gruoch had said guile was not in their nature; perhaps that meant they couldn't overcome it either.

Black, black eyes, he thought, striving to think of nothing else so she could learn nothing more.

Rage distorted her face into a mask of fury. "Do not hide your thoughts from me!" She screamed at him, but he kept staring, keeping his memories to himself. She stormed back over the crest of the hill, but gave a flick of her hand so that her men remained behind.

And the attack came, in her absence. Three guards ganged up on him to beat him hard and the fourth wrenched the axe from his grasp. He fought them with a fierce rage, finally able to use everything he had against them, with neither the captain nor Morgan there to control the Rigellium. Whatever they were, their powers seemed limited to the physical plane.

He spun, kicked, punched, and dove at them, turning from one to the next as they flailed against him. He had learned their moves by now and knew how best to overcome their defenses, formulaic as they were. In the end, he was beaten only because he was exhausted while they remained tireless, but he gave as good as he got, his one to their four. His ability to think ahead and vary his attacks limited their success.

Then he felt her slip out of his mind; he was sure of it. She'd been there the whole time, as he was pummeled and beaten. She neither interfered nor withdrew. She reveled in his torment. Gruoch had called it shameful, this lust she had for the sensation of his suffering. Well, a desire for pain was just as sick, by human reckoning.

That evening, as he swallowed several more drops of the potion Philip had given him, he thought about her words. Copper. He remembered Gruoch saying copper could block the chains, but he didn't understand how to use it.

It was the middle of the night when he sat bolt upright. The shawl! It had to be the green shawl. He knew about cloth of gold; could there be such a thing as cloth of copper? That would explain the sparkle. He might have realized it sooner, but there'd been so little sparkle. Still, it was the only thing he could think of. The pale green shawl. He hoped the lass returned so he could ask her about it. Well, of course she would! She still needed what she had come for. She would be back. And he had so many questions.

## 22 – Liam

*"At first he changed all in her arms into a wild wolf…"*
Child Ballad 39: Tam Lin

A quiet voice coughed from the edge of the trees. Tam looked up and was surprised to see a wild-looking man. The man beckoned to him urgently and Tam ambled to where he stood.

"This clearing is usually empty. Is Gruoch here?" the man asked.

"I've not seen her for some time," Tam answered, then waited for a response.

The man's eyes flicked nervously back and forth between Tam and the direction of Morgan's stone tower. "We need her advice!"

Tam raised an eyebrow. "On what grounds?"

The man looked indecisive.

"If you're looking for the Sh'eyta, you've found us," Tam said, guessing at the cause of the man's reticence, and wanting to move the conversation along.

The man paused just a little longer, then appeared to make a decision. "We need her help with another man who has lost the ability to transform. It seems to be consuming him, and he will not survive another month if we cannot help him. We spoke to her of this, and she promised to look into it, but we're running out of time. Carry a message, if you would—"

"Why would I?" Tam tried to hide his alarm. The man before him must be one of the beastmen Gruoch spoke of since, apparently, his affliction came with an ability to transform, and Tam assumed that meant to transform into an animal. Selkie, perhaps? This far from water?

The man frowned at him. "Why would you not? A man is dying!"

"A beast is dying," Tam answered warily. He didn't like the Sh'eyta, and he didn't trust the creatures they made. The man could assume he was Sh'eyta, he might as well play the part. Would this man become a demon animal before his very eyes?

"Hold your tongue!" The man drew a dagger from his belt, and Tam stepped back, reaching for his axe. "He's merely man now, anyway; I told you he's lost the ability to transform."

"He is blessed, then," Tam said firmly, lifting his left arm slightly to better block the man's small weapon, should he try to use it.

The man shook his head in dismay. "You're no Sh'eyta! We're under oath to report to Gruoch."

Tam crouched down on his heels, ignoring the blade that the man still wielded. If the man were trained at weapons he'd have changed his grip when Tam shifted his arm. It was clear the man was no warrior, and Tam was sure he could disarm him before he took any cuts from the rust-spotted blade. The man's eyebrows drew together and his countenance fell.

Tam began to feel pity for the poor forester. "I'm told I'm half Sh'eyta, half man. Enough to know Gruoch and

Morgan," he offered the second name as evidence that he was, indeed, of the Sh'eyta.

The man appeared to be renewed with hope. "We need to speak to Gruoch! Come, you wouldn't revel in a man's death, would you?"

Tam watched the man's eyes. The man seemed to be earnest. "If you would have me carry your message, you'll prove yourself to me first."

In truth, Tam needed to know more about these shapeshifting humans. If other nations really did use shapeshifters, it would be good to understand what they could do, and how to defeat them. Was it a condition that simply turned him into a beast, yet he remained the same man, inside? It was quite a leap just to consider that a man could turn into an animal. But what if? He eyed the man, ready to leap away if need be. What if they remained human inside, while others called them demons and set out to execute them?

Then a horrifying thought came to him. What if THIS was the devil's ruse? Not to condemn a man with the form of a beast, but to condemn an entire village for murdering an innocent man! The crafty brilliance was just the kind of thing Satan was known for. The devil would only collect one soul if it was evil to become an animal, but the souls of an entire village could be collected if killing an innocent creature was the evil act. The devil would rather collect more souls.

"I just need you to carry a message to Gruoch," the man implored.

"First tell me more about this condition you have," Tam said, as he tried to fathom what the devil's game might be. "Are there others? Where do you live?"

"I've said too much! I don't know you. Why should I trust you?"

Tam leaned back. "Aye, we're at a standoff. Well then, I'll carry your message to the tower in good faith, and it will be your turn to prove yourself to me."

"Come tell me her answer—"

"Nay… I'll not trust you as far as that." The man seemed unaware that Tam couldn't go beyond this field. "You'll have to come back to see if there's an answer."

The next day Tam went up to the gate and gave the message to a guard as he'd promised, fighting the temptation to get revenge for the beating they gave him, now that it would be one-on-one. He had no intention of going inside the tower walls again.

Every evening thereafter, Liam came to find out if there was an answer yet. Tam had no idea what had happened to Gruoch, but in time he found himself looking forward to Liam's visits, having grown lonely in his isolation. He asked about Lord's Dunbar and Douglas, but the man was a mere woodsman with no access to men of high station.

"How are you coming through to this side of the veil?" Tam asked one evening when Liam appeared to see if Gruoch had come yet.

Liam shrugged. "Gruoch tells me all lupans have some Sh'eyta in them. We can open the doorway with some effort, but it was open when I arrived, and since it's not the solstice or equinox I thought you opened it."

Tam frowned. Had he? He understood so little.

Tam cooked the rabbit Liam had brought, which became a ritual as Tam continued to receive daily visits from Liam. He even asked after the man's kin, starved for company as he was. The man asked him about Morgan and the others, hoping he could find a way to motivate them to come to his aid. They both learned about each other's conditions and gradually came to respect each other.

Liam touched the chain around Tam's neck one day. "You say she controls you with this?"

"Aye." Tam pushed Liam's hand aside.

"And you can feel them in your mind?"

"Aye."

"If you were one of us, it wouldn't fit in beastform."

Tam pondered the idea. If he were a seal, would the chains slip off? He shook his head. "I have no desire to become a creature that could never go among my peers again."

Liam snorted. "There is nothing that keeps me from my peers. I live a normal life."

"What do you do when the beast comes over you?"

"We've learned to control when we become a wolf and when we don't, as long as we don't go too long between changes. It helps that we're a small group of forester. We live deep in the wilderness. Once a month we let the animal loose, then return to ourselves again. But for those of us who share the condition, we must keep the knowledge from those that don't. The townsfolk I trade with always appreciate that I bring rabbits for their stewpots when I visit them, and don't ask me how I took them. There are advantages to being an animal once in a while, and in time you can control your form and remain conscious, use the claws and fangs, the four-legged speed; in honesty, you can take venison if you choose. The king's decree is only for humans."

Tam's jaw dropped in astonishment. He would never take the king's deer without permission. Would he? Well, if he were a wolf, he'd have no use for laws, he supposed.

Tam heard the clop of hooves and looked over to the graveled road that led to the tower.

The mounted guard gestured toward them. "Liam! Gruoch has called for you. Come with me."

Liam leapt to his feet.

"Wait!" Tam cried, and Liam looked impatiently back at him. "Come back to me when you are finished with her," Tam said. Liam nodded, then jogged over to the horsed guard and slapped the horse's flank, running alongside the trotting animal until he disappeared over the crest of the hill. Tam hoped the friendly, if beastly, woodsman found an answer for his troubles. If Gruoch could find it in her heart to help the cursed man, then maybe there was still hope she could get Tam away from this place as well.

## 23 – No Regrets

"And he has took her by the hand, took her by the sleeve,
And he has laid this lady down, among the grasses green."
Child Ballad 39: Tam Lin

A week later, on the afternoon of the summer solstice, Janet found herself slipping away from the others again, more discreetly this time. She pretended to have an upset stomach and told the ladies she would lie down until the evening meal and hope she was feeling better by then if she could be left undisturbed to rest.

And so she found the field, the horse, and the stone hall. Should she go to the door? Or would that be too bold, too beseeching? She pulled at a pink rose from one of the bushes, lifting the sweet-smelling flower to her nose.

"What are you doing picking my roses?" he asked, from behind her.

"These are my roses!" she protested, turning toward him.

"Don't I have a say in who comes and goes from my field?" He winked.

"My field!" she insisted. "This land is part of my dowry!"

"Ah," he laughed, "then perhaps I should give you a tithe…" he chuckled and led her to sit on his cloak again, then stopped himself, noticing the way the sun fell on her fair cheeks. "Where is your shawl?" He asked, not wanting to see her skin burned in the ever-present sunlight of this place.

"Safe at home," she said archly, but she was staring into his eyes as if she were hungry. He turned and led her to the shade, and they talked for several more hours, sitting on his cloak. Janet felt a growing longing, and crept closer to the dark, handsome young man, who eventually slipped a hand under her skirt and stroked her bare leg. The heat of his touch enflamed her, feeding a need that slowly enveloped her senses. She was mesmerized by his grey eyes as he pressed her shoulders to the ground, then lifted her skirts up her thighs. She gasped as he caressed her flesh and for a moment he stopped as if surprised, then he ran his fingers between her thighs, and she gasped again. She moaned and closed her eyes as he continued to caress the soft, moist folds of her flesh, then leaned over to kiss her soft, pink lips.

Pleasure? He kissed her again as he loosened his own garments. He'd begun to think maybe the charming young lass was purely human, but she showed up today and he knew he hadn't tried to open a passage since the day before. She could only have come from the tower. Gruoch had told him all the Sidhe were part human and had even mentioned that Morgan seemed more human than most, which was hard to believe. If the Sh'eyta were part human to varying degrees, perhaps this one was more passionate, which enflamed him more. He pretended the lass was human as they both sighed when his flesh entered hers. He insisted on going slow, refusing to make this the chore the Sh'eyta claimed it to be. He found himself wanting her to stay and held himself back, lifting himself up on his arms to watch the way her chin lifted toward him as she moaned softly. The sweet bliss as he penetrated the yielding, tight silk of her downy flesh had them both straining against each other, but he moved slowly, continuing the lingering pursuit of their mutual pleasure as if somehow he was getting through to her. Perhaps, if he did it right, she would come back to him again, and they could talk… his body rocked ever so gently against hers until the sensation became insistent and he increased the pace gradually, holding back the rapture as long as he possibly could until her moans rose in power and he felt a surge crest over him; he could hold back no longer. In sobs of sweet ecstasy, he lowered himself down upon her and they gripped each other tightly as he drove into her like an ocean wave pounding against the shore, and he felt as if it would go on forever, yet all too soon it passed. He continued to rock against her for a few more moments, holding her close to him, burying his face in the rose-scented locks of her hair. He wanted to hold her forever. As soon as he released her she would go, and he desperately wanted her to stay.

But she didn't leave him. He leaned back to see that she was staring up at the sky, the expression on her face impossible to read. Her mouth was open, and she seemed quite dazed. He'd surprised her. Had he reached her, somehow?

"Lass?"

She turned to look at his face, and slowly her wide eyes focused on him. "What have you done?" she whispered.

Her query puzzled him. "Lass? This is what you came for…"

Now the look on her face turned to betrayal, and shock, but he could see the tendons of her neck tighten as even then she seemed to lean upward toward him, and he leaned down to kiss her beautiful face again, then leaned back as she pushed against his chest.

"Tam!" she said, and suddenly pulled her skirts down.

Confused by her conflicted actions he pulled away from her. Her kiss had been eager, and her body as well. He was sure she had found pleasure in this, though the pleasure was needless and so strangely human. Then shock overpowered him. He must have missed something! How could a human be here if the passage was closed?

"Lass! You're Sh'eyta, are you not? You came for this!" he insisted as horror sank in. He remembered something about certain days his people could come to him. Had he just defiled a virgin maid? He tried to remember just what she had said and done when he first touched her skin. Had she resisted? He'd assumed consent. He'd assumed she was Sh'eyta.

She shook her head numbly, eyes wide open. "I don't know what you mean."

His heart dropped like a rock as he watched emotions cross her face while she came to terms with the possible reality. "Oh, no, lass… how did you come to be here? You must be Sh'eyta! I remain hidden to any other…" He took her in his arms and held her tight.

She shook her head against his shoulder, then tried to push away, resisting him, until she relaxed in his arms as he rocked her. "Lass, tell me you came here for this. Tell me you're Sh'eyta."

Against his shoulder she mumbled, "What's that?"

"Sh'eyta. Sidhe."

"I'm not a Faery!" She protested, and after a few seconds added, adamantly, "And I came here for this."

He stopped rocking her and leaned back to look into her eyes, where her expression of wonder was transformed to one of resolve. Her jaw was set, and there was a tiny crease between her eyebrows. She pulled the cloak around herself, then began to speak proudly. "I came here for this. I didn't think about it, but it's true; I came here for this. There was only one possible outcome if I came to Carter Hall, and I knew that. I may be a fool, but you took nothing from me that I didn't give you, of my own free will."

He frowned. "But lass…"

She shook her head with determination. "No. This was my choice. And I'll not have you saying it wasn't." Then, with a sly smile, she continued. "I thought about bringing my brother's light sword and confronting you over your transgressions, but I kept forgetting, for some reason. If I'd meant to defend myself I'd have brought the sword."

Tam snorted at the suggestion that the slender lass could best him, but marveled at the fierce way her jaw moved as she insisted on his innocence. HIS innocence! And what was this about transgressions? He was confused. But more than anything, he wanted to know more about her. "Lass…" he said again, this time with admiration. Then he frowned. "Do you do this often?"

She gasped. "You impertinent wretch! Never before!" Then, more solemnly, "I should not have, but I'll not be betrothed without at least once choosing my partner."

"It's hardly a dance, lass…

"Janet," she sighed. "My name is Janet."

It was Tam's turn to gasp, as he cupped her chin in his strong hand and turned her face to him, looking into her soft brown eyes in the waning light as the sun began to set. He eyed the curve of her cheek, the arch of her brow, the spread of freckles across the bridge of her nose, then leaned back suddenly, in horror. "Janet! Dunbar's lass?"

"He's my father."

"Janet, it's myself—"

As the last rays of sunlight slipped away, Janet cried out, "Oh! Its late!" She leapt to her feet and ran. Clutching his trews he ran after her, but she passed the rowan tree before he could pull them up and reach her. Then the world tilted sideways, and she wasn't there at all. Tam stumbled forward, grasping for her, seeking the folds of her gown, the silken strands of her hair, the curve of her waist… but there was nothing. He tied his trews quickly and ran toward the hedgeline where she'd disappeared, but he was brought up short by the bite of chain around his neck when he tried to pass through; his vision went black as he tried to pull air into his lungs, past the constriction of the sharp metal rings. He stopped and backed up until the chains released their grip. Tam fell to the ground and pounded it in fury.

He had to get away from this place. His life was in the other world. His family, his duty, all back where he came from. Janet was back where he came from. Not here. Janet… Janet was there.

He looked at the chains that bound him. He couldn't remove them, couldn't resist them. He dug at them once again, but they refused to yield. He was trapped, and he hated that fact more than anything else he endured in this hell-born place. He was a free man; he wouldn't rest until he found a way to remove the chains and get back to where he knew he belonged.

Dunbar! Surely Janet would return, and all Tam need do is have her tell her father that Tam had been taken by the Sh'eyta, Lord Dunbar could come and rescue him! Then his stomach tightened and he felt sick. Tam had just taken his daughter's virginity. Would the fiery lord rescue him, or murder him? Tam wasn't sure which, and realized that was a conversation he wanted witnesses for, preferably several strong enough to hold the man back if it came to that. Lord Dunbar had been fighting in wars for longer than Tam had been alive, and he was well known to be quite cunning, as well as powerfully built. Tam was at a disadvantage here. He had to find his way out of this place. He wasn't ready to give up yet.

## 24 – Ware! Wolf

Tam sat in the field staring toward the woods as the evening turned from dusky twilight to full darkness, his thoughts wandering in circles, but always coming back to the fiery redhead who had visited him twice. Even before he knew who she was, he found her enchanting. He loved her fierceness, her energy, her delight in all things wild and open. He thought her only fault was that she wasn't human. To find that she was not only human, but the very lass his memories had returned to time and time again as he grew up, had filled him with such joy… and then she was gone. He kept looking along the trail toward the woods, the direction she ran when the world shifted on him.

Tam looked up as he heard the crunch of hooves on gravel and saw the captain as he appeared at the top of the small hill toward the tower. He wore black leather armor from neck to toe, and his gloves were studded with steel; Tam had never seen him so thoroughly prepared to fight. Tam glanced at the axe on the far side of the field where he'd been chopping more wood for his fire. Could he reach it in time? As if in answer, the black-clad Sidhe spurred his steed to a gallop, closing the distance between them.

"Morgan tells me you're hiding metal," he said as he dismounted. "Where is it?"

Tam scowled. "There's no copper here."

The captain strode forward, grabbing Tam by the neck with his left hand, his right hand on the hilt of the short sword hanging from his hip. "We know you hid from her! There is no way to do so without iron or copper. Tell me where it is or this evening will not go well for you!"

Tam twisted out of the man's grasp. "Keep your filthy hands off me, you hedge-born mandrake!"

The captain whisked his sword from the scabbard, and they faced each other.

Tam had never been so furious. "You've taken me from my lands, my work, my allegiances, my family, you've taken my weapons, and now you face me with sword, and I unarmed, and ask me to yield to you what I don't have! Where are your powers, faerie bobolyne? Your queen can still me with a glance, and now needs less than that, but you can't even hold me with your bare hands, nor overcome me in fair duel, but you must come at me with steel, you lymmer son of a whore, while I, but a man with nothing but flesh and bone against you, have bested you yet. Where is your honor, demonspawn? Come at me if you will, but I'll not go down without a fight. Come at me, you foul misbegotten waste of flesh, and don't use your mind to still me first!"

"Your mind is foul, it sickens me to enter it without need, and I've no need when your skills are no better than those of a trained beast." The captain lunged forward and Tam sidestepped with astounding speed, slamming an elbow down on the other man's leathered wrist. The *crack* of bone on bone rang out in the stillness of the night, and Tam swung a fist against the back of the man's head. The captain was accustomed to obedience, and to weaponed fights, but Tam had been trained to win a duel no matter how he was armed. With a sweep of his leg, he upended his opponent, then lunged down and tried to wrench the short sword from his grasp, but the captain pulled back and Tam fell flat on him. They wrestled on the ground, rolling and kicking at each other as Tam kept trying to get the sword, but the captain's grip held.

"Pfaugh! Give it up, you foul creature!" Tam growled. "Your people do what they're told regardless of what is right, you've never had to fight for what you believe in." He'd surprised the man with his first quick volley of moves, but they were more evenly matched now that it was a test of strength, and Tam had lost the element of surprise.

"Behave yourself!" came the grunted reply. "You dishonor yourself with this disobedience."

Tam leaned down and bit the man's wrist, between glove and sleeve. The captain cried out in shock and pain as Tam tried to wrench the sword from him, rolling away to rise to his feet, the rowan tree at his elbow. He took a step back, then stood in a defensive crouch, watching for another opportunity to disarm his opponent.

The captain declared, as he rose to his feet and tried to reason with the wrathful Tam, "You prove yourself no better than a dog! Your fight is futile, give it up."

"Give yourself up and agree to leave in peace, or I'll put you in a shallow grave," Tam growled.

"You would not dare to soil your honor so! You are half-Sh'eyta, at least, and you are bound to service." The captain lurched toward Tam, but just as he did, Liam materialized between the two, one hand on the rowan tree.

"Liam!" Tam cried, and jumped back, but the captain's blade slashed deep across Liam's thigh before coming to a stop on Tam's shin.

Liam wailed in pain as Tam fell into the hedge at the edge of the field. The chains bit into him, and he gagged. The captain fell back in shock as Tam choked, rolling back toward the field again, trying to free himself from the tyranny of the metal.

Liam dropped to the ground, his flesh writhing as a gradual transformation elongated his face, and a downy velvet covered his skin, growing in length until, by the time his arms and legs had become legs and paws, he was covered with the thick pelt of a wolf, and a full wolf body to match it. The blood that had cascaded down his arm disappeared into the animal he'd become. The wolf edged toward Tam, then shifted back to the man again, to pull Tam from the bushes before dropping on his side, panting, but with no wound, no bleeding, just the drenched, slashed leg of his trews showing where the cut had been. The transformation had healed him, just like the tablet had said.

Tam had little time to sit slack-jawed, staring at his friend, while a thin thread of blood traveled down his leg.

"WHERE IS THE METAL?" The captain yelled at Tam, who was stiff with shock at the entire tableau, still trying to catch his breath.

"There is no iron," Tam stared wide-eyed at Liam.

"Copper, then!" the captain prodded.

"Can't you read my mind? She can."

The captain's lip curled with disgust, and Tam felt the tickle in his head that indicated the presence of one of his captors. It was if slender tendrils wormed their way through his thoughts, then suddenly withdrew with a clap.

"She said you found a way to block our minds," the captain muttered, then his gaze dropped to look at Tam's bloody leg and his eyes grew wide as he gazed in horror at the wound he saw there.

"I'm not blocking you now!" Tam shouted. "Take the knowledge and be gone! I told you, there's no copper, no iron but my pots, no steel but the axe!"

The captain eyed him sidewise, edging away from him. "I saw that," he grudgingly admitted. "But your thoughts tell me there WAS copper here, from the human woman who visited you. It was her copper you used."

Tam was sick at the thought of the dark man hunting Janet. "She's beyond the vale, you've no business going to her—"

"We have business wherever we choose." The captain spat. He seemed to have regained his sense of authority. "But I have no desire to soil myself further by passing into human lands. My place is within these grounds, by duty and by choice. You are bound to remain here, but I warn you, do not hide from the lady. You will be punished. You bested me this time, Tam Lin, but when I return I will not be alone. I know your measure now and will not be surprised again. I have the answer I came for, I'm done with you for now."

Tam stood still, shocked to hear the name "Tam Lin." He had told the first breathless lass he was "Tam of the Glen," and she and all the others had henceforth called him "Tam Glen," as had Janet. He thought about it when the captain was in his mind. But the Sh'eyta officer's strange accent distorted the moniker, and he wasn't sure if he should correct the man, who spun on his heel and mounted his horse. Spurring the animal cruelly he galloped away, leaving Tam and Liam staring at the dust that hung in the air.

"Tam…" Liam whispered, "are you wounded?"

Tam looked at his leg and brushed at the shallow cut. "It's nothing, it will heal soon enough."

"That's not what worries me, friend. My own blood has soiled you; the blade plunged into me before it cut you. My blood will have entered your body."

Tam shrugged. "It's possible, I see it. Your wound was the greater—"

"I'm fine. The transformation healed me. It's you we must think of now."

Tam went cold. "What do you mean, Liam?" Then in a higher pitched voice, "What's in your blood?"

Liam exhaled. "If our blood enters your body you become one of us. We must get you to water, and quickly, so you can wash it away. You might have time—"

Tam cursed as he dashed to the hall, grabbing the pitcher of water to pour it over his shin, where the blade had grazed him.

Liam said nothing as Tam tore his shirt away, pouring more water on his wound and scrubbing at it with a bedsheet. When the water was gone and Tam was just scrubbing with a fresh corner of the dry sheet, Liam stepped closer, reaching out to still Tam's frantic activity. "Enough, Tam. There is no more to be done."

"Am I... changed?"

"Metamorphosed. We won't know until the full moon. Either you will transform, or you will not." The quiet certainty of Liam's voice stilled Tam, and he dropped to the cot, where he sat staring at the ground in silence. Liam stared at him for a while, then turned to walk away, leaving a rabbit on the stump near Tam's axe.

"Liam..." Tam spoke, setting the sheet aside.

"Yes?" Liam turned back to look at the fearful expression on Tam's face.

Tam's mouth seemed to struggle as he tried to put his thoughts into words, until he sighed. "Was the passage open when you arrived?"

"Ah, well, I had hoped to get here during the day so that I could use the solstice thinning of the veil, but since I arrived after the sunset, I had to open it myself, which took some effort, as always."

Tam paused. "Today was solstice?"

"Yes. Solstice and Equinox, the veil grows thin, we can pass without effort."

"That's why the veil was open, and why it closed so suddenly?"

Liam looked at Tam and nodded.

"But..." Tam felt rudderless on a sea of rules that changed with every tide. "I thought a Sh'eyta had to open the passageway. And you, you say you can open the passageway if you try, because you're part Sh'eyta..."

"That's right. But it's easier to just come when the passage is open. I told you, on solstice and equinox the passage opens, at sunrise. It closes when the sun goes down, and those who find themselves in the passageway are taken back to where they came from, no matter how or when they crossed, until it is opened again."

Tam pulled on his wispy beard and looked toward the tower. He remembered hearing Liam say it earlier, and he had filed the information away to ponder at a later time.

Tam stood up and started pacing. Liam was part Sh'eyta as well, but only the slightest bit. Until recently, he thought the world was the solitary realm of humans and animals. It had expanded drastically, in a short time, to become peopled with creatures from fairytales that he neither believed in nor understood. But it seemed Liam did.

A thousand thoughts tumbled through Tam's mind. What else had he neglected to ask? "What do you know about Rigellium?" Tam looked deeply into his friend's eyes.

"I've never heard of it."

Tam returned to pacing. It wasn't the answer he wanted. He tried again. "Can you overcome the constraints of Rigellium?" he asked, but, as could be expected, the answer was the same. If Morgan was to be believed, he was more Sidhe– Sh'eyta– than Liam; if Tam couldn't do it, neither could Liam. There were rules that bound this new world he stumbled into, but he didn't know them well enough to find a way around them. He had to keep searching for answers. At least it would also take his mind off watching the moon as it waxed toward full.

## 25 – The Highwayman

"None can pass by Carter Hall but he demands a pledge: rings of gold or shawls of green or else their maidenhead"
Child Ballad 39: Tam Lin

Tam stood stripped to the waist, resting the axe on his bare shoulder as he stared at the log perched on a stump before him, imagining it as an enemy. He lifted the axe and swung downward with a blow that would cleave a man's head in two if he sat waiting to be slaughtered. Which of course the enemy never did. The two halves flew apart and Tam grunted as he yanked hard on the axe that was now stuck firmly in the stump. In battle, this was the most dangerous moment, when the weapon he held in both hands was temporarily unusable, and the effort it took to pull it from the dead man's body made him vulnerable to attack by others. He broke the axe free of its fibrous imprisonment and sighed. Hours dragged on, one after another, in this ethereal world of the elves where it was hard to feel any sense of urgency no matter what he did. The stump would never attack him and he knew it. He retrieved one of the half-rounds of wood and set it on the stump again, determined to yank the axe out in a single motion this time. He lifted the axe high and swung—

"Egad!" a shrill voice interrupted his swing, and he startled so that the axe missed the log and stuck even more firmly in the stump. Tam whipped around to see a young woman in a bright gown who had halted her progress through the trees toward him. He left the axe in the wood, disappointed that he let himself be surprised and, worse yet, had missed his swing because of it. The battlefield would never forgive such mistakes, and the fact that this wasn't a battlefield was little solace. If he couldn't focus on a task when there was no threat, how was he to do it in the confusion of war?

The woman stood stock still, staring at the axe, in a gown cut so low he was surprised it contained her at all. Janet spoke of "transgressions," and he knew now that his attempts to open the passageway had been successful. Ever since her abrupt departure he went to the rowan tree each morning to reach for the world-tilting sensation with his mind, then let it play out until it seemed done shifting, just like he'd done when he thought it wasn't working. There was only one pathway into the field, but beyond the rise, one road led toward Morgan's tower, and the other led to the hold that was now property of the newly named Lord Turnebull. He could see what looked like a turret rising above the tops of the trees if he backed away from the canopy and stood in the middle of the field where he chopped wood.

He suspected that was where this woman had come from; he didn't think the Sidhe would be alarmed to see him chopping wood. It also had to be the same place Janet had come from. He marveled at how obvious it seemed, now. The Sh'eyta were always coldly imperious, these other women were, well, women. He bowed low. "Milady, I'm sorry to have startled you," he said, then pulled himself upright, somewhat self-conscious of being half-nude in front of the woman marveling at his physique. "How can I be of service to you?" he asked, hearing a slight edge to his voice. He was disappointed that it wasn't Janet, and irritated that his exercise had been interrupted. He tried to relax.

"Ah, prithee, may I have a cup of water?"

Tam had noticed that was the first thing the presumably human ladies said, as if performing a ritual. Every single woman who had visited since he came to Carter Hall. Not a single one was Sh'eyta, if his suspicions were right. With a sigh, he went inside his tent to find the wooden cup he kept there, as always, then filled it with the cool water he gathered from the creek that ran along the far edge of the field. It was good that he had an endless supply. They barely touched the cup to their lips while staring at him, taking in his broad shoulders and trim hips, letting their eyes dally below his waist before continuing to travel down his muscular thighs.

How could he have mistaken these wanton harlots as anything but human? The Sh'eyta had little care for his body, only interested in what he could do for them, not how he appeared. But the women who came through the woods and asked for a cup of water always seemed very interested in his appearance. He shook his shaggy hair away from his eyes as he watched her watching him. When her eyes returned to his face, he wore a sardonic smile. "Have you come to talk?"

"Oh—" She breathed shallowly. "I thought…" her voice trailed off as she stared into his grey eyes. "Um, prithee…"

He took her hand and led her to where his cloak was spread out on the grass, in the shade of the stone hall. "Here," he said, "I wouldn't want to see such fair skin turning red with the harsh sunlight. Please, have a seat here and rest a moment. I'm sure you've been walking for some time, I'd hate to send you away without at least a chance to catch your breath." He pulled her arm over her head and twisted it so that she had to turn around, just as he would in a dance, and pressed her shoulders down so that she sat abruptly.

Many of the ladies who came had worn green shawls of the same fabric as Janet's brat, but this one didn't, to his disappointment. Did she really come from the same place? "Do you know the Earl of Dunbar?"

"Oh," she said with surprise, "That's the lord I serve. We're staying at Philip Hall until the Earl's castle is rebuilt."

"Oh, I thought the ladies there all had shawls of green. Are you sure you're from Dunbar's house?"

"Oh yes! I have one myself. Do you like them?"

"Very much! If I had such a favor from a lady, I'd defend her with my life," he answered, and watched her eyes grow bright.

"Well that would be a far better use for them than we've found yet, I'm sure. They've become no more than a sign of our folly to us. Perhaps we should bring them to you."

The offer shocked him. He just wanted to learn more about them, but a new plan began to form. He considered the audacity of these women, coming to him with a clear expectation that he would ravish them, then going back to Dunbar and describing the encounter as a "crime." Perhaps it was, but they kept coming anyway, it seemed. The way she leaned in toward him, undressing him with her eyes, made her intentions clear. The first visitor had likely cast him as a mere character in her fantasy, declaring her innocence to her employer while sharing a different story with her friends, in titillated whispers behind closed doors, so that they came to him one by one, seeking him out for their own pleasure. Well, he was hardly adverse to giving them what they came for, but he'd extract payment if he could.

"I think it would be fair, but only if I can offer something in return. Let me see what I can think of," he said, gently laying her down. "I would want to know that you would leave satisfied." He pulled the hem of her gown up and stroked her leg, paying attention to her every response, noting how her breath caught in her throat when his touch was light, and how she became restless if he went too fast, or too slow. He played her like a lute, applying himself to this lesson as he would any other skill he had learned. If this was his new occupation, he would master his technique, and perhaps he could extract further payment in shawls, if they were going out of fashion in Dunbar's house. It would take more than one shawl to equal the length of Janet's brat. But would they still come if they knew it would cost them a garment? He would have to see to it that he fared well in their stories.

She yelped, and he lurched back, only to lean in and kiss her to take her mind off whatever he'd done that had been too much. She moved his hand back to where it had been, and he was more gentle this time so that she was soon sighing in pleasure again.

He assumed she wanted sex, in full, not just heavy petting, but he had much to learn yet. He ran his hands over her entire body now, noticing what pleased her and what distracted her. He pressed gently, and he pushed harder, noticing what made her chest heave. He was surprised to find so many different places that made her moan, but not every time he touched it. It was as if he chased a moving target. He squeezed a breast and brushed a nipple and she gasped, then he moved the other hand to the downy space between her thighs, watching her eyes roll back in her head as she tilted her neck up to him. He recognized this position from some of the other women. He wondered if all women were the same; was it like a horse, that responded like any other horse did, or more like different armaments, each needing a different approach? He would learn. He couldn't go to Dunbar's hall, he couldn't steal their shawls away, nor even buy them if he had the funds. He had nothing but this, the power of his body, and his knowledge that this is what they came for. Human or Sh'eyta, this seemed to be his lot in life, as long as he lived according to the whims of the Sh'eyta. He found it odd that human women came to him for the same reason as Sh'eyta; he was told women were shy about sex.

But while the deed was the same, he had to assume it was passion that brought the humans, not duty. That's what separated humans from Sh'eyta: passion.

She began to raise her shoulders and he pressed her back down, reminding himself of the work at hand. He needed to keep his mind on the task; it wouldn't do to have her return with a bad review. He needed the women to come to him and bring him their shawls willingly. Then he would use the shawls to escape.

"Come, lass," he whispered before kissing her gently on her lips, then her ear, "I'll not have you go away dissatisfied." She relaxed again. More like a horse, he thought; responsive to what was on his mind. He wouldn't get distracted again. And so he made love to her, much as he had Janet, but with a different motive. With Janet, he had been falling deeply in love. In the case of this nameless woman, he was perfecting a technique.

By the time he finished, they were both gasping and covered with sweat. He rose to his feet and wet the corner of his shirt from the mug. He knew he preferred to wash when he was sweaty and assumed she would, too. Whatever he could do that might please her, he must do.

"Shh shh shh shh shh," he intoned. "We've become too hot in our activities. Let me wash you down and get you dressed again." He bathed her quietly, washing her from head to toe, as she watched him in amazement. He flipped the shirt to find a dry patch and dried her body, then pulled her gown back on, lifting her in his arms and carrying her to the edge of his field, where he set her on her feet, still speechless at his ministrations. "You mustn't be too late getting back. I'd not want you on these roads after dark. You never know what kind of rogue you might meet." As soon as he saw the questioning look in her eyes he pulled her into an embrace and kissed her again, leaving her breathless and wide-eyed, but unmoving.

"Lass, you can't stay, they'll be looking for you," he said, and waited. What if the guards came to find her? He didn't want any interference. "But come back. I'll be thinking of you."

"Oh?" A tiny smile crossed her plump face.

"Yes! I'll imagine you wearing the beautiful green shawl, and if it pleases you, you'll leave it as a token of your affection for me, that you will remain in my thoughts whenever I see it. This is the new covenant between us, lass; the shawl will mark our affection for each other."

She frowned, and for a moment it looked as if she were going to speak. He drew himself up to his full height. "You wouldn't deny me this, would you? Have we not shared enough to call ourselves close? Did I not earn a token of your affections? Any knight would be honored to receive such favor from a bonny lass like yourself, and go into to battle to defend your honor," he said, placing particular emphasis on the last word.

"Oh," she said with surprise that turned to delight, and he knew he guessed right. She might be a lady of some sort, but not of high enough rank to bestow her favor on a knight. Only ladies of high rank were sought out by knights; by referring to it as the favor of a lady, he was drawing her into another fantasy. In this one, she no longer attended the needs of another lady, but stood at the edge of the field tying a bit of cloth onto his lance as he vowed to defend her against any threat. She giggled. "Oh, if it means so much to you—"

With a devilish grin he answered, "A green shawl is the price of my passion." He swept her into another embrace for good measure, then leaned back and looked at her, hoping he got it right. "Go now. Come back whenever you wish, but don't forget to bring me the token to remember you by."

He released a deep breath as she skittered down the trail, doing as he told her to in the end, and turned to walk wearily toward the hall. He felt like he'd been through a wringer, desperate to leave her yearning for more, and strongly enough to be willing to pay. He hoped a single shawl would be enough, and if not, she'd tell the tale and leave others wanting the same deal, in case one wasn't enough. Did it have to cover him head to toe, or just cover the Rigellium? If there were any other ladies with shawls of the same type, he had to have them; if the shawls were as effective as Morgan and the captain said, then it was the only way he knew to overcome the Rigellium. Janet's had been several times the size of this one, and it had covered both of them.

He thought through every moment of the day since the woman had arrived. She came because of the first lady's story. She knew what had happened and wanted the same. So the stories of Tam were favorable. Favorable enough, he hoped, to bring shawls in exchange for his attentions. He did all he could to assure it, at least with her; attentive to every nuance of her body, doting on her from beginning to end, promising to always treat her as his lady. He hoped it was enough. If not, would Janet come back? Could he convince her to give him her own, as well? He wasn't so sure of himself with her. He didn't want his time with her to become a transaction. But Janet might help him by choice. For that, though, he'd have to tell her his plight.

He sighed and thought of all he learned about a woman's body today. He hoped women were like horses, and every woman responded to the same subtle cues. If he had to learn to handle each one differently, the way he had to adjust to the balance of every sword, every cudgel, every axe, it would be a tedious study. For a moment he found himself wishing human women were more like Sh'eyta, with no care to how it made them feel. He looked up at the clouds, where the light shining through turned golden as evening fell and remembered Janet. She was a woman he would cherish studying. He closed his eyes as he imagined running his fingers across her jawline, then down her neck, learning her body the way he had the lass that had come today. Janet was anything but tedious; Janet was enthralling. He indulged himself with the memory of her, and night fell as he drifted off to sleep, dreaming of Janet, forgetting how tenuous his situation was, if only for a short while.

# 26 – Change

"And I will change all in your arms into a wild wolf but hold me fast and fear me not, I am your own true love."
Child Ballad 39: Tam Lin

Tam was stripped to the waist again, working himself into a sweat with exercises to keep his strength up. He set the heavy stone down a final time and lifted a thick stick to practice weapon skills. A swing then a step and a lunge and leap, assume his opponent would feint then attack. Without a thinking opponent his skills would languish, but he could at least work on strength and agility. The fight with the captain would have been a welcome relief if it weren't so desperate. Even the rigors of the pell yard were never quite enough to prepare for the field of battle; the safety of knowing one's opponent isn't trying to kill is just enough to set it apart; adrenaline always ran higher in actual warfare.

It had been a little over two weeks since the disastrous encounter with the captain, and he had looked for the moon every evening, watching as it grew larger. Tonight was the last night of the waxing gibbous moon, tomorrow night it would be full. Liam had told him there would be three nights in a row that he would change. Tam's blood felt like it was full of thousands of tiny fish swimming through his veins. He swore he could smell the squirrel on the beech tree twenty feet away. It could be his imagination, and it could be that the change had already started. The anxiety had him rushing through the moves and he tried to slow himself down. He focused on his exercises, trying to take his mind off the nagging worry that his life might never be the same.

There was almost no time to register the unpleasant sensation of Morgan's presence in his mind before her voice filled his head. *You attacked my captain.*

*You're only learning this now? That was weeks ago. I would think you'd have been watching as it happened. What are you here for this time, really?*

*You recalcitrant buffoon! I have more important work than to babysit a bumbling derelict.*

Tam scowled. *I've done as you asked. You can't fault me for dereliction of duty.*

*You have a duty to be obedient to my demands, and those of my captain. It is time for a reckoning, my son.*

Tam was unprepared for the swift pain that accompanied her words, as all three pieces of jewelry stabbed into his flesh, though he was able to breathe freely. This time, she just wanted his pain, and the chains merely stabbed him without constricting. He felt as if he could hear a deep moan of pleasure emanating from her, revolted by the sensual gratification the pain brought with it and hoping it was hers. If she could feel his pain, it must be her own pleasure he felt in return. Or was he going insane? He recalled the knights talking about men who took pleasure in their own pain, and the stories never ended well. Any fighter who welcomed injury could find more than enough and was not long for this world.

The pain intensified. He recalled the metal biting into him when Liam had bled on him, and for a moment the fear of becoming a wolf numbed him.

Suddenly the pain stopped, and bitterness overwhelmed him. *He told me you allowed your body to be soiled with the blood of Homo lupanthrus. Tonight we will know if you've ruined yourself.*

He'd hardly allowed it. Liam appeared inadvertently between himself and the captain while they fought. It was the captain's sword that had shed Liam's blood before striking his own leg.

*And that is why you should not be fighting my officers.*

Tam took a deep breath. *I thought it was because it's disobedient—*

Tam couldn't breathe. He tried not to panic, teeth clenched against the growing pain, hating the parasitic rapture that came with it. The pleasure was hers; he was sure of it. He'd never been so deviant. She, on the other hand, was the epitome of deviant.

His vision began to swim as he spasmed, trying to draw air into his lungs, and soon he was falling.

As he became conscious again, he whispered, "Do you never get tired of this unimaginative game, Morgan? Where is this great intellect you lay claim to? An intelligent woman would know more than one way to cause pain. Many castles have entire cellars dedicated to the craft."

The delight she felt at this revelation made him bite his lip. He realized belatedly that he should have guarded his thoughts better, but he had little experience with people who could turn his mind into an open book. For a long while he didn't move, chilled at the thought that this knowledge could be deadly in her hands. Or worse.

He felt her thoughts withdraw from his mind, grateful to be left with just the pain, a sensation more familiar to him from all the hours grappling and weapons training. There were things a person should draw pleasure from, and injury wasn't among them. *An entire lifetime spent learning to fight men hand-to-hand and I meet an enemy who fights with her mind*, he thought. *How ironic.* He froze, fearful for a moment that these thoughts were unguarded while she was still in his mind. He had no idea what made her come and go, or by what reckoning he might know when the next "visit" might come. So much time passed between them he could almost believe he was free of her.

Tam slowly rose to his feet and picked up the stick again, getting back to his weapons practice, a reassuring routine for five years, learning the skills of a knight from Sir Gregor and the other knights and lords who took an interest in his progress. He stepped into the first position of the first form he'd learned and moved through the steps, stabbing, swiping, blocking. Then he stepped back into his original position, took a moment to close his eyes and picture the stick as a different weapon, one that was only sharp at the tip, then moved through the steps stabbing and blocking, there was no point in swiping with a weapon that couldn't cut. Once he finished all the moves he could recall for a pike, he stepped back into his original stance and thought for a moment. A mace then; with such a cudgel, neither slicing nor stabbing would be of use, it had to be swung like a club. He lifted it and brought it down, but it felt too long and too light. He stood back for a moment, staring at it. Could he strap a rock to the end of a shorter stick to give it the proper weight? He didn't want to lose the skills he worked so hard to perfect, out here so far from his own people.

He heard the distant thunder of hooves coming toward him at a gallop. It was more than one horse, and it came from the direction of the tower. It had to be guards, most likely coming for him. Was that why Morgan had "visited" him? Well, she was gone now. But she probably knew that tonight would be the test; if he was infected, he would turn into a wolf tonight. If not, he would remain a man.

He glanced around, then ran for the far side of the field, in the direction of the hoofbeats, and grabbed the axe. He knew he couldn't go toward the hedge, the chains would stop him, but he had no desire to be out in the open when the riders arrived, nor trapped in the hall. Still holding the axe, he ducked behind the wide trunk of an oak tree and tried to relax so he could hear over the beating of his heart. Pressing his back against the rough bark, he listened as the galloping hooves thundered past him, then suddenly became the pounding of hooves on grass, some prancing, the jangle of reins and saddle scabbards. Several gentle thuds he presumed to be men dropping to the ground. They were close, but the trunk of the tree and a few yards of underbrush stood between them. Nothing for a moment, then the crackle of a number of feet walking through bushes and over twigs. They were coming straight for him. Uncanny. Some kind of eldritch sense they had, as if they were bloodhounds. When he heard the steps draw even with his tree he launched himself right in front of them, using all his momentum to swing the axe as hard as he could, catching the first man across the ear. He shot past the others, turned, and swung again, with all the force he could muster, and the blow landed with a hard crack across the back of the last man's shoulder.

He yanked the axe back as the other two jumped on him, bearing him to the ground, but he squirmed to the side and they found themselves holding nothing but grass and leaves. He leapt to his feet and feinted at one, then swung at another, but his opponent had time to block the move, grabbing the axe and yanking him forward. He had to release his grip and he spun away, putting a birch between himself and the four solid men that now encircled him. His eyes went wide as he saw that the two men he should have felled with such blows seemed perfectly fine. Again he fought them all for some time, but soon enough he was panting with the effort, while he couldn't even hear them breathe. He wasn't sure they did. In time, they wore him down, his attacks merely causing them to pause before resuming motion. He never actually tried to kill them before and he wondered if it were even possible.

Setting aside his fears, he reveled in the opportunity to fight, jumping and kicking as well as swinging and punching. When one of the men swung an arm toward him, Tam grabbed it and twisted so that the man was flung into another man. By then he'd been kicked, and he jumped and rolled to reduce the impact to the blow, rolling to his feet and catching his breath while the four advanced on him together. Kicking, punching, rolling, grappling, he would feint, spin away, feint, block, feint, attack, shove one man into the next, take an arm that came at him and hang on as he dropped onto his back, kicking upward as the big body flew over him, launching the man higher into the air so that he landed hard several feet beyond Tam, who leapt up, still looking for the axe; none of them wielded it. They weren't using their swords, either; they were likely under orders to bring him back without any permanent injury.

He wasn't sure how long it had gone on when he felt the seeping presence of Morgan in his mind. She was probably wondering what was taking them so long, and might paralyze him, so he dropped to roll under a bramble, knowing she could stop him if he didn't get away first. The thorns tore his flesh. He didn't get deep enough before his hands were stilled and his breath cut off. Soon big hands pulled at his ankles and he was dragged back through the bushes, his skin torn again. He felt nauseatingly delirious with the awful combination of pain and pleasure that came with Morgan's presence.

*You are twisted and vile,* he thought, and sensed only her silent laughter.

*And you are a fool, Tam Lin,* she used the same strange-sounding name the captain had used, pulled from his memory of the first woman who had visited here in Carter Hall.

The guards carried him to the field, where the captain had put a new saddle and reins on Honor. Tam saw the sunlight reflecting from gold trim on the pommel as he was lifted onto the broad back of his horse. The captain touched the gold chains on Tam's wrists to the gold trim on the pommel, and they stayed there as if welded into place by a blacksmith.

As he regained his breath and felt all the scratches from the brambles, the cuts from the chains, and the bruises from the pummeling blows, he was grateful to have had the chance to get a good workout, but the new indignity was infuriating.

He felt her loitering in the back of his mind, and a chill came over him as he sensed her assessment of the different textures of his pain; the sharp and specific cuts, the broad ache of the deep bruises. She was tasting his pain as if cataloguing flavors for a recipe she would enjoy again. The invasion of his very thoughts, the most private thing he had, was violation enough, but the sadistic pleasure she took in his pain was revolting.

When they arrived at the walls of the tower, they kept going, passing under the portcullis where the captain stood aside to watch Tam pass. A guard lifted Tam's hands from the saddle and he was pulled down and dumped roughly on the hard-packed earth of the courtyard, the same as before.

The portcullis scraped against stone as it was lowered into place. He rose to his feet, not sure there was any point in preparing to fight whatever came next.

"Come," The captain said, and strode into the keep. The men slapped Tam and forced him to follow or be flogged. They had him surrounded and would likely drag him if he resisted. Within the grounds of the tower, he knew he was beaten.

*This should not be a fight,* her voice whispered in his head. *You have a duty.*

*Several, it seems. What now?*

He was surprised to find that they directed him off to the side of the tower rather than the front. They went past a window from the spiral stone staircase to arrive at a separate entry. He assumed the side door of the tower was a root cellar. They opened the door and shoved him roughly inside, closing the door behind him. The room was glowing with light, but he couldn't tell what the source was. It was as if the air itself was imbued with it. It was just an empty room, the door made of heavy planks. There were no shelves, no barrels, no piles of vegetables. Where did they keep the food they served? And why had he been shoved in here? He thought Morgan wanted to punish him, but she didn't even seem to care that he had arrived. She'd disappeared from his mind at some point. He paced back and forth, waiting for something to happen, but as time crept onward he began to think no one was going to come before night fell. She would want to see him then, to see what happened to him. Why else would she bring him here when she could spy on him at will? Perhaps she couldn't, if he changed. Perhaps, as he hoped, the chains would fall off and she wouldn't be able to when he was not close enough. If so, would she keep him locked up here, captive to her demands?

He checked the door. It was locked, of course. He stepped back, then landed a hard kick against it, right where the lock appeared to be. The door was built to open inward, of course; he'd have to kick the door as well as the doorjamb out if he wanted to succeed. Several more well-placed thuds had no effect on the door, and his leg ached. He considered throwing all of his weight against the door, ramming it with his shoulder, but he'd seen men dislocate their shoulders doing so, and he wasn't sure he could get his shoulder back in place without help. He'd never tried. He wondered if an out-of-place shoulder would be healed in the transformation, should it happen.

The thought of transforming unnerved him enough to try it. If he was to be at the mercy of the moon, he would prefer not to be at the mercy of the lady. He stepped back to the far end of the room, took several running steps, and threw himself against the door.

"AAAGH!" He grunted in pain, then held his arm. He reached up and felt his shoulder. It wasn't dislocated, just badly bruised. He decided not to try that again. He was securely imprisoned, with nothing to do but wait for night to fall, and no way to know when it had, unless he found himself exchanging his skin for a shaggy coat of fur.

The minutes dragged on as he waited for some sign. He wondered how she thought she would know what was happening to him in the well-sealed room. He didn't feel her presence in his mind. Would she return at dusk? If she waited until morning and he became a wolf, but changed back, would she even know? Would he? Was she reluctant to be in his mind when he changed form?

Suddenly he itched all over. His mouth ached, and his nose felt like it was slowly breaking. From the inner corners of his eyes he could see it lengthening, and he struggled to stay on his feet as they grew longer from heel to toe. His hands shrank while the skin on his palms thickened, and his fingernails drew together, lengthening slightly to become claws as his head tilted forward on his neck and fur grew out of every pore. He writhed in pain as his body changed, his breeches pinching against an elongating spine that projected further and further from his lower back, and his thoughts became foggier, more feral.

## 27 – Observation

Tam felt as if he were emerging from a deeper sleep than he ever knew and tried to hold onto the strange dream of four-leggedness. He sifted the scent of pine and hay for that of small animals and found himself flat on his belly on the dirt of the courtyard, his legs folded uncomfortably under him. He rolled onto his side and stretched out his arms and legs as he tried to remember what had happened. He turned to see the near end of the tower; the door of his cell was open, and he was outside it, in the courtyard.

Every bone in his body ached like he'd been thrown around in a small wagon for days while traveling on a rutted road, and his teeth and ears hurt intensely, as if pulled on, hard, by a very strong child. It wasn't surprising; he felt as if his skin didn't fit him anymore. He felt an unfamiliar exhilaration that was not his own and recognized Morgan's presence in his mind. He looked around to see her standing, licking her lips as she stared at him and sensed his pain. He scowled at her; he could feel her delight in his discomfort. He glanced at his wrists, hoping to see that the chains had fallen away when he changed, but the chains were in place. He touched his neck and found it chained as well. He realized he had no clothes, and he tucked himself into a ball as disappointment set in. The chains had clung to him through the entire change. He had been hopeful that the curse of changing into a wolf would at least be useful in setting him free, but they were still there.

"Well, Tam Lin, you have disgraced yourself even further," she spoke with swift viciousness. "You have indeed soiled your blood. You are not fit to be breeder. The one task you've been given cannot be completed without infecting your offspring with the curse of lycanthropy." She spoke aloud, perhaps so others could hear her, but the pleasure he sensed told him she was in his mind as surely as his skin was bare for all to see. It amazed him that her delight in his pain was so much greater than her dismay at losing him as her breeder.

Tam drew a sharp breath. "So you have no further need of me," he said. Realizing she was probably pleased with his humiliation, he rose painfully from the ground, refusing to be ashamed of his nakedness. He wavered with exhaustion and the extraordinary aches that lingered from his transformation. His fingernails and toenails felt as if they been peeled away, reshaped into claws.

"I've discussed the matter with our scientists; they plan to formulate a regressive to correct your perverted anatomy. If they succeed, you will be expected to resume your responsibilities, but for now you are useless to us." The word "useless" had an element of disgust that suggested there was nothing worse she could imagine.

Tam didn't bother to ask what she meant about the scientists as his shoulders drooped. Somehow they were going to fix him for her. That was unfortunate; if he could continue to sire the next generation, they still needed him. The only other possible benefit of the curse would be shot as well. But they had a solution even for this; their arcane spells would undoubtedly return him to his original self. That would be a bittersweet relief.

Tam saw Gruoch out of the corner of his eye; she stood near the stone walls of the tower, watching Morgan. He recognized the texture of Morgan's presence in his mind, but it was different: fuller, more golden. Then the goldenness withdrew. Gruoch had been in his mind at the same time as Morgan, he was sure of it. Gruoch turned toward him at the same time Morgan turned to Gruoch with a scowl.

Tam watched her as he tried to discern how deep her loyalty to Morgan ran. Gruoch herself had sent Tam to Carter Hall, to get him free from Morgan. She had also said higher ranking Sh'eyta would disapprove of Morgan's actions. Was Gruoch protecting Tam from Morgan, or was she protecting Morgan from her superiors? Was this a weakness he could exploit? Did she care enough about Tam that he could count her an ally?

Two guards stepped up from behind him, and he stumbled forward in an instinctive but clumsy attempt to escape them, but his body felt unfamiliar to him and didn't respond as it should. They grabbed his arms. He was still dizzy and disoriented from whatever had happened through the night. They pulled him forward and he stumbled so that they ended up dragging him on his knees back to the small room on the side of the tower. They pushed in on one of the stones that made up the walls and thin rods of black metal slid forward, releasing a cable that they looped around his neck and drew tight enough to secure him, leaving him on his knees in the bare room. They didn't bother to close the door. He checked the strength of the cable; he was too weak to break it, but then he wasn't sure he had the energy to speak. The loop around his neck refused to loosen, and he decided to try it again later, when he felt stronger. He hoped. Right now he was disoriented, sore, and ravenously hungry.

He turned around to see that he was alone. He'd hoped at least to see Gruoch, his only support in this increasingly menacing place, but she wasn't there. Perhaps she would arrest Morgan and come back for him. He wondered if he was to be fed; he suspected some of his weakness came from how hungry he was. As before, though, these creatures had little care for him aside from how they could use him.

Tam watched the shadows move across the courtyard when he wasn't exploring how the cable that tied him was anchored into the wall. He noted that someone was in his mind periodically and expected that it was Morgan at least some of the time, particularly when he noted the perverse pleasure that often came with it. He knew the captain found the mental connection distasteful. Did they all? Before he could formulate the question the presence was gone, as if playing a game of cat and mouse. When Roscoe arrived with a platter of food he felt faint at the thought of relieving his hunger, and was so grateful he barely had a moment to feel disappointed it wasn't Gruoch before devouring every morsel on the heavily laden dish. After finishing the meal, he noted that it must be around noon by the way the shadows had progressed since morning, and he went back to tugging at the cable, both around his neck and where it disappeared into the wall. The cable was a tight enough fit into the hole it came from that it was barely stressed when he pulled on it in a circular motion around it's point of origin, attempting to grind it against the stone that surrounded it.

By evening he was restless and frustrated as well as hungry again. The pain had faded, leaving him with just a shadow of the aches that had haunted him throughout the day. The sun was low in the sky when he saw Morgan step into his chamber, along with three others, one of which was Gruoch. His teeth began to itch, and his skin prickled as if he sat in a field of dry grass. He spasmed, and realized the change was coming over him again. She timed it to the minute. He raged in despair and fear at his inability to stop the process.

"Ye Gods of Alba," he cried out, "Where are your weapons against these otherworld heathens that mated us with beasts of the field?" His distorted feet wouldn't hold him upright and he fell forward to his hands and toes, still refusing to yield with grace, invoking with impotent fury the mythic forces that forged his people. "Derga, Beira,

Finn MacCumhall, you taught me to believe in …
owwww… owooooo…" he tried to hang onto his
consciousness, but his thoughts were fogging over like the
moors on a cold morning. "Haaaaag yoooou ha'nt ta'en
me yet…" he barely mouthed through his newly grown
snout, then dropped his head in reluctant verbal defeat,
yielding his ability to speak now that his lips refused to
form the consonants he took for granted, but he clung to
his consciousness with renewed ferocity. *I am Tam,* he
insisted. *I am Tam. I am man.*

Crouching with his tail between his legs, he fought the
fog that tried to swallow his mind. *I am Tam, I am man,* he
repeated, clinging to whatever humanity he could find in
himself. *I am Tam, I am man,* the mantra focused his mind
and kept his baser instincts at bay. *I am Tam, I am man*—

The thread of a guarded thought distracted him, and he
lost his tenuous grasp of consciousness. When he became
conscious again, he was still tied by cable to the wall of
the small, stone room, and the sun had risen again.
"ATTEND ME, YOU ABSCONDING MIND-
THIEVES!" He shouted into the courtyard.
"BEDSWERVING FIENDS OF HELL, COME FACE
ME ON FAIR GROUND!"

*Tam,* he felt the golden presence of Gruoch's mind in
his own. *Don't make a scene. You shame yourself.* Tam
noted that there were two dark-skinned men standing in a
corner of the room watching him.

*I'm not the one who created this horror of inhuman
mating!* Tam thought. *Who gave you leave to change
God's own creation, that you recreate it at whim? I was
human! What am I now, and who created this travesty that
has been visited upon my flesh? The only bitches I've had
congress with walked on two legs and called themselves
Sh'eyta! This curse is not of my own making. You fiends
have done this! You have no right.*

There was no reply, but he felt her there, still, and
waited, livid with impotent rage. He paced back and forth,

a few feet each direction, limited by the metal band that tied him to the wall, as the men jotted notes in the strange books they held. He said what he had to say and refused to speak further to the passionless presence that lurked behind his thoughts, watching him as if he were no more than an animal locked in a cage for observation.

"Tam," Gruoch said as she stepped into the room, and he swung around to face her.

"Take this off me!" Tam spat at her, tugging at the cable around his neck.

Gruoch shook her head with a frown. "Morgan has ordered you restrained so the scientists can find a cure for you. You're hardly giving her reason to trust you if she set you free," she admonished him.

Tam lurched to the end of the cable and was brought up short, coughing at the strain on his neck. "YOU must set me free!" he said, as he backed up, angry at having to give ground.

She shook her head. "I can't go against her orders, Tam."

"But you watch her. There is something going on between you. There is something she is doing that you disapprove of. What of her superiors?"

The men scowled at Gruoch. She pursed her lips. "That's not your concern! As long as she is ruler, her orders stand."

Tam stared at her as she stood in the doorway. She neither left, nor came closer. He still didn't know whether to count her friend or foe. "What are you doing here, lass? Why have you come here to stare at me, caged as I am? Do you enjoy seeing me beaten?"

"Your status is precarious," she replied, then added grudgingly, "As is Morgan's. I have a job to do."

"What are they doing?" Tam gestured toward the men.

"Observing you. And they'll need a blood sample from you."

"A blood sample. What do you mean?"

"They took a sample of your blood when you were in wolf form. They need to analyze—"

"Don't give me your words! Tell me what it means."

Gruoch paused for a moment, then went on. "They'll put a needle in your arm and draw blood—"

"They're going to make pictures of my blood?"

"Remove your blood," Gruoch said with a sigh.

Tam stared at her for a moment, then said, "No, they won't."

"Yes, they will."

Tam glowered defiantly, then sighed in resignation. "You'll do what you will, then. Why bother telling me?"

"You asked."

"Why bother with an answer?"

"I'm part human. I care about you and your kind."

Tam leaned his back against the wall as he looked at her, wondering just how human she was. "Your kind" she had said, contradicting her own claim that she was part human. He turned to look at the men, perhaps an easier enigma to solve. One watched him while the other pulled a cloth sack of some sort from a vest pocket and covered his head with it so that he appeared to have pale skin and two huge, dark eyes. It was large around the top of his head and small at the bottom so he seemed to have a tiny chin. Then he pulled thin white gloves on and removed a container out of a bag, from which he drew a slender cylinder. Tam felt a pressure inside his head just before his legs folded underneath him as if he were too weak to stand, and panicked as he tried to move, but couldn't. If it was so easy to paralyze him, Morgan's choice to control him with pain was purely evil. *Quickly now, before it learns to reverse the mind invasion,* he sensed the words; they weren't Gruoch's. He watched in horror as the man holding the narrow device pushed the slender steel shaft deep and painfully into the skin on the inside of his elbow, then pulled back on a loop of metal, then the second presence exited his head and he found he could move again as the two men left. Again, this suggestion that somehow he could damage their minds when he entered theirs. The thought was of enough concern that the scientist let it leak, but he still had no idea how to do it. Unlike opening the passage, which he seemed to be developing a skill for, this was more than reproducing a sensation. How did he get his thoughts into someone else's head?

*Perhaps the skill is beyond you. As for Morgan and her choice of pain, she seems to like it when you fight back, and she likes to feel your injuries. Indulging in the senses is wrong, but she does it through you and so escapes breaking our law, but barely so. She claims she is learning of your sensation, not indulging in her own bestial urges.*

*Why do you let her?*

*I've no grounds. It's a technicality; it isn't her own senses she's indulging. She claims it's for research purposes, and perhaps it is. You're the first half-human Sh'eyta in hundreds of years, and there's much for us to learn about you; it's allowed because she is learning your limits. Your defiance makes this information essential for us to know.*

She discussed Morgan's pleasure in Tam's pain with such cold logic he wanted to find the limits of Gruoch's pain. She had to be aware of this thought, but she didn't respond. And why should she? There was nothing he could do to her.

Gruoch's presence disappeared from his mind and she turned to leave. "Don't go," Tam said, and she turned around. Tam grimaced.

"What do you need," she asked.

The words had come out of him without thought, and now he wanted them back. He didn't like the way he wanted the comfort of her presence. For all her strangeness, she had cared for him enough to help him get away for a while. But she was Sh'eyta. She was no friend, no matter how kindly she had behaved toward him once.

"It is nothing," he grated through clenched teeth. Her presence in his mind was gone, she didn't know what he was thinking now; he could lie to her with ease.

"Why don't you remain in my mind?"

She looked thoughtful, then he felt her presence again. *Entering your mind opens my own to you. It's wise to be wary when we have thoughts we don't wish to reveal.*

Tam made a point of feeling her presence in his mind, and tried to find its source. Could he read her thoughts? Or better yet, control her?

*Tam!* In a flash her presence disappeared. Her voice was cold. "Don't even think about it, Tam. The Rigellium is trained to attack you if you try to assault one of us."

He watched her as she walked away. Her pale skin, the golden hair; it was a ruse. Her people were dark-skinned, darker than himself. He couldn't expect honesty from her, and he wasn't fool enough to trust her. At times like this, she showed her true colors.

## 28 – Failure

Skaal peered through the eyepiece at the highly magnified cell, in which a genetic microservant engineered ten thousand years earlier was invading a tissue cell so it could edit the chromosomes of its host. When his people had come to this planet, they thought to colonize what looked like a rich paradise. After landing and assessing the life forms, it was clear that the most intelligent of the life forms were surprisingly similar to the Sh'eyta in build and metabolism, providing them with a unique opportunity to advance their research on blending local DNA into their own chromosomes so that they didn't need as much technology to survive in what might otherwise be a hostile environment. And so, rather than colonize, they had turned Earth into a research facility where they hid their own existence from the creatures they experimented on.

Skaal leaned back and flared his nostrils as he considered what he would tell Commander Morgan. No matter how he came at it, it seemed the tiny creatures couldn't remove the entire wolven DNA from the human cells without leaving the host's chromosomes in tatters. Tam wouldn't survive the process. The overlords didn't leave documents detailing how they engineered the change agents, and none of the Sh'eyta scientists knew how to make adjustments to them.

"Skaal . . ." The voice penetrated his thoughts and he turned to see one of his peers entering the laboratory. Skaal nodded, irritated at the interruption.

"The answer to this dilemma won't be found under a magnified lens," the scientist continued. Skaal tried to recall a name and gave up. Under normal circumstances, they would be speaking mind-to-mind, where names were unnecessary. The past millennium had brought more and more friction between the extraterrestrial community, and it was increasingly rare for them to expose their minds to each other. Too many secrets, too much vulnerability. Scientists were normally so isolated that they rarely had need to speak to each other at all, so names were particularly rare among his industry. Most scientists couldn't remember their own names, if they even had one. Skaal had chosen a new one when he was elevated to chief scientist, knowing that the promotion brought a greater need to communicate with Sh'eyta from other departments; that would require verbal speech, to match his need to control the flow of information from one industry to the next. Without the requisite education, that information could be confusing to others and lead to poor decisions. Mindspeak wasn't possible across great distances, either.

Skaal finally gave a brief nod. "I agree. We know of no way to safely remove the wolf from the human once the metamorphosis has occurred. The original virus was crafted to alter the DNA in every single cell of the human body—"

"It's not a virus," the other being interrupted contemptuously, and Skaal bit back a hot retort. Being part-human was an advantage, physically, but the emotional weakness it brought was humiliating, and they all avoided showing any of it.

"The purpose of words is to communicate meaning, and this word did that well enough that you know exactly what I was saying. Or are you saying you can't determine what

I meant?" Skaal was pleased to see the slightest thinning of the other's lips, and decided to placate him, now that Skaal had undermined his argument.

"You are right. It can't be undone any more than I can sew a head back on after decapitation and bring a creature back to life. The last advance in this mechanism took a century to perfect; this feature will likely take three times that, and we can't wait that long to replace the lives we lose. We must bring more into the world within the next thirty years or we are doomed." Sh'eyta were long-lived, but the chromosomal adaptation required to live on Earth would eventually delaminate, and the breakdown would result in a rapid aging that was horrific to witness.

"Ironic that our own inventions can outlive us."

"They're not inventions," Skaal said, and immediately regretted it. Verbal sparring was as remedial as physical combat, and he should be above that. It was a beastly thing.

The tiniest of smiles appeared and disappeared in a flash on the other's face. "If you can't find the answer in the mechanism, can you find it in the flesh of the beast?"

"He is the offspring of our commander, I advise you to be careful with your own words," Skaal warned, despite his agreement with the term.

The other made an odd noise in his throat. "If you can't remove the lower life form from the human, we will have an opportunity to reproduce the research of our ancestors."

Skaal felt himself sitting up straighter. "But there are laws against harming the hybrids."

"We wrote those laws for the benefit of science, so that we didn't lose important data. The populations are sufficient now; too large, even. We should rewrite the laws. Consider how much we can learn if we can observe them as they disassemble."

It was an intriguing thought. Much could be learned by dissecting the animals while they were still living. Cadaver autopsies were always disappointing in that what had happened couldn't be manipulated; while you could see what had occurred, you weren't able to witness it as it was happening. A living specimen would be far more rewarding.

## 29 - Vivisection

It was an hour later that the light in Tam's room increased until it was blindingly bright. Tam felt as if he were floating, then a disorienting flash blinded him and he lost consciousness. When he awoke, he was lying on his back in a brightly lit room; the walls were white, and tall, pale slender shapes stood around him, all with the hoods and gloves that the one scientist had worn before. He couldn't move nor speak, but he winced as they stabbed him with needles like the one they used to steal his blood.

His head felt strange, like when Morgan or Gruoch was communicating with him, but more foreign, and fuller. He couldn't make out words, just intentions. They seemed to be curious about the mechanism that caused his body to change from a human to a wolf, then back. The unpleasantly familiar presence of Morgan's mind slipped into his awareness just before a blade sliced into his arm, and he watched in horror as it cut his skin away from the muscle underneath. For several moments he felt nothing at all, then an excruciating agony forced his jaws wide in a silent scream of terror. He strove to ignore the torment as he watched the long, slender hand deftly pull the skin back. He recognized the cuts of a butcher; he made just such incisions when removing an animal's hide. The searing pain was making it hard for him to concentrate, but he found he couldn't take his eyes off the carnage to his limb, fearful he would be left with nothing but bone when they were done, but it seemed they just wanted to explore the space inside his body. Stopping short of detaching meat from bone, the blade separated flesh from flesh, peeling the skin back to expose the raw meat of his muscles. His voice still refused to work, paralyzed along with the rest of him, save his eyelids and some movement of his head and jaw, though both responded sluggishly. He saw another blade, wielded by a different entity, as it moved toward his face, and he tried to escape, helpless, as it was placed against his cheek. He was enormously relieved to find that the sharp blade merely shaved him clean, the wispy beard and mustache that had been growing since he arrived now gone. When a third creature started removing his fingernails the torture drove him mercifully senseless.

He found himself waking up in such throbbing agony as he could never recall. He was back in the cellar where he started, the loop of cable secured to the chain around his neck rather than the neck itself, and his stomach lurched as he saw many skinless patches over one side of his naked body. The sun was low in the sky, and he felt feverish as the change began. He glanced around and saw the tall, lean, dark-skinned men watching him, books and pens in hand as his body reshaped itself, every twitch a surge of agony. He fought the stinging and confusion, trying to hold onto his identity though part of him was desperate to retreat from the suffering. But he didn't want to lose consciousness again; who could know what they would do to him next?

He compared his two hands; one was turning grey with the downy precursor of fur, but the skinless one took longer; he looked away and fought to remain conscious as the pain overwhelmed his ability to concentrate. He focused on the change in the left side of his body, where it was a familiar itching and stretching, trying to ignore the fading pain in the right side where skin grew, then fur. Slowly his form reshaped itself until he looked out from the eyes of the wolf. A horrific memory was all that was left of the pain. The chains were slightly loose on his furry wrists, but the paws were almost as large as his hand had been and he couldn't pull them off, nor bite through them with his new fangs. The circumference of the wrist chains had shrunk to fit his new form. He couldn't see his neck but he didn't feel the tightness of the chain choking him. He thought the neck of a wolf was larger around than that of a man; if so, the chain had conformed to the new creature there as well, the individual links lighter than the heavy cords they had been.

Tentatively nosing the fur apart on his flank he could see none of the cuts that had been made to his skin. The process had healed him.

He smelled Morgan before she stepped into the room and whirled to face her. She was flushed. She looked him over, then her presence slipped out of his head. His thoughts were his own, for now; she'd been the only one willing to experience what he'd just gone through, and she'd been there the whole time.

"He is still conscious!" She blurted, and the men turned to her.

"Nonsense," one said.

"Is his body truly restored?" She asked.

"We never damaged him."

"You DID remove body parts," she noted.

He dismissed the charge with a wave of his hand. "We pulled out some collagenous tissue, most of it dead, but the skin we merely pulled away; it moved back to its former place. As you can see, the transformation process hasn't mutated; it's just as described in the books."

"But it could have."

Another man gave a slow nod. "The process is due for a spontaneous mutation, I had expected it. Nothing remains the same through eternity."

The others nodded as well. Morgan lifted her chin. "Yes. That's why I asked you to test the transformation to its limits."

The first man's face remained blank as he said, "Madame, do not think for a moment that I believe you when you say you have no interest in his pain. You've made it clear you care nothing for our science."

Morgan made as if to lunge toward him, but the other two men moved between them and she stopped herself.

"I'm sorry they stopped you. You would be in better hands if we imprisoned you for attacking me. You are not of sound mind, Morgan; time will betray you in the end. Nothing good will come of your fascination with these... senses."

Morgan sneered. "HIS senses, not mine. I have only an academic interest in how humans experience pain."

The second man turned to the first. "It's important that we understand how humans are motivated, Skaal. I think it would behoove us to indulge her interest in this."

A smile flirted across Morgan's mouth, and Skaal admonished her, lip curling in disgust. "Do not think this means we will not see you imprisoned if you cross the line, Madame. You are fortunate to have a subject for your folly, but I do not doubt you will find yourself entrapped by your desire to experience the limits of his pain." He turned to the second man and nodded. "It is the human in her; it's far too strong. I believe she will entrap herself just as I believe the base human emotions will entrap this man into the beast's form, if he is pressed hard enough, for long enough. Humans can be reduced to their most primitive selves by their emotions, she and he included."

"Nonsense," The first man said. "It's the pull of gravitational forces that causes the change, and the change removes the human consciousness. We inserted a strand of Sh'eyta material into the creatures to verify it could survive the process, and it benefited the savages by our body's natural proclivity to balance forces, which gave time for the animal material to actualize itself, but only when the balance of gravity between the large, distant sun was perfectly balanced against the gravity of the near but small moon. It's a physical response, their primitive emotions have nothing to do with it."

"You underestimate the power of human emotion. It is a force to be reckoned with," Skaal objected.

The second Sh'eyta shook his head. "You could ply your skills for a millennium, he'll not change but at the turn of the moon's phase."

Suddenly Gruoch spoke up, and Tam was surprised to realize she sat in the dark corner of the room, just watching. "You haven't read Skaal's report on the new development among the hybrids, then."

The man turned to her, his face expressionless. "I find his theories preposterous. Why would I bother with his words?"

"That's a grave oversight," the third man said. "Gruoch reported to Skaal several centuries ago that the creatures have learned to change at whim." Suddenly they all stared at Tam, two of them wide-eyed with interest.

"Change," Skaal commanded, but Gruoch stepped forward.

"They can't do it so early in the metamorphosis. He isn't even conscious right now."

Morgan smirked. "Ah, my little rogue, that's where you're wrong," she said with glee. "I told you, he is FULLY conscious!"

Tam's tail tucked itself between his legs as they all stared at him, and his mind filled with one presence after another. He recognized the texture of Gruoch and of Morgan, but the other three were new. His mind felt too full, and he shook his head in distress, stumbling over all four feet as he tried to edge away from them. He was himself, and he wasn't. It confused him, and he wanted to figure it out before dealing with the mental invasion.

"It's difficult to detect a difference between human and wolf. Both are so remedial!"

Tam growled at the insult, and Morgan smiled with triumph. "You see, he understands you! He's conscious."

*Can you change, Tam?* Gruoch asked.
*How?*
*Just focus and intend to change.*

Tam looked at his paw and tried to change it into a hand, hoping he would succeed, but nothing happened. It was hard enough to remember who he was, with all the thoughts that skirted his own. Impossible to perform magic he didn't understand. He felt Morgan's triumph and Gruoch's curiosity, though the other presences seemed grey and blank. He focused on his paw and tried again, concentrating on seeing it become naked flesh, but no matter how hard he tried, nothing happened.

Gruoch waited just a little longer before withdrawing from his mind. "Well then. In time perhaps he'll have that skill, but for now he seems preoccupied with remaining human in intellect only."

One of the men sighed.

"That would have been good to see," said another. "Still, it's remarkable that his mind seems to be human despite the physical change. I didn't realize they have the will, much less the talent."

"Can he be forced?"

Morgan smirked. "Shall we try?" Suddenly the chains were chewing into Tam, and he howled and snapped in distress, tucking into a ball.

When he looked up, the room seemed empty until Gruoch crept toward him after making some marks in the book she carried. Had he blacked out? He felt her presence skip across the surface of his mind and turned to her. His body ached, but not as much as it had the previous days. He realized he was naked. Of course. Then it dawned on him that he was human. Time had passed, then. But fear gripped him as he recalled the dispassionate conversation of the previous night.

"Lass, am I to be butchered while I'm still alive?"

A crease appeared between her brows. "Your body will be preserved for some time. And if they can cure you, your original value will be restored to us. Until then, you're a curiosity to be explored."

The hopelessness he felt at her cold logic must have been obvious, because she leaned toward him and took his shoulders in her arms. He pushed her away, enforcing discipline over his emotions. He was still a man. Whatever else he was, he was first and foremost a man, not a child to be coddled. And she was a demon, he reminded himself. "They'll take me apart, then, and watch my body put itself back together, will they?" He refused to look at her. If she nodded, he didn't see it, but he knew what the answer was. "Well, that was the third night. They'll have to wait. Liam says the change only happens on the three nights of the full moon. I'll be free of their ministrations for a while."

"There are other ways to test you," she answered aloud.

Tam swung around to glare at her. "They seemed only interested in how my body reshapes itself! I was left alone the entire time before the moon matured. You said they would not harm me yet, just cause great pain that falls short of what this… curse… can repair!"

Her head dropped as if it were too heavy to remain upright. "Before the full moon, they weren't sure you'd been changed. Morgan asked what effect another hybrid virus would have on you. Two thousand years ago, the hybrids separated from each other because humans can only survive a single hybrid form. A second form will cause the flesh to tear itself apart when the transformation occurs. They intend to find out if this is still true."

Tam's stomach lurched, and he felt nauseous. "Why would they do this to me?"

"Morgan is very angry with you."

"Sh'eyta don't get angry."

"She's very human for a Sh'eyta, as I've told you, which is why she's being observed. It's also why she finds mind control more challenging. It takes a great deal of practice to master the ability to control humans with the mind, and none of us can do it when the subject is out of sight unless we use Rigellium, but the amount of time she spent studying it she should be far more adept at it. The scientists put her to shame." Gruoch leaned back against the wall. "But there are very real concerns about her humanity. There is suspicion that she has or will break the law against primitive behavior by acting on desire or out of fear." She sighed. "It's a shame. Her humanity is why she was chosen to create this generation's breeder. It was thought we would get the highest concentration of human traits if we offered our most human progenitor. We want to go longer before having to breed back in with humans; this last interval has been quite short, and we had offspring that were gasping for air much sooner than we expected. But if they also have her sensory motivations it might be for naught. As it is, unless you can be salvaged we've wasted our time on you. The scientists are trying to get as much information out of you as they can; they don't believe they can reverse the mutagen. And so they're using you to test any theories they have on how the mutagen works, which could help them improve the mutagen."

"Or the experiments could help me now."

"That's unlikely. You probably won't survive them."

Tam glanced at her face and was surprised to see intense sorrow. Her voice was steady, but her eyes shone with unspilled tears. "Lass, you betray yourself," he said.

"No. I only feel it. It doesn't motivate me."

Of course, Tam thought. It was a subtle distinction, but an important one. His thoughts returned to his own plight. It appeared he was sentenced to death, and worse than that, he was to be tortured first.

That afternoon he was sitting against the wall when a paralysis came over him again. One of the scientists stepped into the room with a satchel and a tiny clear cylinder, covered in the pale suit and strange hood that made his head look more like that of a mantis. Tam's eyes were wide as the man shoved the needle at the end of the cylinder painfully into his arm, then pressed down on a plunger so that whatever liquid was in the device was forced into his flesh, with a sting like a wasp big enough to eat a man.

Gruoch came running into the room, then stopped herself as the scientist turned to her.

"I've made note of your refusal to inject the mutagen. I'll advise you not to shirk your duties a second time. You'll lose your position as head xenobiologist if you can't perform the appropriate tasks." He pulled the device from Tam's arm and dropped it into the case he brought, then left the room, and Tam found he could move again. Gruoch ran to his side. "Oh Tam! I'm so sorry. I couldn't, but I should have. I could have made it less unpleasant."

Tam was leaning over, holding his arm, grimacing against the sting of the needle and the growing ache where the fluid had created a small lump under his skin. He shoved her away. "Unpleasant? Gad! I find boar taint in ham unpleasant. He drove steel into my arm while I was held motionless! I'd love to see how he would fare if we both had swords and neither of us was held fast against his will."

"I'm sorry. I should have at least—"

"Stop!" Tam spat. "I have no faith in your feigned concern. What did he put into me?"

Gruoch's eyes were wide and her mouth hung open. She closed it slowly. "Homo ursanthrus mutagen."

"In English, if you would," he snarled.

"Human bear metamorphosing agent."

A lungful of air whooshed from Tam as he collapsed against the wall. "Human bear." He knew those words, and what they meant. "And you think it would be better if you had done it?" He asked incredulously.

"It wouldn't have been so painful."

"Death will be painful! The sting of the tiny dagger is nothing compared to that!" Tam corrected himself internally, though; the pain in his arm seemed to be growing, and he wasn't sure when it would stop.

"It can't be helped, Tam. You're lost to us now. Once they determined they can't change you back, you have no purpose but to satisfy their curiosity. There's nothing I can do about that. When the full moon rises again, your body will tear itself apart, trying to decide which to become: wolf or bear."

## 30 – The Bear

"And then I'll change all in your arms into a wild bear, but hold me tight and fear me not, I'll be your husband, dear,"
Child Ballad 39: Tam Lin

Aside from occasional painful explorations of Tam's body, which Morgan was always in attendance for, they had left him alone except to feed him. The minutes had crept into hours with such maddening slowness he had taken to singing tunes he couldn't fully remember, creating new verses as he went. He had exercised as the cable had allowed, stretching against it until he coughed. Day after endless day had passed until he had nearly lost track of time. Tonight should be the last night of the waxing gibbous moon, if he had counted right.

Tam twitched, then spun around as he heard footsteps approach. His fists clenched and he dropped to a crouch as the steps grew closer, praying they would give him even an instant to knock one of them flat on the back and wrench his silly neck right off his Sh'eyta shoulders.

Three forms in white suits with large white heads, big dark eyes, and tiny pointed chins stepped into the room, followed by Morgan, who licked her lips in anticipation. She had to suspect that whatever would happen would be painful and she wanted to be there to enjoy the agony of his dissolution.

Tam lunged to the end of the chain that still held him, and his hand barely missed the arm of the second man, who stepped deftly aside.

"Stand and face me, cumberworld!" Tam cursed him.

Morgan laughed. "Ah, see how fresh his spirit is now! He believes he has some control over his destiny. Let us see what the new transformation does to him, Skaal."

Skaal leaned in towards Tam. "Face you? Listen to the creature; he thinks himself our equal."

The other suited scientist was jotting notes. "There's not much left for him to be concerned with, of course. If his stubborn body had responded to any of the reversal agents we prepared you wouldn't need to give him the second mutagenic agent to keep him useful to us."

"Do you still think the second transformation could eliminate the first?" the third one spoke up.

Skaal scoffed without looking up. "I never thought it likely. What I want is to see his body tear itself apart. The old studies are unclear how this happens, and I'd like to get a proper record of the event."

"A remarkable thing to witness," the third scientist said. "Brilliant idea, salvaging what we can of this creature by getting more accurate data. But his constitution is half-Sh'eyta, which makes him a stronger being. Perhaps he'll actually transform first to one or the other of the animals or take on traits of both. If so, the features could blend, or they could have regional dominance of one form over another. I look forward to getting some answers. I only hope that his body holds together long enough that we have something to witness."

Tam pushed himself to the end of the chain, more carefully this time, and tried to reach them, but they knew just how far he could go and stayed a maddening inch or two beyond his reach. He cursed and lunged one more time, but the cable caught him up short and he landed on his back, hard. As he tried to catch his breath, head ringing from slamming against the stone floor, he looked toward the door, hoping to see Gruoch. It remained empty. A spasm contracted his leg, and he went cold with dread. In seconds, his skin was shifting and trembling, lumps forming then receding. One moment he saw bare skin, the next a powdery grey down, then a thick coat of short black fur, then the grey down again. His body fought with itself as he twisted and lurched in confusion. The pain of having his skin peeled off was no match for the excruciating convulsions his body endured for what seemed like eternity. His bones would lengthen, stretch muscles so taut he was sure they would tear from their bed, then suddenly the same bone would shorten, leaving the flesh loose and tender. His heart would push against his ribcage, then the ribcage expanded before something in his belly shifted and he lost what little was in his stomach from the pain. Fingernails became small claws, then huge claws, wrist slender then fat, and he couldn't remember where his tail was, or if he had a tail, or where his teeth ended and his jaw began. For a moment he had the strength of an ogre and eyesight as sharp as his hearing, then he was almost blind, then it was his hindlegs that seemed ready to tear away from the rest of his body, then come to rest just in time for his back to straighten, then curve, and he was sure he would soon be torn apart just as they said he would. He was out of breath when the twitching subsided, and he lay on his side, panting with exhaustion as the pain receded. He just breathed, praying that it was over. He saw the men jotting notes in their books, then looking up at him. He could feel Morgan's presence in his head. She had been there the whole time, as his body stretched and strained almost past its limits.

"Remarkable!" Skaal said. "He is intact! What do you make of this?"

The other two were staring, rapt, and didn't answer him.

He looked down at the thick black fur that covered his body. His front paws were huge. He glanced back at the rest of his body. It was that of a bear. But just the one animal. There was no sign of the wolf, nor the man, except that his thoughts were clear. He remained conscious through the transformation with little effort somehow, but now he had to focus as his mind wandered. He was distracted by smells and had an urge to hunt things down and kill them, hungry as he was now. The scent of prey was maddening. *I am Tam*, he reminded himself, as he struggled to remain conscious.

Gradually he stood on his four legs, then rose up on his hind legs and roared. He lunged to the end of the cable, using the bear's strength to fight his restraints, and the chain choked him. He backed up to get slack again so he could breathe, looking at the chains on his forepaws; they fit his bearpaws just the same as they had fit the wrists of the man and the wolf.

Morgan's presence slipped away, and she left the room without a word. She had what she came for; now that the pain was no more than a memory she lost interest in him.

Another presence paralyzed him, and one of the men came forward to shove a cylinder into his arm, as they'd done every few days. In a fit of rage, he bellowed, and smashed the man across the room with a loose paw. The slender body hit the stone wall hard, then crumpled in a heap at its base.

The other two men gasped, then one ran to his colleague and placed a hand on his neck and leaned over to put an ear to his face.

"What happened?" Morgan shrieked, running into the room.

After a few seconds the man leaning over the crumpled form looked up. "He's alive but unconscious."

Morgan turned a narrow set of eyes to Tam. "Look what you've done!" She spat. "Have you no decency? One of our most respected scientists!"

She took several steps toward him but stopped just short of his reach. The chains tightened on his wrists and neck, but his fur was too thick and it seemed they couldn't find their way down to his skin to cause him pain. Tam found himself panting in what passed for laughter, for a bear. He sat on his haunches, panting so hard he coughed, but he couldn't stop. They had subjected him to a form that could dominate them.

Morgan looked confused. "Is he still conscious?"

The two men looked at her. "You want us to enter his mind NOW, madame?" Skaal asked. "I don't think it wise; look what just happened. Our minds are stronger than any Terran, but a bear's mind is unfamiliar. I'm confident a human could never overwhelm me, but a bear's mind is too foreign. We can't know how the encounter will affect us."

She snorted, then Tam felt her presence in his thoughts again. *The scientists are cowards. I find your mind fascinating. And I'm sure you have no power over me but in the physical plane. There is no bear here, just a frail human. Your mind is weak.*

*I will break free,* he said.

*You'll break nothing more! The Rigellium can't overcome your fur, but even a bear hasn't the strength to break it, and in time you will be a man again.*

Tam lunged, but she stepped out of his reach, and he sat on his haunches, tucking a claw under the chain on one of his wrists to tug at it, but it seemed she was right. He leaned over and snagged it with a tooth, then pushed his foot away from his head, but the result was the same. The guards came and dragged the body of the scientist from the room. The others stared balefully at him, but soon they left as well.

*Just you and me, your ladyship. Shall we dance?* Tam laughed.

She scoffed and left as well, her presence in his mind snuffed out like a candle.

Tam was surprised that it was now no effort to remain conscious. Whether it was the result of his efforts, or his new circumstances, he was glad, but it made for a very long night. The bear seemed not at all inclined to sleep. The night dragged on, as the days had. For all the interest they took in his transformation, it seemed they had none for his changed form. Or perhaps they were cautious. He tugged at the chains and lunged against the cable that held him tied to the wall, then dropped to the ground coughing at the sudden choking tightness of it. It seemed his breath couldn't be entirely stifled while he was a bear. In the end, though, even the superior power of the bear still couldn't free him of the Rigellium, and he sat back on his haunches again to wait for the sun to rise. No, it was the setting of the moon that ruled him now. Moonset, then. He finally lowered himself down to rest his huge head on his heavy front paws and waited for the change to come, as he was sure it would.

Many hours later, the two remaining scientists walked into the room with Morgan, careful to give him a wide berth. It wasn't long before he felt the now familiar crawling of his skin, which shifted to a grinding agony, and he wished he could relinquish consciousness, but he was all too aware of his bones, his skin, his muscles, his nails, and his organs as his entire body writhed in waves of misery. Again, he would see what looked a bit like wolf, then turned to bear, then back to wolf, and felt his flesh and bones lurch and twist, spasming in a bizarre shapeshifting progression between bear, wolf, and man. He roared in pain, then howled, collapsed against the wall, and began to think his body would, indeed, tear itself apart. It was as if the animals were trying to burst out through his skin, destroying him in the process, much like a man he'd seen torn apart on the rack. Then he prayed for death, wondering why his mind now refused to fade into unconsciousness. "Aaaauuugh!" he screamed, hearing the bellow of a bear, and finally merciful silence as the room went black and he dropped to the floor, unconscious at last.

When he awoke a naked man, the sun had risen and he was alone with his thoughts. For several months the pattern continued; occasional visits by the scientists who blinded him with light then paralyzed him for their experiments on his flesh, then Morgan invaded his mind on the nights of his transformations. He resolved not to eat, but he awoke with a full belly after the blinding lights and invasive inspections of his body. His throat would be sore and new tracks of needles appeared on his arms. Other pains made him wonder what all they did to him while he was unconscious, though it was probably better he didn't know.

## 31 – A Royal Pain

*"And then I'll change all in your arms into a lion bold, but hold me tight and fear me not, the father of your child."*
Child Ballad 39: Tam Lin

Skaal stepped into the clean white chamber where Morgan was using a long, bony finger to draw shapes on a glassy surface in front of her. On the wall, images surfaced and retreated with every move, until she found something of interest, and she stared at the strange lines and swirls that defined a language so foreign to earth that it had never yet been seen outside of the Sh'eyta dimension.

Skaal tapped his foot quietly to announce his presence without startling her.

"What is it?" she asked, without turning from her study of the figures.

"The others are calling for dismemberment and necropsy, madam."

Morgan's finger became utterly still. "A complete end to the research, then."

"Some say it is a beginning."

She turned so suddenly Skaal was startled. "Once he is dead, there will be no more change to witness!"

Skaal was ashamed to find his mouth hung open. He snapped it shut, then voiced what he'd been trying to find words for, for several weeks. "Madam, you can't keep him alive for your own amusement. We must continue the research!" His hands began to quiver as he faced the gradual scowl that appeared on her smooth face. His adrenaline response dismayed him, but it was necessary to be part human to conduct his extraplanetary research. It couldn't be done on his home planet, and they had to be part human for their metabolism to respond to this planet's resources. It was distasteful, but expedient. He held his ground as she took deliberate measured steps in his direction. "Who says I keep him alive only for my own amusement?" She came to a stop much closer than he'd have liked.

"They all believe it, Madam, but—"

"As do you!"

He faltered, then lifted his shoulders. "It's hard to deny that it seems so, commander."

She nodded briefly at him, then turned away and walked back to the glass screen, rapping out a pattern of taps that brought up an image of Tam, who was jumping in place.

"I haven't given up on him, as you have."

"We've used every method we know of to eradicate the beasts from the man, as you well know."

She folded her arms as she watched Tam exercising. "We haven't seen his body tear itself apart."

Skaal sighed. "His body resists dissolution, madam. It won't deconstruct."

She turned toward him. "But you DO want to witness the deconstruction, don't you?"

Skaal pursed his lips as his pulse quickened. "We had hoped to . . ." then he couldn't trust his voice not to crack in his excitement, and he tried to picture the remarkable vision of a body turning itself inside out. He yearned to witness a biological process that no one living had ever seen.

"What if you applied a third form?"

Skaal's brows lifted in astonishment. "A THIRD beast?"

She nodded with a smirk. "Imagine his frail human body attempting to stretch into the shape of a lion while warring with wolf and bear . . ."

Skaal's eyes widened with delight as he pictured the morbid scene. "To witness the remarkable events we've only read about . . . I have dreamed of filling in the details on that process. Our early researchers were too sparing with words, and I have so many questions! It would be a fantastic thing to see . . ." but his own fascination with the idea seemed a dim reflection of her own. Her arms quivered, as his had only a minute ago, though it seemed to be more desire than fear. It sickened him; not only was it repulsive to see how she indulged in emotion, but that she actually found pleasure in pain was not only primitive but perverse. A creature that indulged in pleasure was to be pitied. A creature that enjoyed its own destruction, that enjoyed pain... well, that wasn't just primitive, it was absolutely wrong. He turned away, not wanting to face the leader before him. She was a masochist. But the purpose defined for her was to be their leader. He couldn't go against purpose, but he had begun to wonder if her extreme mental aberration called for a change in Sh'eyta law. No Sh'eytan had ever been so repulsive. He shook it off and went back to his work. It wasn't his problem; he had his own purpose to pursue. Let someone else deal with the leader.

The following evening Tam felt her slip into his mind just before he endured the searing pain again as his body twitched and writhed in progression from one form to another and finally panted in exhaustion as he found himself entirely wolf this time. All night long he paced back and forth, watching for the scientists to come, but he remained alone. In the morning it was a much simpler reversal as he became man again. That evening he howled in pain as he convulsed, eventually becoming bear.

He breathed heavily as he felt Morgan's presence slip away from his mind; he sensed her through each transformation, but he hadn't seen her in person since the first evening. She had no interest in the phenomena itself, only relished his suffering. He bellowed in anger and lunged against the cable that tied him to the wall, then turned to swipe impotently at the wall with a huge paw. One of his claws caught on the cable and he heard the metallic twang as if he were playing a harp with a single string. Furious, he beat at the cable with one paw after the other, then turned his head to take it in his mouth and chew on it, grinding the cable between his teeth. After an hour his teeth began to feel tender, but he was sure he felt a weakness in it, and he kept pressing it between his teeth, sliding his lower jaw back and forth against it. Another hour went by, then a sharp edge bit into his tongue, and he roared an objection before he realized he'd weakened the cable enough to break one of the strands. He placed his teeth over the cable, then crushed it again, grinding back and forth, hour after hour. The sky began to lighten, and he kept grinding in spite of the pain. He eventually felt the now-familiar crawling sensation under his skin and realized he was about to lose the benefit of his newfound strength. He gathered himself against the wall and heaved to the full extent of the cable one last time as he felt a ripple of change rip through his body. He grunted and coughed as the chain snapped tight against his neck, straining against the metal yet as it choked his breath. Despair took over, and he closed his eyes. The fur pulled back into his body, and his neck shrank, the Rigellium chain cutting into him, still strangling him, then suddenly he was falling forward as the cable snapped. The heels of his hands struck the hard ground just after his knees, and he barely caught himself before his chin struck the earth. He was free! He gulped air, shaking his head as he lurched to his feet, then looked around, but there were no weapons, of course. His automatic response was no use here. He crept to the doorway and peered around the edge to see who was in the courtyard; it was empty. He took a deep breath, then walked out boldly into the courtyard, crossing to the stables, where Honor greeted him curiously, snuffling against him for a treat.

"And where do you think I'd be hiding anything, you big fool?" Tam whispered as he rubbed Honor's neck. He was naked, of course.

There were footsteps behind him, and Tam instinctively grabbed Honor's reins off the wall, slinging around with them so that the hard bit struck Skaal square in the temple. The scientist lurched backwards, hitting his head against the wall, and dropped to the ground. Tam swung the reins against him again, beating him about the head with the leather and iron, and Skaal screamed. Tam struck him twice more before he felt the scientist's presence in his mind, then fell to the ground himself, paralyzed, as the captain ran in through the doorway.

"NO!" Skaal cried, as the captain grabbed the reins from Tam and looked as if he would hit him.

"But Sir, he attacked you--" The captain began.

"It is no matter. I should have been more careful. He doesn't know any better."

Tam tried to fight the stillness that had come over him, but it was useless. Skaal had the captain and the golems carry him and drop him onto a cold metal table in the white room with the bright lights.

The captain stood back as Skaal opened a cupboard, taking out a vial. "What's that?"

"It's the leonid metamorphic. The transformation between human, wolf, and bear nearly ripped him apart. Morgan suggested we add one more metamorphic; that should allow us to see if the descriptions of ancient multiform dysgenesis are accurate."

The captain stared for a moment and Skaal glanced at him. "We want to see how the transformation tears his body apart."

The captain nodded, his eyes lighting up. Skaal filled a syringe from the vial, then injected Tam, who strained to get away. His eyes were wide and the tendons stood out on his neck, but he couldn't force any other muscles to move at all.

Gruoch appeared at his side, a worried look on her face. "I'd have done it, Skaal."

"No mind, it was easy enough to do it myself."

Gruoch looked sadly at Tam. "Well, what will be will be. Not for another twenty-five days, though. Will you need him here before the final transformation?"

Skaal frowned. "I think we have all the data we want on his current condition. He refuses to stay in the cell we gave him, but he's too violent to have him roaming free."

"Then you'll want him outside the gate."

Tam was furious with her. His only desire right now was to destroy Skaal. If he were outside the gate, it would be much harder to get to the scientist and tear him apart. If Skaal wanted to know what it looked like to see a body torn apart, Tam would be happy to oblige him by ripping his own body limb from limb.

The needle slid into his arm, then withdrew, while he strained to resist.

Skaal looked at him. "We need to have him here for observation."

"But not for a month."

Skaal stared at Tam. "We can't spare the time to have one of us keep him subdued, but how can we retrieve him if he resists capture?"

"He resists capture only because Morgan allows him to do so. She lets the golems pummel him, rather than subduing him with her mind. Isn't that why he was fitted with the Rigellium? So she can subdue him and enter his mind at any distance?"

"And to keep him within the boundary. The Rigellium is too valuable to allow it beyond our borders. But remember, his mind is no longer solely human—"

"He is fully human aside from the solar-lunar gravitational opposition that forces the metamorphosis."

Skaal grunted in agreement. "True. His form is governed by the moon's phase. Well, having to reacquire him is more complicated . . ."

"Keeping him captive is complicated. Did you not find him in the stables? I came when I heard the commotion."

Skaal sighed. "We'd have to bring him back ourselves, rather than leave it to the commander."

"We're due to convene the Sluagh Sh'eyta."

Skaal paused to think. "Has it been so long?"

"Seven years. The order has been given, we ride at Samhain. The moon will be full. That's when the ley tides are strongest. We have to retrain the Rigellium to recognize our borders."

Skaal shook his head. "I have too much to do! I would prefer it be later."

"It has to be done when the greatest ley tides change."

"I'm well aware of that!" he snapped. "And the damnable Rigellium is excruciatingly sensitive to routine." He sighed. "Well, it has to be done. Every single one of us, every single one of our steeds, every single ounce of Rigellium, all must go around the boundaries of our land here, to see that the barriers are made strong again, that we can pass while it blocks all others. The last thing I need is a human disrupting my research." He peered at Tam. "Of course, he'll have to ride with us, since you've installed the Rigellium on him." A look of surprise overtook Skaal's features. "Oh, well, I suppose he won't be alive at that point."

"He has to go with us, and it must start before he is due to change. He'll rupture while we ride, carried by his horse, which also wears Rigellium."

"Let me think for a moment."

Tam tried to move, to speak, but he was still bound by the invisible hold the scientist maintained. The Sluagh Sidhe? He knew of no one who had ever witnessed it, but it was said that spirits rode the skies once every seven years, on Samhain night, and any who were seen by them were whisked up by the riders, never to be seen again.

Eventually Skaal nodded. "And if he is torn apart, he can act as the blood sacrifice. Your logic is unassailable. You may take him, we have no need for him until then and no desire to manage him. We'll release him to Gruoch," he said, turning to the captain, who looked as if he were going to speak. "If she considers him so easy to control, she is free to prove it."

Tam tilted and stumbled as his body was returned to his own power. Skaal was beyond his reach, and the captain strode after him. He was alone with Gruoch.

"Where have ye been, lass?"

"I have many tasks that await completion. I can't watch over you every moment," she said.

Tam drew back, then grinned. "But ye wish ye could, don't ye?"

"I wish I had. I was too late to stop him."

They stood for a moment, contemplating the injection he just received. Tam drew himself up. "No matter. My body can withstand two, why not three?"

She shook her head. "Barely two. Unlikely three."

Tam stretched. "Then I have a month to live. And I don't want to spend it here. Get me to my field, lass. If I'm to die in a month, I'll spend it there." He watched for an opportunity to grab a scientist, a guard, or the captain, but they were nowhere to be seen as Gruoch saw that he was clothed and rode back to Carter Hall with him.

## 32 – Expecting

"Father, if I go with child, I must bear the blame; there's none among your gentlemen shall give the babe his name." Child Ballad 39: Tam Lin

Several weeks later in the ladies' tower, Janet's hand moved the needle across the fabric while she looked out the window to the garden. She winced in pain as she pricked herself again and flung the shawl down with a scowl, along with the needle and thread, then looked up when she realized the women had gone silent.

"Did you hear one of the milkmaids is pregnant?" someone said, resuming the gossip. There were gasps as the hands of the other women stopped stitching seams and they all turned to the speaker with feigned horror. Janet could see the delight they strove to hide as they all waited, transfixed with anticipation, for the next revelation about the plight of the poor milkmaid.

"It's that elf, Tam Glin!" Another said, and their heads all turned toward the speaker.

"No doubt. Someone needs to stop him. He's a rogue!" The murmurs of objection rose to affronted cries of repudiation.

"Has the Lord forgotten about him? Are his men so busy watching the border?"

Janet leaned down and picked up her shawl as the gossip continued, noticing that her most recent stitches were crooked. She sighed, pulling the thread from the needle, and gently pulled the last stitch out, then the one before that, as she listened to the ladies discuss the scandal.

"Who would be foolish enough to have commerce with the Sidhe?"

Janet's cheeks grew warm and she bent down to hide her face, peering at the crooked seam as she continued to pull the poorly placed stitches out of the fabric.

"I doubt she was willing. He has his way with any who comes by."

"She was probably bespelled."

Janet almost leaned back in astonishment to look at the woman speaking but caught herself in time, not wanting to let any of them know how interested she was in what they were saying. Her hands went still as she listened, still leaning over her sewing.

"She'll have to end it! We can't have a demon born right here in the Lord's keep."

"A demon!" Janet broke into the conversation, too loudly, and the ladies all turned toward her. "I thought he was an elf?" She remembered how he appeared so suddenly out of nowhere, twice.

"Aye, elves are the devil's own get. Any child fathered by the Sidhe will destroy the clan foolish enough to let it live."

"It's just a child!" Janet protested, and they all went silent again, gazing at her with pity for her innocence.

"It's no human child," The eldest said. "It's a demon. It mustn't be allowed to live. The only time a woman has any control over the creature is before it's born. That's when it must be put to death."

The ladies' murmured their assent, but their eyes were bright with the salacious vision. Janet was disgusted. *Children should be cherished,* she thought, *not murdered*, then stopped herself. If it wasn't a child, then it wasn't murder. One didn't speak of murdering a chicken for dinner. *Inhuman,* she considered the word, then went cold with fear. She would be sure to count the days to her next cycle. The thought of having an inhuman creature inside of her was horrifying.

"The laurel rose grows only in Carter Hall at this time of year," spoke the first woman, eager to have the ladies' attention again. "She'll have to go back and face him if she wants the herb." She described the leaves and blossoms of the plant that, when brewed as a strong tea, would end any unwanted pregnancy.

Janet felt so foolish. What had she been thinking, going out to see the mysterious man that lived out in the weeds of Carter Hall. A landless peasant at best, a ne'er do well who had his way with any lass that he found. Ashamed, she leaned over her stitches again. "Pooh!" she murmured. She'd removed all the stitches, even the ones that had been perfect. With a sigh, she started over, remembering how enchanting the handsome young man had seemed. He never spoke a word of who he was, or what he was for that matter. The more Janet thought about it, the more she became positive he was exactly what the ladies had said. An enchanted being: an elf. Faerie. Sidhe. Who else would live in a field of grass? How could she have been so foolish?

She thought the very same thing a week later when she realized her cycle was late. She waited another week; perhaps that was it, she was just late. And then another week. Well, she had to change her life around to sit in the dusty room with the old ladies and learn to embroider. They told her her cycle would likely change, and their bodies would all come to be on the same schedule.

When the second month went by, though, and she still had seen no blood on the cloth she used for her monthly cycle, she began to panic. Still, she thought, perhaps it was merely that her body was confused, what with being cooped up all day inside the keep. She hadn't been eating as much, with so little appetite. And this morning, she was nauseous. How could she eat anything when she wasn't sure she would keep it down? If she ate something, it would come up again. She went to the kitchen and found a crust of bread to nibble, taking it back to the room where the ladies sat, embroidering and chatting endlessly about useless things. She felt her bile rise, and put a hand over her lips, trying to keep the bread down.

At lunch she found that she was starving, so it must have worked. She helped herself to a huge pile of pickled beets, which had never appealed to her before, but she discovered they were delicious. And they went very well with the sharp tang of the deep orange cheese that had been put out on the sideboard with the stewed goat's meat, which she smothered with peppers.

And so it went; mornings nauseous, afternoons ravenous, and with a taste for foods she had never considered before, but she remained adamant that her body was just learning a new routine, that once she felt better it would all straighten out and her cycle would begin again.

Several months went by until one evening when all the ladies were sewing in the great hall near the roaring fireplace to warm their cold feet, and the men-at-arms who weren't currently on guard drank their beer while playing chess. Her father stared at her for quite some time, unnoticed, until he suddenly spoke up, having seen the glances the men were casting at Janet as they whispered behind their hands.

"Janet," he called out to her, and she looked up.

"Yes father?" she said, easing her back, which had begun to ache for no apparent reason.

"Are you well?"

Janet was puzzled. "I'm fine, father, thank you for asking."

There was a murmur of amusement, and her father looked angry. "Are you quite sure, Janet? I see you've loosened the laces of your bodice."

Janet looked down at her belly, realizing that the laces she loosened before eating the noonday meal were still untied. They were too uncomfortable when pulled tightly enough to fully close the gown at the front. It cramped her belly. She was getting fat, but then, she always gained a few pounds as the weather got colder, and she sat around a great deal since her father insisted she learn to sew.

Her eyes flew open wide as she looked in shock at her father; she'd forgotten how long it had been since her last cycle, so sure the crusts of bread and full meals would cure whatever ailed her, and she realized that no amount of food would fix the condition she was in right now.

"The ladies are whispering about you, you know," her father's voice cut through her thoughts, and she looked furiously at them, "and the men have said some unsavory things. I've had to correct their choice of gossip. Do you think that's fair, Janet? Have you given them something to gossip about? If you have, they can't be held at fault, can they?"

Janet's cheeks were burning.

"Is it true, Janet? I'll have you answer here and now, in front of all who slandered you. I'll have you answer; is it true you're pregnant? If not, there are a number of men I'll punish for their loose tongues. But if so, I'll need to know which one of them, or the visiting lords, will be held to account."

All eyes were on her, and Janet tried to come up with something to say, but she couldn't think of anything.

"Eogan, I heard you claiming that my daughter is pregnant. If she says she is not, I'll have you flogged. Rise, Eogan."

A man rose to his feet, looking straight at Janet, and she realized his fate was hers to command. And the truth was the truth; there was no hiding it any longer. Not from herself, not from the people who were gathered in the room. She was furious with herself for continuing to wait just a little longer, then longer. "It could be true, father."

"Could be, or is, Janet?" His voice was soft in the immense silence that had taken the room.

Janet bowed her head and whispered, "Is, father." But everyone in the hall heard her words. They could have heard a mouse stirring in the straw.

Her father nodded. "You may sit down, Eogan. It seems you were only recognizing the truth. But I'll have you mind that in the future you will come to me with such truths, not the rest of the men. It is unfair that we have to clear this up in such a public place because it has been bandied about by every mouth."

Janet wanted to creep from the hall, but he wasn't done with her yet. "And who is the father, Janet? Is it one of my men, or one of the nobles that have visited us? It seems you have chosen your husband and gotten on with starting a family much sooner than I expected. I would prefer it be a nobleman, of course, but I'll not have the babe born out of wedlock. Who will your husband be?"

Janet looked up. Straightening her back, she scowled at him. "Aye, father, you've called me out in this room in front of all, but I'll tell you this; I've still not seen a single man in this hall, whether among your men or among those who have visited, that I would marry, nor even kiss! And certainly not…" her voice faltered. "No, father, it's none of the men in this keep, nor a man that has passed through. This child is mine and mine alone to bear the blame for. I made a choice, indeed, but it's not a man I will be marrying in any church." She strode from the hall, then went running to her room to hide herself away for the rest of the evening. The next morning she rose before dawn and slipped out through the small door in the gate, before the gates were opened. The guards were in the hall grabbing a bite to eat, except for the one at the top of the wall, but he was looking for incoming strangers, not the Earl's daughter, who went around the corner of the wall to disappear into the trees, following a circuitous route to get to the path that led to Carter Hall.

## 33 – Poison

"What makes you pull the poison rose? What makes you break the tree? What makes you harm the little babe That I have got with thee?" Child Ballad 39: Tam Lin

Janet hurriedly searched the ground at Carter Hall, praying that she wouldn't see the dark, handsome creature that had seduced her months before. She took courage in the fact that she hadn't seen him through the window even once since then, though she thought about him a great deal. She'd given up on looking for him weeks ago. She found the plant that had been described to her, but it was behind a thick rose bush. She knelt down on the gravel that covered the path into the grassy glen, reaching through the rosebush where the canes were more sparse to pull at the delicate flowers that clustered at its feet.

"Lass, what are you doing?"

Janet's heart lurched as she looked up at the beautiful monster she'd trysted with, what seemed like ages ago now. He wasn't there a moment ago! "I'm gathering herbs," she replied, but didn't move.

His gaze fell. "I studied a book on herbs a short while ago; the one you hold has a terrible use."

Janet stood up and threw her shoulders back. "Yes, it's a terrible use, but it's none of your business what I do with it."

He grabbed her by the wrist and pulled the plant from her fingers. "If you intend harm to a child we've made between us, it is my business. Why would you do such a thing?"

Janet tried to pull her wrist from his iron grip, but he was far too strong for her. "I'll not bear the child of a demon, Tam o'Glen!"

He released her wrist and she tumbled backwards, surprised to be freed so suddenly.

"A demon! What makes you call me a demon?" He dropped to her side.

"You're an elf, and I'll not bring an elf child into my father's keep."

Tam went stiff. "Lord Dunbar's keep."

"You know of him?" she asked cautiously.

"I tried to tell you just before you disappeared, lass. How could I forget the little warrior princess that dropped from this very tree when I was but a lad…" he took a deep breath. "Janet, I'm a man… it's myself; Tam, son of Randall, the Earl of Murray. Do you remember when we played together, in this very field, with sticks and wooden swords? Climbing trees as if they were the ramparts of a castle?"

She could barely hear his words over the beating of her heart as he spoke, but she nodded as she looked at him anew, comparing his appearance to the little boy from so many years ago. His jaw was wider, his cheekbones sharper, and the wispy hairs of new growth on his face disguised his cheeks, but those were the same mischievous eyes of the energetic lad she shared that day with.

"Tam?" she whispered hesitantly.

They stared at each other, she in confusion, he in despair. "Lass," he said, "We're not wed. Had I known it was you, I would never have presumed… and here you are…" He looked at the weed he held in his hand and rose to his feet as he flung it to the ground, grinding it under the heel of his boot. "You can't do this!" Then he gave her such a desolate, miserable look that it seemed her heart itself would weep for him.

Janet thought quickly as she eyed the handsome stranger that was far less strange than she had imagined. He was a nobleman's son, and therefore a nobleman himself. He'd talked about all he learned of swords, armor and warhorses while studying to become a knight. She squared her shoulders, then spoke with quiet resolve. He met the two requirements her father had named. And she grew warm at the thought of spending her life with a man she'd known as a child, and loved. "Would you never consider marrying me, then? We'll have a child, if you insist on destroying the herb I've come for. Will you have it be raised as a bastard, condemned to act as a servant in his mother's hall while you continue your play out here, a foul highwayman?"

"Hold your tongue!" He blurted. "I'm no brigand! I'm here as a captive, and I've only done what the Sidhe demanded of me." He grabbed her wrists, both this time, and pulled her toward him. "I'd marry you, yes; I'd raise the child in my own house, as my heir. I'd teach him the arts of governance and of war, or, if it be a girl, you'd teach her to grow into the finest lass in the land, just like her mother—"

She fell into his arms with a sob, unable to handle the shock any longer. "By the stars, Tam, is it really you? Do you mean what you say?" she mumbled against his shoulder.

"Aye, lass. Janet. I mean it," he said as he stroked her hair, "But it means not a thing if I can do none of it. Marry you I can, but escape this place I cannot. I'm held here by the… the Faerie Queen, as you would call her. And I might not have long for this life. The child you will bear might be all that this world knows of me soon enough."

Janet drew back to look at his face again; his dark grey eyes were glistening under brows drawn together in pain.

"What do you mean?"

He pulled away from her then and turned to look up at the peak of the tower that stood beyond the trees. "She will be taking my body apart on Samhain eve, seeking to drive the beasts out of me or kill me in trying, and I'm sure it will be the latter. I'm no more than a scholar's specimen to her at this point; I served my purpose long enough that she thinks she can discard me, but she'll try to salvage me first, and they say there's little chance my flesh will survive her attempts, though I hold hope that I might. If I survive that, though, surely they'll destroy me at last. This is my last day on earth, I'm sure of it. Our child will have no father…" his words trailed away as he glared furiously at the crenelated wall barely visible in the distance.

"Isn't there anything we can do?" Janet implored.

Tam turned to look at her. Her eyes were wide and sorrowful. "Nay, she comes today to take me back to her tower, where she'll put an end to my life."

"No!"

He embraced her swiftly, his hands pressed against the back of her head as he pulled her upwards and pressed his lips against hers, exploring with his tongue as he kissed her deeply, as if he sought to be consumed by her. Her stomach roiled with a delicious yearning that took her over. She clutched his broad shoulders as tightly as he pulled her body against his, feeling the hard strength of his muscles under her soft hands as she lowered herself to the ground and pulled him down on top of herself eagerly. They both lost themselves in the groping, the sweetness of tongue on tongue, hand on waist, belly to belly, thigh to thigh.

The embrace seemed to last for hours, or seconds, it was impossible to tell. When he released her lips and drew back to look into her eyes, she was panting as if she had run the entire way to his grassy field.

"I'll rescue you," she whispered.

He shook his head. "Ye cannot, lass," he whispered back as he stroked her hair and seemed to drink in every inch of her face as if taken with a mystic thirst.

"I'll hide you away from her."

"And how will ye . . ." his voice trailed off. "The shawl!" he said.

"What?"

"The shawl is copper, isn't it?"

"Yes, but—"

"Copper blocks her magick!"

Tam looked up at the sky, and the smile escaped his face. "Ah, but the sun is already begun its path down toward the horizon. They'll come for me before the sun sets, I'm sure. They should have been here by now, I'd think. And it will be the lot of them, on their wild steeds, from the sound of it. They'll have me mindbound on my own horse. If you can't get home and back before then, ye'd have to pull me down off my own horse to hide me under your shawl."

"I'll do it."

"Nay! I'll not have ye handling me at that hour," he answered with horror. "It'll be not long after that their foul plans will force me to change, lass. I'll go from man, to wolf, to bear, to lion. I can't vouch for your safety!"

Janet went cold at the thought, then shook her head. Clearly it wasn't his choice, so it wasn't his fault. Her child would know its father if she had any say in it. "You can't stop me, either, Tam," she said quietly.

He drew back and looked deep into her eyes. "I'll not have ye do it," he repeated, but without any force to his voice.

"You'll not stop me, Tam," she said again, and pulled his lips down to hers to kiss him deep and long, then pushed him away as she sprang to her feet and ran for Dunbar's keep.

## 34 – Dead Man Walking

"But aye, at every seven years, they pay a fee to hell; and I a human full of flesh, tonight 'twill be myself." Child Ballad 39: Tam Lin

Tam stared after her, unable to follow across the border where the Rigellium cut off his breath. Had she heard him? That he would change from one beast to another as the moon rose in the sky? Surely she misunderstood him. He looked up toward the sun, tense with fear for her. The golden globe would soon be dropping fast. Searching his memory, he recalled this clearing being far from Phillip Hall, the new domain of Turnebull. Is that where Dunbar had said he'd just come from, months ago, when he'd called Tam into the fateful discussion that had led to all this? Phillip Hall was surely the nearest place that could possibly hold the Dunbar, the Earl of March, and all his retinue. But it was too far, it would take her too long to go there and come back. When he was young, they'd run through the woods, playing, for hours, hadn't they? He paced, his heart racing. Perhaps she was swifter of foot than he feared. Certainly swifter than young boys who were easily diverted with every new discovery.

And Morgan would come for him any time now. It would be before the moon rose, of that he was sure, but how long before? He nodded. He would be taken before she returned. She would be safe from him. She would come back to find him gone from this field. He pictured her seeking him in the stone hall, looking for him in the nearby woods, and finding him gone. Nodding again, he assured himself she would be safe. They'd come for him soon, and he would be safely away from her when his body betrayed him. He would die tonight, but only himself; she was safe. She would never meet the fiends who had abducted him what seemed ages ago now. Breathing easier, he went to chop more wood. It would loosen his tension and give him a weapon to wield when the devils returned. They would take him in the end, but he would not go down without a fight.

As he chopped one log after another, he couldn't keep his fear at bay. What if she came back on a swift horse? What if he survived the transformation? What if he was freed from this imprisonment and took her hand in marriage? The thought buoyed him, then the brief moment of elation was dashed. He hadn't told her the best he could hope for was that a beast would come out again, every month, for the rest of his life. What kind of a father could he be?

A father. He would be a father. Did it matter what kind he was? Three nights a month he could reside in a dungeon if the rest of the month he was allowed to be her husband, the father of her child. Did anything else matter? But no, she wouldn't be back in time. He wouldn't survive.

He chopped the log into kindling. If he did, though, how would he remain free? He would still bear the chains. He couldn't live his entire life draped in her shawl. If Janet returned before they came for him, he'd send her safely away. No man would put his wife and child in danger. He steeled himself to resist her if he must. She couldn't be allowed to take him away. She couldn't take him against his will, of course. He felt sweat trickle down his cheek as he thought of how he would turn her away and go to Morgan if that was what he had to do. He struck the log so hard the axe went straight through the section of wood and bit deeply into the stump. He ripped it out of the stump and swung again, driving it so deep into the wood he thought the handle would break before he pulled it free.

Janet's lungs ached as she ran back to the keep as fast as she could, feet pounding the earth. As she came into sight of the stone wall, a cry went up from the guards who patrolled the rampart. In an instant, horses were galloping toward her, the men atop them bellowing at her to come back to the keep. Could they not see that's what she was doing? Within minutes, they had her arms and were marching her back home as if she were a common criminal. She was mute with dumbfounded fury until they brought her before her father in a private chamber he normally used for deliberations of war.

He nodded at the men and they released her.

"Leave us alone," he said. He was furious, and no one liked to be near Dunbar when he was furious, but Janet's own fear for Tam and anger for the way she'd been treated gave her extraordinary courage.

"How dare you have me handled like a common thief!" She shouted at him, tears running down her face as she gripped the skirt of her gown in her fists, fearful of what she would do with those fists if she released the expensive fabric.

"You've stolen away with the heir to Carter Hall, and you have the gall to accuse ME of wrongdoing? Where were you, and what do you do when you sneak away from my protection?" His gaze dropped to her swollen belly, and he snapped, "Never mind your answer! The truth is clear. What kind of foul-birthed heathen have you been with?"

"Heathen he is NOT!"

"You refused to even NAME him, much less speak for him when I commanded you to do so!"

"I had no answer then, but I'll tell you now, he will be my husband. He meets your requirements; noble born and experienced in war. Or did you lie when you told me you would let me choose such a man?"

He stared at her in astonishment. The silence between them grew, and she released the folds of her gown as the truth caught up with her. "Father," she whispered, "he will die if I don't return to him soon. I must go back—"

"You will not!" came his swift reply, then he looked at her as if he'd never seen her before. The silence grew again, until he whispered, "Janet, what on earth have you gotten yourself into? Where is the freckled girl I once bounced on my knee?"

She sank to the stone floor in a puddle of silk and began to weep. He strode over, but she shook her head and resisted his attempts to lift her to her feet. "No! Let me speak," she whispered as she gathered her thoughts, then spoke in a firmer voice, ricing to her knees. "Father, do you remember our cousin Tam Randall?"

His eyes narrowed. "Your mother's second cousin. What do you know of him?"

She nodded. "He's the father of my child."

Dunbar lowered himself into the chair behind him. "Oh for the love of . . . right here on my own grounds! Here lass, tell me the tale in complete—"

"I haven't time—"

"You'll make it!" He bellowed, and she sat back so quickly she found herself falling backward, but she caught herself just in time to spare another ungainly prostration.

"Janet, tell me, what is all this you speak of? Randall's son disappeared months ago. No word has come of ransom, so we've been concerned for him; it's good to know he's well enough to be siring a child." The last few words were delivered with a growl.

"He's alive, father, but taken by . . ." Janet faltered as she realized how impossible it might sound to her father, who thought fairies were nonsense. She hadn't believed in fairies herself since she was a child. Peasants would believe their entire lives, and even many of the dukes and earls, but most, including her own father, refused to hear of it.

Her father waited for her to complete the sentence, but she couldn't do it. "Never mind," he said. "I expect I know who he was taken by."

"He must be rescued, father."

"He must NOT!" Her father gave her a sharp look. "Janet, you must keep your distance. There is more afoot than you know. You are putting your nose into matters that don't concern you. I'm disappointed that he forces me to choose between what is best for my grandchild and what is best for Scotland, but he must stay right where he is until it is time for him to return."

"And when will this time be?" Janet asked, wide-eyed.

He rubbed his bearded chin and stared toward the southern wall. "Well, perhaps I should send scouts to see what we can learn. Once his mission is complete, perhaps he'll need to be sprung. If he is so nearby, we'll get a report from him."

"Then you'll send men right away?"

"Don't be silly!" he scoffed. "We can bring him back when the time is right, but I must know where he is, and how many men I'll need to overcome them. His father will be in our debt, which is a good advantage for us. Randall has the ear of the king even more than I."

"There isn't time! He'll die tonight if I don't return for him!"

"Nonsense. What makes you think tonight is the end of him? Why, it's Samhain, Janet! No one goes abroad on Samhain eve. Most think it's bad luck, and even those who don't believe have no desire to rouse the rabble. Fear not, daughter, he is safe for now, but be sure if he is so concerned, we must act quickly. Tell me, who has him, and where?"

Janet shook her head, lips held tightly together.

"No mind, if you can reach him and return in a few hours, he must be near." Lord Dunbar still looked to the south, as if he could see through the stone wall of the tower toward Aikwood, the only other keep in the vicinity.

"Send your men now!" Janet wailed. "He won't be alive past this evening!"

Her father chuckled and patted her hand. "Don't be silly, Janet. He'll be fine! Your worries are misplaced. I agree that we must act quickly, but not so quick as that. You leave the planning to me. I'll send scouts in the morning to see what we can learn of the situation. Tonight there is a feast to attend to, or do you forget what day it is in your besotted imaginings? There are forms to observe. Our people will expect the blessing to be given."

Janet's jaw had dropped in astonishment. Finally she nodded in mute agreement, eyes wide, but she steeled her resolve to rescue Tam without delay. All she needed was to retrieve her shawl and run back to the grassy meadow. Time was rushing past, but she would find a way. She had to.

Lord Dunbar began to turn away, but stopped. He must have seen something in her expression that betrayed her. Suddenly he turned back. "You are not to go anywhere near there until this is resolved! Do you hear me?"

Janet squared her shoulders as she rose. A grim determination replaced the pallid astonishment that had been there a moment before.

His eyes narrowed. "You will attend the festivities with an armed escort, or you will be banished to your rooms until the morrow. Do you understand?"

Janet clenched her jaw and could barely speak through her gritted teeth. "I'll not let the father of my child die at the hands of his captors."

"Guards!" her father bellowed, and in a moment the doors slammed open. "Take her to her room, and don't leave from her door. She is not to step out of it until I rescind this order."

"No! Father! What about the feast?"

"You surrendered your right to attend when you declared your defiance, daughter." Then, more gently, "It is for your own good, Janet. You have far too much of my determination in you. It isn't safe. Don't you see? And you are in no condition! You aren't even thinking clearly. It must be the motherhood descending upon you. These are decisions better made by men. No matter how protective you may feel of your child, and of his father, it isn't safe, my dear. Trust in me. If he is so close at hand, and ready to come back to us, I will prevail. Really, Janet; with your own mother a Randall herself, do you think I could do anything less? I only count myself fortunate that my own castle is being rebuilt, and Turnebull is not yet ready to defend his new home, or we'd be many a mile from here; I'd never thought of Phillip Hall as more than a resting place when we traveled. If he was taken away too far from us, we'd have never learned where he went. I can only hope his capture has yielded knowledge worthy of his sacrifice. You're to be commended, child, for bringing such news. Now go, and try to behave yourself. I'll send food up when the roasts are done turning on the spit. There, there, it will be alright soon enough, you'll see," he patted her on the head as tears began to stream down her face. Then he nodded to the men, who once again held her arms so firmly that she could barely stay on her feet as they steered her away.

How would she get back to Tam if she were locked in her room? "Nooooo . . ." she wailed, but no one cared what she had to say.

## 35 - Escape

"She's taken her mantle her about, her coffer by the band, and she is on to Carter Hall as fast as she could go." Child Ballad 39: Tam Lin

Janet wished she could see behind her as she lowered herself to the ground on the drapes she'd tied together and flung from the balustrade. There was no help for the way they hung down from her balcony; they had to support her weight, so she tied them too tightly to pull them down and hide them now, but she drew them into the shadows to hide them for the rest of the late afternoon, then she scurried toward the garden and hid behind a shrub as she caught her breath. Her silk gown was pulled up to her waist and tucked into the trews she stole from her brother, along with his black hooded cloak and his boots; she had to stuff cloth in each toe because they were much too large for her. The shawl had been too much, she held it folded in her hand, so she could attach it to the saddle once she got to the stables. The rapier that hung at her side completed the look, but she knew she'd have to keep the hood over her face and try to not turn toward anyone to keep her face hidden. Hopping over to her balcony to his room had been simple, the two of them had done so since they were young, it was the descent to the ground that she never contemplated until now, the ground being a long way down. Steeling her resolve, she strode toward the stables and was relieved to see that no one took any notice of her.

She strode up to the stall of Darkness, her father's hunter. She reached toward him and jerked her hand back as he snapped at her, ears folded flat against his mane and chin up. "Stop that!" she cried, then held her breath as she waited to see if anyone had heard her. Darkness whinnied and chuffed angrily, and she questioned whether he was the right horse, then drew a deep breath and grabbed the reins from the hook by the stall door. Darkness was the fastest horse in the stable, and the one thing she needed most was speed. He could bite her if he chose, but she had to take him; by now the sun was low in the sky and she knew she only had an hour, maybe less, before Tam was taken, if he wasn't already. This was her only chance. She grabbed a handful of grain and held it out to him, then pulled the reins over his head as he lipped them up, shoving the bit between his teeth, barely escaping the powerful, grinding teeth before he chewed on the treat. Once she had the reins firmly in place, she pulled his head around and tied it to the hook so she could get the saddle on, but this proved to be more difficult, as the saddle was heavy and she'd spent all her strength on the heavy fabric of the drapes that she had torn and knotted for hours. Tears of frustration ran down her face the third time she tried to foist it high enough to reach his back. He stamped and blew at her, whinnying again.

"Hush, you fool," she sobbed. "The stableboys will come to check on you," but no one came. She wondered if perhaps they had escaped early to partake of the mead that was always poured liberally on Samhain, hoping that they were in their cups. By now, Darkness was becoming excited. While it was nice to think he might be eager for a run, she wished he would just stand still as she tried to get the heavy saddle onto his moving back. "Stop moving about, you big bruin, or we won't be going at all!" She thought of Tam being taken for sacrifice and her vision blurred as tears welled in her eyes as another sob escaped her. "Stop, Darkness. Oh, stop, you fool. We'll never get out in time if you can't stand still." With a burst of desperate strength she slung the saddle high into the air and it finally landed in pace. Perhaps her word had gotten through to Darkness because the long-legged horse stood stock still and she was able to pull the cinch around his barrel, drawing it tight as she'd seen her brother do so many times. He believed it was best to handle one's own horse and refused to let the stable hands do it for him most of the time. She buckled it, then checked the reins again, and pulled hard at the saddle to see that it was secure before climbing up on the slats of the stall to lift herself into place. It felt strange to have the heavy cloth of the trews between her thighs and the leather saddle. She arranged the fold of the tucked-in gown, the long fold of the shawl, and the cloak over herself so that her body was hidden and all that showed was the black leather boots and the hooded cloak, then pulled the reins around to lead Darkness from the stable. She felt the reins tremble and he lipped the bit, so she slapped him between the ears to keep him from taking it between his teeth. She walked him into the courtyard and prayed that the hood hid her face well enough as Darkness kept fighting the bit.

"Who goes there?" A guard called out from his position by the gate, and fear flooded her as he looked right into her face, but he quickly looked down. "My pardon, my lord, I didn't expect to see you on your father's horse."

Janet's heart was beating like a hammer as she wondered at how the clothing seemed to identify her as her brother; in this light her face was shaded. She nodded briefly as she passed, but the man didn't look up again, and she fought with Darkness as he continued to struggle for control of the bit. She was hardly fifty paces past the gate when she lost the battle. Once the bit was firmly between his teeth, there was nothing she could do as the stallion thundered into a fierce gallop straight down the narrow road away from the hold, and it was all she could do to stay on the back of the huge animal as it ran like the wind toward Aikwood tower. Janet pulled at the reins, and slapped the beast's neck, but mostly she just held on for dear life, every moment fearful it would be her last as she was thrown wildly up into the air, to come down hard on the saddle. She prayed no harm would come to the babe and cursed furiously, pulling again on the reins, but as long as Darkness had his teeth clamped shut she had no control over the frenzied dash. Bouncing and gasping, she sawed sideways with the leather straps, and managed to pull the edge of the bit far enough to one side that his teeth came open slightly. She pulled back hard, getting the bit back into place against the horse's mouth and tongue, and Darkness suddenly slid to a stop as the bit dug into the corners of his mouth. She held it another moment before releasing slightly, not wanting to hurt the foolish animal but determined not to lose control again. She hardly noticed the pain in her bottom and relief gave way to determination. She kicked him to a gentle trot, then canter, holding the reins so tightly in her hands that they began to cramp. The sun was falling fast now, so close to the horizon it was. She caught glimpses through the trees as she sped toward Carter Hall, and Tam, and was relieved to see the sun falling on grasses ahead. She prayed that he would be there.

As she came thundering over the rise, her heart leapt into her throat; the field was bare. A pile of chopped wood was strewn around a split stump. She reined in, and Darkness slowed to a trot, then a walk. The head of the white gelding peered around the stone wall at her, but she didn't see Tam anywhere

She swung wide to see if he might be beside the stone building, but he wasn't there either. Was her lover gone? Oh, dear lord, was she too late? She slid down from the saddle and led the horse behind her as she searched the grounds, stepping into the stone hall to see if he was there, holding tightly to the reins lest Darkness should try again to control the bit, but it seemed he was done running, The long-legged horse paced patiently behind her as she looked everywhere for the man she loved, but he was nowhere to be found.

## 36 – The Wild Hunt

"The morn is Halloween night, the elfin court will ride, through England, and thro a' Scotland, and through the world wide. They begin at sky setting, rides a' the evening tide." Child Ballad 39: Tam Lin

Gruoch looked around at the mass of people and animals; at least a score of Sh'eyta had been joined by another dozen or so golem servants. Then all of the horses, most carrying a passenger but some carrying huge bags laden with all the Rigellium that wasn't secured in place. Of course, the telepathic nature of the metal organisms meant what one experienced they all experienced, but the more they brought with them the stronger the bond would be with the borders of the Sh'eyta land.

Several thousand years ago Morgan's father had thought to simplify the task and took only a portion of the Rigellium, three of the golems, and a third of his people on the Sluagh Sh'eyta. The borders had become permeable, humans coming and going from Sh'eyta dwellings, and they had to post bespelled guardian ornaments that confused their human senses so that they returned to their villages without even realizing they'd been turned around. But when two minds connected, thoughts traveled both ways, and the humans absorbed some of the Sh'eyta knowledge while they were being mentally controlled, learning enough of the secrets that some had to be assuaged with caches of gold, so much that they were given pots to carry it in. The lesson was painful, but impressed upon Morgan how essential it was to commit to the ritual. Morgan had faults, but ignoring the imperative of the Sluagh Sh'eyta was not one of them.

Gruoch looked around. The light was turning golden, and she worried that there was little time to get to Carter Hall before Tam changed. The timing couldn't be worse. If they were to salvage anything of what they did to Tam, beyond using his blood for the ritual, they must be in time to witness the change. It distressed her to know that he would die tonight, but there wasn't a thing she could do about it. She set the feelings aside; emotions were to be expected from a species that was part human, but being Sh'eyta meant you didn't act on them.

With a jangle of reins, impatient barks from the Sh'eyta hounds from the south quarter, and a final glance to see all was in order, Morgan cried out, "Sluagh!" and her people roared, "Sluagh Sh'eyta!" then plunged after her as she galloped across the causeway and between the trees, going straight to the nearest edge of her lands.

Galloping through the trees, Morgan thought back to the last ride as she flexed her legs and clung to the back of her steed. The last ride had been just as disorganized. She had envisioned a timely process of orderly ranks, but more and more time was slipping away. Soon the High Anunnaki would arrive from the home planet and want to inspect her rule. She cursed as a branch whipped her arm, and drove her heels into the sides of the beast. There was little enough time left, none for tending to a bruise. If she couldn't control her realm, there would be more than bruises for her. She enjoyed pleasures no Sh'eyta should be drawn to, much less indulge in, and she had to hide her masochistic decadence; she hid the truth from her people, but the Anunnaki were harder to deceive. She thrilled in the wild run as her body rose and fell with the plunging gallop of her horse, which leapt into the air, almost floating with the others. The Rigellium horseshoes repelled the minerals in the earth, making the steeds lighter of foot than they were without the intelligent metal. When given their heads, the horses exulted in what seemed like flight. It suited her that they'd circle the border swiftly. The Sluagh Sh'eyta was a nuisance, but it couldn't be postponed.

Steeds leaping like winged mounts, dogs baying in the joy of a run, the host was mindful of their travel to the border and soon they came around a bend in the road where blackthorn hedge defined the edge of their lands. Morgan began to rein in, slowing down to allow her captain out in front of her. The rest of her people galloped in circles as the captain stepped forward on high alert. She scanned the field for Tam but he wasn't there. He had one use left in him, after all the time and planning she put into creating the perfect mate for her people. Her fury at finding he soiled his genes found satisfaction in knowing they would use his blood to mark the perimeter of her domain. If he wasn't torn apart by the transformation, she'd do it herself.

Tam's horse was tethered near the stone building. Morgan used her senses to feel the Rigellium he wore, and almost smelled the sharp tang of the metal creatures as they swarmed on his flesh. She detected the ones around his neck and her mind slipped past skin and skull to find Tam's thoughts, which were riddled with fear, anger, and determination. She stilled him.

"He's at the other end of the hall, in the bushes," she called out to the captain over the pounding of hooves as the host continued to circle the field, and withdrew her mind from Tam's trusting the captain to handle it, while she turned to scan the area for the faint traces of the borderline, so they could ride the fine boundary between the Terran world and her own Sh'eyta realm.

Tam felt the ugly threads of Morgan's mind in his where he crouched in the bushes, and knew he'd been found. He focused on the darkest thing he could imagine: a pool of water deep in the forest, on a moonless night. He heard the captain's voice giving orders to the guards, then felt the rough grasp of hands on his arms and legs. He was thrown heavily onto the back of a horse. The glint of gold trim told him it was the captain's horse, and the captain himself in the saddle. The threads of Morgan's mind slid away, and Tam exploded into motion, jumping down from the back of the horse and slapping the beast's haunches. The captain's horse leapt away, and Tam swung around to face two guards. His axe was several feet away, and he lunged for it, but a booted heel struck his thigh. His feet slid out from under him and he fell heavily onto his chest, driving his breath from his lungs. As he tried to recover, another boot struck his head, but he was ready for it and already rolling away toward the axe. He grabbed its handle and leapt to his feet with a grunt at the pain in his leg and turned, swinging the axe into the chest of the guard behind him. It bit deeply through the bones, and Tam yanked hard to break it free. But he had little time to think about it, as he saw the second guard driving a sword toward his chest. He parried the blow and swung the axe at the man's legs, forcing the man back toward the stream. He heard a crackling of branches behind him and dove to the right, rotating so he could see both the second guard and whatever else might be coming at him. The captain sat astride his horse ten feet away, just watching.

He was shocked to see the first guard lumbering toward him, chest split open and showing a gold lump of metal where a man's heart should be. The second guard lunged at him, and Tam almost casually drove the axe toward his head so that the man seemed to split his own head open on the axe rather than the axe striking him down. The guard's moves were so formulaic it took Tam little effort to then launch a high kick at the first guard, driving him to the ground with a boot to his groin. But was surprised by a blow to his kidneys, driving him to the ground again. By who? He rolled over and looked up, to see both guards coming at him as if one didn't have his chest split open, and the other, his head. But that gold lump slid out of the gaping hole in the first guard's chest, and the man crumbled to the ground, no more than a bundle of sticks and lumps of clay.

Tam swung the axe into the belly of the second guard just in time to stop the man from getting a good punch to Tam's head. It didn't slow the creature a bit. This is not a man, Tam realized. This is some magickal beast.

A tattoo of hooves was all the warning Tam had before the captain struck Tam with a boot from the back of his horse. Tam rolled several times, trying to collect his wits before he got back on his feet. He heard the thud of the captain's boots landing on the ground and rolled once more, then jumped up to face his eldritch foe. A scowl of fury passed quickly over the captain's face, then disappeared, and Tam tilted his axe across his body to block the sword that would have cut him in two if he'd been a moment slower. The golem was at his back, and Tam had to dance quickly sideways to have them both in view. The captain lunged again, backing Tam against the trunk of a tree. The golem pressed forward more slowly, and Tam had to swallow his horror at the ghastly sight of what appeared to be human, but with one half of its head tilted sideways.

"Surrender, you fool! You've no way out," the captain hissed.

"Surrender to what, death? What's the point of that!"

"Death comes for all beasts. If not today, then tomorrow. Let your death be meaningful. Your blood will assure your people's security in this wretched place."

The golem rushed at Tam, but he'd been watching out of the corner of his eye, and he swung the axe straight into the creature's chest, burying it deeply as its body was carried past him by the combined momentum of its lunge and Tam's strike. The weight of the body pulled it off the blade of Tam's axe, and Tam swung full circle to parry the captain's immediate attack, barely staving off the blade of the sword, which took a small bite of his wrist. He heard the the scuff of gravel behind him as the thing rose to its feet again, but more slowly this time.

"Nay, you hellborn heathen, I'll have your liver on the ground before this evening ends, or you may waste my blood right here," Tam said, breathing heavily. He lunged forward to force the captain back, then swung around and dived into the golem, driving his fist into the beast's chest to pull the golden heart out and drop it on the ground. The rapid dissolution of its body was rewarding, but he had little time to celebrate, turning swiftly again just in time to parry the heavy sword that came straight toward his head. Down to one foe, but the captain was a canny opponent.

Tam circled to the right, then to the left, watching the captain's hands and feet out of his peripheral vision, staring into the devil's eyes, watching for his next move, but the captain was simply watching in return, unmoving, braced unflinchingly for Tam's attack. It was disconcerting, made no sense, and Tam didn't trust it. With good reason, he thought, as the chains he wore bit into his flesh and he fell to the ground.

"If you'd come a bit sooner, my liege, we'd not have lost two of my guards," he heard the man admonish his queen.

"Easily rebuilt," she answered.

"It takes time to train them. Their memories are ever lost, we must start over, and I tire of this repetition."

"Hush, you dolt. It is not your right to question me."

Tam wondered at the rebellious words. He knew the captain was often displeased with the way Morgan handled Tam, but the blatant criticism was new. Surely he could use this, somehow, as he felt the captain heave him up onto Honor's back, his hands drawn around the thick neck so that his wrists met below it. The chains affixed themselves to each other, and he held on tightly with his thighs; if his body slid, he'd be under the hooves and dragged.

"To the border! The sun falls," Morgan cried, and turned to gallop away.

The hoofbeats of a dozen other horses pummeled the earth behind her as Tam's mind fought with her for a minute or two, but it made little difference. She wasn't the reason he couldn't move; the chains had done the job. Honor still wore the Rigellium horseshoes, had no choice but to follow the Sh'eyta horde.

Morgan was half a mile away when she felt Tam's mind suddenly go blank.

Stunned, Morgan tried to turn her horse, but too many other horses were right behind her. She struggled to get past them and sped back toward the field, scanning for the white horse that carried him.

## 37 – The Curse

"Oh, had I known, Tam Lin, " she said, "what this night I did see, I'd taken out your two gray eyes, put two in from a tree. Had I known at early morn that Tam Lin would be gone, I'd taken out his heart of flesh, put in a heart of stone." Child Ballad 39: Tam Lin

Heartbroken, Janet had begun making her way back to her father's keep when, in a dazzling display of lightfooted leaps, an entire herd of horses and a bevy of hounds swept past her, faeries on the back of every flying steed. Shocked, she watched as several went to the far end of the stone building, grabbing Tam's horse as they went. She tried to gather her courage, but there were so many horses, hounds, and fiends that circled in front of her that she wasn't sure how to get past them, or around them. When they finally stopped circling and began to leave the field, stretching out in a line along the stream, she could see Tam's form astride the broad back of his horse, the grey of his eyes surrounded by the white sclera of fear in the last golden light of the setting sun. She barely had time to pull the shawl from where it was wrapped around her waist as she kneed Darkness in front of the poor animal, who reared, spooked. She flung a long loop of the green fabric over Tam and pulled sharply, but the pull of the cloth wasn't strong enough to break the tight grip Tam had on the horse. Fortunately, though, the horse stood still with indecision, nose toward the rallying horde, but ears turned backward, as if listening for a command from Tam.

"Let go, you fool!" A large bundle of cloth in her hand, she grabbed at Tam's wrist, and the copper-laden cloth made a hissing sound as it touched the chains. Tam's hand fell away from Honor's neck, and Tam fell to the ground, then lunged to his feet, reaching to his hip as if expecting to find a sword. It took Janet less than a moment to pull the rapier she wore from its scabbard and toss it to him as a tall, dark man in black leather galloped from around the back of the ruins toward them. Tam grabbed the blade out of the air, then took a moment to wrap the shawl tightly around his neck and over his arms. Janet pulled the tails of the fabric behind him and made a swift knot that would keep the length from tangling in his legs or pulling the rest away from his golden chains.

"Filth!" The captain spat from the back of his light-footed steed.

"Get down here and make it a fair fight!" Tam shot back, as Janet grabbed the dangling reins of her own horse. Tam's white gelding shot away toward the building, desperate to find safety.

The two men circled, the captain wielding a heavy sword from the back of his horse, while Tam stepped quickly from one side of the man's horse to the other, holding his slender blade lightly and watching both horse and man to see how they moved. Suddenly he grabbed the near rein and jerked the horse's head down. It reared against him, trying to free itself, and the rider had to lean forward to stay on its back. Tam thrust the tip of the blade toward him at the same time and there was a yelp as several inches of the rapier found its way into the man's chest. Tam pulled the blade away and struck again, lower this time, the sharp steel sinking in the same amount. Tam released the reins and grabbed a booted leg, yanking downward once more, and stepped quickly away as the heavy body fell to the ground with a thud. Tam stepped on his wrist and yanked the heavier blade from tight fingers with his left hand, stepping back now with two blades rather than one.

Janet had found her own reins and wrapped them around her hands with worry as she watched for a chance to help if she was needed, but Tam was methodically dispatching the fae warrior with such alacrity she hardly had time to take a breath before Tam stood before a motionless body. He turned to her, barely panting, then looked sharply beyond her as they both heard a voice scream "Tam Lin, you will pay for your foul deeds!"

Tam held the rapier toward her, and Janet took it by the pommel. Releasing it, he bent over the captain's body and unbuckled the belt that held the sword's scabbard, buckling it over his own hips quickly as the banshee howl of an angry woman came louder and louder toward them.

"Tam Lin, if I'd known you would betray us so, I'd have ripped your heart out and replaced it with that of a golem! I'd have pulled your eyes from your head and replaced them with smithed stone!"

"Lass, are you waking?" Tam snapped his fingers in front of her face as she swayed on her feet, her furious race through the woods and the thought of the hideous curse catching up with her. She stumbled toward her horse, but she must have been moving too slowly for Tam's liking, because his powerful arms had grabbed her by the hips already and he was poised to fling her up into the steed's saddle.

She slipped out of his strong grasp. "I'm perfectly capable of riding myself!" She shouted at him.

"Get ye gone, lass, the demons are going to take me."

"Not if I get you first, you idiot," she snapped, fighting against him as he tried to lift her into the saddle. "You've got the shawl over you, get up there, you fool of a man," she barked. Tam stood stock still and stared at her with his mouth slung wide. "I'm not moving an inch without you! If you want me to escape, get up there and ride with me!"

He seemed to gather his wits and accept her threat as real. Rather than lift her into the saddle, he slung her up behind it and grabbed the plastron at its front, crouched down, then propelled himself up into place in it, folding a leg up and over the horse to the other side with the grace of a cat.

Janet slipped the rapier into its sheath, then felt his strong grips close over hers as he yanked the reins out of her hand. "Not enough time, you damn fool of a woman," Tam muttered, and Janet grabbed his waist as he kicked the horse and steered it away from the dead body it was nearly stumbling over. "Home!" he shouted.

Janet prayed that the shawl was enough as Darkness sprang into a sudden gallop. She clung to Tam as he powered the huge stallion toward her father's keep. They thundered toward the still shrieking madwoman and nearly made it past, but her steed leapt in front of them and Darkness reared. Janet slid rapidly down the hips of the horse and landing painfully on her ribs.

She looked up and saw Tam pulling the reins back and down, so that darkness nearly sat on his haunches, and Janet barely had time to roll out from under him, but he leapt forward first, his chest hitting the woman's shoulder, and Tam swung the pommel of his sword down on the top of her skull with a resounding crack. The woman grabbed his wrist, and he twisted free. "Janet!" he shouted.

"I'm here! Go! I'll follow!" But Tam looked back at her, and she knew he wouldn't. Furious, she drew the rapier and dove forward to drive it into the woman, who stepped deftly away. She turned and swung the blade high, slapping the woman in the face with it. Bad luck that she'd hit with the side of the blade, rather than the edge. But the woman grabbed the blade, and Janet drew backwards, the sharp-edged blade slicing through the woman's hand.

"Up, Janet," Tam shouted, and she saw the hand that reached down for her and grabbed it. His grip was painful as she felt her body lifted into the air and she landed sideways against Tam's back. She grabbed his shoulders and pulled a leg over to get seated properly, but her head snapped backward as the woman screeched again, trying to pull her down by her hair.

"Release me, witch," Janet screamed, pulling herself forward to press against Tam as Darkness danced under her thighs.

Suddenly everything was still. The lady's grip on Janet's hair was gone, and Darkness danced in a circle, giving Janet a view of the woman, whose jaws were wide as she stared at her bleeding hand, a long, thin welt turning pink on her cheek.

Tam wrenched their steed around and gave a heavy kick, and Darkness lurched forward, away from the woman and her dark horde, which was nearly out of sight. Janet whispered a prayer, her eyes squeezed shut as Darkness sped down the gravelled path.

As the last rays of sunlight limned violet clouds in a glowing gold, The horse slowed down and Janet felt Tam's body convulse, then stiffen until he felt like a marble statue. His muscles seemed to ripple as he turned around toward her, and she squeaked with alarm as his nose grew longer. His hand was turning grey where it came out from under the loop of shawl that covered his wrist. The grey was replaced by yellow fur. But no, his arms grew very thick, covered with coarse black fur, and the shawl peeled away from the heavily furred paw that had replaced her lover's hand.

"Lassshh –"

He was changing. He had said he would. And he said the shawl would be the only thing that saved him. She pulled it over his wrist again and wrapped her arms around him, pinning the fabric to his body as he writhed and shuddered under her grip. She clung to him with all her might. He fell forward as his body twisted and turned against itself, and for a moment she lost her grip on him as he squirmed away. Janet ripped the reins out of his spasming hand and gripped him tighter with her left arm. "Stop fighting me!"

"Unh –" he tried to pull away.

"Stop it! I'll not let go. If you wish me to get safely home, you must ride, I'll not go without you."

"Unh," he said again, then the bellow of a beast roared in her ears. A bear. She was sure she held a bear. Then suddenly she held an even larger beast with soft fur on huge, tawny legs that stuck out past the now much too small shawl, which was frightening. But she held on, clinging so tightly he yelped. Then he was a grey dog of some sort, and finally he stopped changing.

Janet gripped him tightly as she rode on toward the keep. "You'll not have him as long as I live," she whispered to the fading shrieks, her hands gripping the reins until her knuckles turned white. The dark woman had raced after them briefly, then the hoofbeats stopped, and turned, but the piercing cries continued until they could be heard no more. Janet's heart was in her throat as she kicked Darkness to greater speed.

Tam's wolfen body bounced precariously against Janet's thighs, but her arm held him with a fierce strength that warmed his heart. He listened for the shrieks to grow louder again, fearful that at any moment the dark lady's hand would reach out and pull them down off the horse before they could get away. The black stallion kept racing toward home until he wondered if it might run itself to death and leave them stranded. He knew this would be their only chance to escape; if he was recaptured, there would be no further leniency.

When they came racing toward the stone walls, they could see that the gate was closed.

"Rouse, you fool," Janet called out to the guard who reclined against a parapet. "Open the gate, quickly!"

The soldier stood, mouth wide open, and she cursed as she brought the horse to a shuddering halt, then paced fretfully in circles as the great wooden doors were unlatched. It seemed to take forever for the gate to open, and the horse was trying to dash away the entire time. As soon as there was an opening wide enough the animal plunged between the big wooden doors, and Tam felt the wood scratch against his nose as they passed between, but Janet still held Tam's misshapen form tightly against her body. Once the gate was closed behind them, she pulled the reins tight and the horse reared in objection, eyes rolling wildly as he shook his head back and forth, trying to get the bit, but she pulled his head around to give him no slack. Another guard ran toward her and took the reins, but she had to be lifted from the saddle by her brother, who had come to see what the ruckus was. Tam dropped to the ground, emitting a yelp as the shawl fell off. His clothes had shredded away underneath, and the belt and scabbard tumbled to the side.

"Janet! What is this?" Jack cried out.

"No!" she cried as he put his knee down painfully on Tam's spine.

Everyone jumped back except Janet, who jumped forward to shove her brother off him, pulling the shawl back over his head and forelimbs, though he twisted to keep it off his head. "He must stay shrouded!" she insisted.

"Janet, a bit of fabric won't protect you from those teeth," he objected.

"Does he LOOK like he's a threat?" She blurted, and everyone looked at the grey animal that cowered in front of her, his tail between his legs.

"It's a wild—"

"No it's not! Listen to me!" she shrieked, and the courtyard fell silent. He lay down at her feet, nose on paws, like a lapdog. She looked down in surprise and he turned only his eyes up toward her, otherwise remaining perfectly still. He wondered what she would say now. Several men had drawn their swords, and he tensed, knowing that even in this moment he was far safer here than he'd been for some time.

"This is... it's a pet. He's tame. He means me no harm." Tam clenched his jaws and snorted quietly, trying to stifle an urge to laugh, knowing it must come out as a bark at best.

Her brother was staring in wonder. "I've never seen the like," he murmured.

Tam's heart ached with love as Janet lifted her chin and turned toward her formidable father, who had just come out of the great hall. The burly, red-headed man scanned the courtyard, taking in the scene before him, and Tam wanted to shrink back as he saw the nobleman glare at him, but he crept in front of Janet, setting himself between the angry lord and his daughter.

"Janet, it seems I must ask you, once again, what is going on." He stared at Tam, then marveled, "I have never heard of a grey-eyed wolf." The black stallion shuddered and blew, and Dunbar looked at the horse. "Bollocks!" he cursed, hurrying over to wipe at the frothy saliva flecks that spattered the steed's neck where it had been strewn while he ran. Tam shrank back as Dunbar stepped over him to take the reins, and the crowd that was gathering gasped.

He looked down. "Janet?"

"It's a gift, father. A wolf that has been tamed to do my bidding," she answered lamely.

Lord Dunbar looked into her eyes, measuring her answer. He looked down at Tam again, and Tam lowered his head to the ground. The man gave a curt nod. "There appear to be chains around its neck and paws. A wolf would have to be tame to accept such trappings. I'll tell you I don't like it, but I'll withhold judgment until I know what the hell is going on. That will wait until tomorrow, when I will get better answers from you. I'm torn between fury with you for running off and gratitude that you've returned. . . safely."

Janet took a step forward, but he stopped her with an icy glare, then looked toward the two guards who had opened the gate. "Put this creature in a kennel! At a distance from my hounds. I'll not have it breeding with or chewing on my hunters." Lecture paused, he led the heaving horse into the stable and barked out orders to the stableboy.

## 38 – Where There's a Will

Gruoch stepped into the clean, white room where Skaal was peering into a microscope. He leaned back, glanced at her, then held his hand out for the vials she carried. "It's a shame your little friend could do nothing for us, in the end," he murmured as he took the vials and set them down, then looked back into the lens of the microscope.

"Yes. I've been thinking about that."

Skaal looked up and let his gaze rest on her this time. "Were you planning to share your thoughts?"

A crease appeared between Gruoch's pale eyebrows. She turned to a solution that had finally come to her, and she cursed herself that it had come too late. "What if we had come at it from a different angle? Curing Tam might not be the only option. I'm not sure, I'm only an observer, but is it possible we could have protected the women he mates with from being infected by him?"

Skaal's eyes widened slightly. "That would be a novel approach. But we know we're as susceptible to the gene-altering agent as the humans are. It's only our care in handling it that prevents it from affecting us."

"Us, yes. But we're not purely Anunnaki, after our ancestors were first altered on Shanadu so that our bodies could take on the Terran modifications. Is it possible to reinforce the original form, that was more resistant to modification?"

Skaal stroked his chin and rose to pace the floor. "It's a good question. If I can eliminate the Shanadu modification, our Anunnaki genes would resist the hybrid modifications."

"And it is clear our genes have also made us strong enough to survive recoding, so it should be safe to experiment on any who volunteer," Gruoch said, quietly.

Skaal glanced at her. "What do you mean?"

"Consider Tam himself. Ever before, when a human hybrid took a second form, they failed to survive the transformation. Tam has not only survived a second form, he succeeded with a third. It has to be due to his half-Sh'eytan heritage."

"Hah," Skaal scoffed. "That is further evidence it can't be done. Our form is far too adaptable. We are MORE likely… but that's the Shanadu variant." Skaal tapped his finger on the table, deep in thought. "I'm not sure if we can be returned to that condition. The whole point of creating the Shanunnaki subspecies was to allow us to adapt ourselves to whatever planet we wish to colonize. Unfortunately this makes us very susceptible to recoding by the agents we performed our research with. Which means we're susceptible to the hybrid mutagens."

"I suppose you're right. It would take a very great scientist to find a way to recondition our Shanunnaki-Terran heritage so that we're no longer susceptible to recoding agents," Gruoch used the full name of their subspecies to reinforce the genetic heritage it carried; Skaal loved excuses to manipulate DNA to see what could be accomplished.

Skaal scoffed. "Oh, I could certainly do it," he waved a hand as if brushing the idea away. "We Shanunnaki that received the Terran genes can simply strengthen the Anunnaki to prevent further alteration," he said.

Gruoch wondered if he was aware he had just voiced her idea as if it were his own. "But wouldn't that keep us from holding the Terran genes we need?" She said, prodding him to argue his point.

"I've isolated the DNA we need for survival. If I see to it that it is duplicated in both strands, we'll be fine. Then it's just a matter of fixing all the DNA against any change. Easier to keep a body from changing than to remove a change that already happened. But it's hardly worth the effort for a single generation. Even if we did, we have no way to track down and retrieve the scoundrel. He escaped." Skaal gave her a disapproving look. It was, after all, her suggestion that he be allowed to live in the meadow.

Gruoch was frightened for a moment by a strange but pleasant lurch she felt in her heart – was this the thing, joy, that she'd heard humans speak of? If so, many things about humans made more sense. If this worked, it was a brilliant solution for the current tragedy. "Oh, I can find him if you can protect our women from his affliction."

Skaal's eyes lit up as he rubbed his chin again, and Gruoch willed him to accept the challenge. She wasn't sure it could be done, but if it could, he was possibly the only Sh'eytan scientist with enough influence to bring the other scientists together for the task. She also wasn't positive she COULD find Tam, in fact, but she was willing to try. She knew Tam would have a powerful urge to contact his family, and his wife's. Humans were very family-oriented, and Tam, in particular, seemed to consider family of the utmost importance. Despite the fact that humans seemed to scurry about like squirrels, he could be found, in time, wherever he had close family.

Skaal continued to pace and rub his chin. "How on earth do you think you can find the creature when Morgan herself seems incapable?"

"Morgan relies on the Rigellium. You yourself have told her Rigellium should be used as a last resort, but she finds it too convenient. I've studied humans and hybrids for several centuries now, and I've learned more about their needs and habits than anyone else. That's why I was brought in first, when he was reacquired, after he'd been raised as a changeling by the humans. Reacquisition has always been a challenge, and we couldn't afford for it to go wrong this time."

Skaal nodded. "Which it did anyway."

Gruoch held her gaze steady, though her heart pounded. Her fault, again, the current failure. And so, hers to find a solution for. And she had, if Skaal would just open his mind to the possibility.

Skaal looked at his feet, lost in thought for a moment. "Well, I've relied on your counsel often, myself, when it comes to the unpredictable creatures." He looked torn. He had never failed, even once, at any given task, and Gruoch knew he was extraordinarily proud of that record. If he started looking for a way to block the transmission from Tam to the Sh'eytan women, he would have to succeed, or accept a blemish on that record.

"Ah," Skaal said, raising a finger into the air. "If only it were safe! But we've seen the effect he has on our commander. I think it best we don't allow Morgan near this Tam again, for her sake and ours. This sensual abomination she indulges in when he's present cannot be allowed!"

"Oh, that will be no problem," Gruoch said innocently. "Clearly he can hide from her, and she doesn't understand humans well enough to find him without the Rigellium, which he has managed to block from her. If we don't reveal his location to her, we can safely secure our next generation without tempting her to pervert herself."

Skaal stopped pacing, clearly shocked at the suggestion of keeping secrets from their commander. But Gruoch could see that he was considering it. She knew his temptation was strong. She decided to push him just a bit farther. "And your leadership in this area would be appreciated by our superiors, I'm sure," she said quietly. The Anunnaki orverlords were already overdue for their periodic visit to assess the Terran project.

Skaal began to nod. "Yes, there is merit in this course of action. I'm sure I can find a way to prevent transmission between the subject and our women. I've never failed before."

Gruoch hid a smile. She'd come to admire the half-human Tam. Once a solution was found, she would have the task of ferrying women to him again, and so she would have to be in contact with him. There was so much more she wanted to know about his new form and how it would affect him. And perhaps, for all that she took pride in understanding the power of human motivations to drive Sh'eyta behavior, she herself was blind to the fact that she, herself, was in love with Tam.

## 39 – Happily

"They turned him in this lady's arms like to a naked knight; she's taken him home to her own bower, and clothed him in armour bright." Child Ballad 39: Tam Lin

Janet smiled at Tam where he lay on the cloak he'd spread across the soft grass of the walled garden. He watched her as she placed stitches in linen while watching their giggling child bat at a butterfly that landed on his upturned nose.

"It's good to see you resting after the long ride you had from Moray. How's your father?" She asked.

"He's well, overseeing the new flagstones in the courtyard that my mother insists on, so she doesn't have to dismount into mud." Lord Dunbar had insisted that he go speak to his own father after they shared the truth with the fiery Scot. Tam had been formally knighted in a public ceremony, his duty to Sir Gregor and Lord Douglas was complete, and he answered now to his father and Lord Dunbar, they were the only other people who knew the truth about Tam.

He peered at the dark fabric around his wrists and Janet held her tongue. She knew he was worried about how delicate the protective coverings were. It was hard not to wear them down too rapidly; the life of an Earl's son, and a knight, was hard on equipment, and the shawl fabric that had covered the chains wore out over time, but the covering was essential to keeping his location hidden from Morgan. As it was, he moved about the country overseeing his father's estate and carrying information from one lord to another, and they kept scouts fielded to watch for her spies. It would work as long as the fabric held and she couldn't find him through the chains, but Janet had replaced one set, and the new one was already going threadbare. The fabric around his neck lasted longer, but it wouldn't last forever, and eventually the replacement fabric would be gone as well. He considered putting actual copper plates over the Rigellium, but wearing metal all day and night would chafe over time.

"There!" Janet said, as she bit off the end of the waxed linen thread.

"What is it?" Tam grinned at their fat little baby playing in the patch of shade. The boy had almost grabbed the butterfly that kept dancing around his head. Janet kept one eye on the child, knowing it would go straight into the mouth if it were caught, though so far that seemed unlikely.

"Come here, I'll show you."

Tam looked over at her and she reached her hand out to show him the linen cuff with the Moray coat of arms embroidered on it. Tam slid closer to her and took it from her hand as she offered it to him. She pulled another one out of the bag at her side, and then a collar with a bit of lace. She had taken a great deal of time to be sure it was both strong and stylish. He handed it back. "What is it for?"

Janet crooked an eyebrow at him. "For you, silly."

Tam chuckled and shook his head. "You should wear them yourself, you're a Randall now. Sleeve ends are good enough for me, love. Fancy is out of place on a fighting man."

"Ah, but you misunderstand. This is for your protection, just as much as a set of bracers would be. You can't keep wearing out pieces of my shawl. The linen upper and lining can be replaced as it protects the green fabric I've placed between them."

Tam snatched it back and looked at the seam; for all her care, he noticed an edge of green thread sticking out where she'd sewn it together. He looked at the linen again; she made it so it would totally cover the Rigellium chain while looking like a cuff for his sleeve. He looked again at the coat of arms on both of them, then placed one over his wrist; it would need very little adjustment once the frail bit of shawl that was already there had been pulled away.

"I think it will be just right," she said. "Do you think you can bring yourself to show a bit of lace at your collar? I know it's not your style, but it will keep people from asking why they never see your throat, while blocking the metal from communicating with Morgan."

Tam looked at the cuffs again.

She sighed at his worried brows. "I know it's not the style you'd choose, aside from weddings and court appearances, but if it keeps Morgan at bay, isn't it worth the fussiness of it?"

He assessed the three ornamental pieces, then pulled the collar around his neck to find that it fit almost perfectly, and seemed to completely cover the chain, with a bit of room to spare in case it shifted. "I'll have to wear these the rest of my life, won't I?"

Janet paused. Did he truly hate it so much? "If you want to go back to Carter Hall—"

"Don't even suggest it!" he fingered the cloth again. "Well, if I must dress the part of a nobleman's son—"

"A nobleman in your own right," she interjected.

"As you wish! I have a role to play, and finery isn't misplaced. As fussy clothing goes, your needlework will be a credit to my appearance." He pulled the new collar away from his neck to inspect it again. "I see you kept the lace at a minimum."

"I thought you'd appreciate that."

"And I suppose without the lace people would wonder why I bothered. I think I understand your design here, my love, and I had no idea you could be so crafty! This is the solution to what I was just worrying about. This will protect the copper fabric, preserve it longer, while looking like something I ought to be wearing rather than this lie I've been telling that I have wounds that are healing. That excuse was about worn out. Oh, Janet, this will do. This will do quite nicely!" He swept her into an embrace, kissing her deeply.

The baby gurgled and cooed, trying to reach them now instead of the butterfly, which had flown away.

"Tam!" Janet laughed, as he released her. "One child is all we can have." For a moment, the dark truth that it was unsafe for them to be intimate loomed between them.

Tam gave a mischievous grin as he said, "Oh, not for long, Janet. There will be more. I've had a visit from Gruoch—"

"Oh no! They found you?"

"Not Morgan. Gruoch understands humans in a way Morgan never will. She assures me Morgan has given up her search for me, but Gruoch knew I would come back here eventually. She tells me there will soon be a. . . some sort of thing. . . vaccine, she calls it, that prevents a woman and our child from taking on my less civilized traits."

Janet pushed him away so she could search his eyes. "Oh, Tam, could it be true?"

He grinned. "They wouldn't send their women to me if it weren't, and I've been told their program will resume in the near future."

Janet frowned. "They're still requiring you to sire the next generation, then?"

Tam leaned back on his hands and watched her. "Gruoch swore to keep Morgan from me as long as I wear the shawl fabric over my chains and keep my promise to fulfill my purpose, as they see it. Does that disturb you?"

Janet considered her answer. "Well, no, not if it means they'll leave you alone otherwise. It's not uncommon for peers to have mistresses, I reconciled with that fact long ago. But aren't you trying to keep your distance?"

"From Morgan, yes. But Gruoch has proven that she can find me. And I've the feeling that she doesn't approve of Morgan's personal interest in me."

Janet fingered her lip as she watched the baby bat at the returning butterfly. "It's the price of your freedom, then?"

"Yes." He paused, then whispered, "does that worry you?"

"Welll. . ." Her voice dropped. "I suppose the upside of it is that we can share a bed again?"

Tam leaned forward, pushing her down to the cloak with his body. "It does. Does THAT worry you?"

Janet wrapped her arms around him and pulled him down for a deep kiss. The baby cooed, and they both looked up quickly, but the butterfly was still dancing in the air rather than in the boy's plump cheeks.

"It doesn't have to be the changelings alone that we'll raise, Janet," Tam prompted, still waiting for an answer.

She looked into his serious grey eyes. They both believed that the babies the Sh'eyta women birthed should be brought to Janet and Tam so they could raise them, instead of being thrust upon unwitting parents whose own babies were discarded. "A true family we'll have, then?" She said tentatively, almost fearful to believe she could have the joy of raising more of her own children.

"A very large one, with some of them our own, some of them changelings."

"They'll all be yours. Some mine as well, but all of them children to be loved." She sighed. "I can't think of any news that could make me happier in this moment." She looked over at the door in the wall. On the other side was once a small medicinal herb garden, but Janet and Tam had convinced Lord Dunbar to build a steel-shielded room for Tam to retire to when he was here, so that Tam didn't have to limit his travels to stay near his father's lands far to the north, where an identical room had been built.

"So you agree there can be more? Our little boy will have brothers and sisters?" He whispered, hardly daring to hope.

"In time," Janet said slowly, then a smile bloomed on her face, lighting up her eyes. "Oh, there will be many more, Tam. Yes, there can be more." Then, more seriously, "In time. Let's just enjoy the child we have right now, love. You'll find it's soon enough that your arms will be full of children and you'll wish you'd waited a bit."

"Never!" He growled, and pulled her into another kiss.

With a bit of effort and a great deal of laughter, Janet managed to fend him off long enough to place the cuffs and collar on his wrists and neck, only pulling the previous fabric away once it was clear the new pieces were snug enough not to shift around on him. His well-muscled arms kept the cuffs from sliding toward his elbows, and gravity did the work for the collar; a brooch with a large gem held it in place over the neck chain.

As long as his scouts stayed on their toes, and she made new linen pieces to protect the copper fabric as needed, Tam would be safe from his cruel mother. They agreed it would be best if he travelled often, even more than most lords did as they managed their estates and people.

When her father had told her she must learn to sew, she never imagined how right he was. To keep the man she loved safe, the work was no burden at all. Tam seemed to be adjusting to the idea, even held his head a bit higher as if he just donned a new suit. He was safe now, from Morgan and her kind.

The evening sun was setting and Tam gathered up his child and his cloak as Janet picked up her sewing basket so she and her son could retire to the hall. They kissed once again at the heavy, metal-reinforced wooden gate, and Tam kissed the top of the baby's head before closing the door between them. Janet strolled through the rose garden, her son hon her hip, and back to the hall. Her place was with the baby, and it would be years before the baby needed to know his father's secrets.

As the sun dropped toward the horizon, a howl lifted up toward the round, silver moon where it rose, sending shivers down the spines of the ladies as they paused their gossip. Janet hid a smile. It was wolf tonight, then. The bear and the lion were too wild to allow anyone else to see, but the wolf was accepted, though grudgingly, when it walked at her side through the garden. She tucked the baby into his crib and strode back to the garden where she would meet her husband, shaggy as he was, and tonight they would be together again.

# The Harrowing of Tam Lin

## *Tam Lin*

"I forbid you maidens all that wear gold in your hair
To come or go by Carter Hall, it's known Tam Lin is there
None can pass by Carter Hall but he demands a pledge
rings of gold or shawls of green or else their maidenhead"

Janet sits in her lonely room, sewing a silken seam,
Looking out on Carter Hall, among the leaves so green
And Janet sits in her lonely bower, sewing a silken thread
And longs to be in Carter Hall, among the roses red.

She's let the seam fall at her heels, the needle to her toe
And she has gone to Carter Hall as fast as she can go
And she has pulled a single rose, a rose but only one
When up appeared Tam Lin, the elf, said "Lass, what have you done?"

Who's this pulls the red, red rose? What makes you break the tree?
What makes you come to Carter Hall, without command of me?
"Carter Hall is not your own, roses there are many;
I'll come and go all as I please and ask no leave of any."

He has took her by the hand, took her by the sleeve,
And he has laid this lady down, among the grass so green.
And he has took her by the arm, took her by the hand,
And he has laid this lady down, among the roses red.

Four and twenty ladies fair sewing at the silk
And out then came fair Janet, as pale as any milk.
Four and twenty gentlemen playing at the chess,
And Janet goes among them all, as green as any grass.

Well, up then spoke her father, he's spoken meek and mild
"Oh, alas, my daughter," he said, "I fear you go with child.
And is it to a man a man of might or to a man of means?
Or who among my gentlemen shall give the babe his name?"

"Oh father, if I go with child, this to you I'll tell,
There's none among your gentlemen that I would treat so well,
and father, if I go with child, I must bear the blame;
there's none among your gentlemen shall give the babe his name.

## The Harrowing of Tam Lin

"If my true love were born of man and not an elfin grey
I'd not trade my own true love for any knight you have.
The steed that my love rides upon Is lighter than the wind;
With silver he is shod before, with burning gold behind."

She's let the seam fall at her heel, the needle to her toe
And she has gone to Carter Hall as fast as she can go
She is down among the weeds, down among the thorns,
And then appeared Tam Lin again, says "Lady pull no more.

"What makes you pull the poison rose, what makes you break the tree?
What makes you harm the little babe that I have got with thee?"
"Oh I will pull the rose, Tam Lin, I will break the tree,
But I'll not bear the little babe that you have got with me.

If he was to an earthly man, not a wild shade,
I'd rock him all the winter's night, and all the summer's day.
Come tell to me, Tam Lin," she said, "What you have never told;
Are you an earthly man?" said she, "A knight or a baron bold?"

"The truth I'll tell to thee, my love, a word I will not lie;
A knight's my sire, I'm human born, just as much as thee.
Douglas, Earl Murray, was my sire, Dunbar, Earl March, is thine;
We met as kin when we were small, which yet you well may mind.

"When I was but a beardless boy my uncle sent for me,
To hunt and hawk, and ride with him, to keep him company.
I lay upon my cloak one day and soon fell fast asleep,
And by the queen of fairies came and took me to her keep.

"The Queen of Fairies has kept me in yon green hill and dell,
and would I never tire, my love, In Elfish land to dwell,
But aye, at every seven years, they pay a fee to hell;
And I a human full of flesh, tonight 'twill be myself.

"Tonight is Hallowe'en, my love, the faery folk will ride
If you would your true love win at Miles Cross you must bide."
"But how shall I be sure, Tam Lin? How shall I thee know,
Among a pack of hellish wraiths the like I never saw?"

## The Harrowing of Tam Lin

"First let pass the black, the black, and then let pass the brown,
but go you to the milk-white steed and pull the rider down.
For I ride on the milk-white steed, and nearest to the town;
because I was a christened knight, they gave me that renown.

"But first I'll change all in your arms into a wild wolf
hold me tight and fear me not, I'll be a gentleman.
And then I'll change all in your arms into a wild bear,
but hold me tight and fear me not, I'll be your husband, dear,

"And then I'll change all in your arms into a lion bold
but hold me tight and fear me not, the father loves his child,
and when I change all in your arms into a naked knight
cloak me in your mantle green and keep me out of sight"

In the middle of the night she heard the bridle ring
She heeded then what he did say and young Tam Lin did win.
Then up spoke the Faery Queen, an angry queen was she
Woe betide her ill-fared face, an ill death may she die

"Oh, had I known, Tam Lin, " she said, "what this knight I did see
I'd taken out your two gray eyes, put two in from a tree.
Had I known at early morn that Tam Lin would be gone,
I'd taken out his heart of flesh, put in a heart of stone.